# Heartless Crimes

ALSO BY MICHAEL HAMBLING

# Michael Hambling

# HEARTLESS CRIMES

*Detective Sophie Allen Book 13*

Joffe Books, London
www.joffebooks.com

First published in Great Britain in 2024

Cover art by Nick Castle

ISBN: 978-1-83526-887-2

# FOREWORD

This is a work of fiction, and none of the characters and situations described in this novel bear any resemblance to real persons or events. Some of the locations in this novel do exist but are used fictitiously.

For convenience, a short glossary appears at the end of this book. It also lists the main ranks within the UK Police Force. You'll also find a short introduction to the area in which the novel is located.

The fictional country of Parantos is a small ex-British colony on the Atlantic coast of South America. It is situated close to Colombia. UK locations are real.

# CHARACTER LIST

*Wessex Regional Serious Crime Unit (WeSCU):*
Detective Chief Superintendent Sophie Allen
Detective Inspector Barry Marsh (Dorset)
Detective Sergeant Rae Gregson (Dorset)
Detective Constable Tommy Carter (Dorset)
Detective Constable Jackie Spring (a trainee detective on loan from Somerset)
Detective Sergeant Stevie Harrison (Wiltshire)

*Dorset Police Officers:*
Sergeant Rose Simons
Constable George Warrander
Sergeant Greg Buller (Fast Response Unit)

*Other Important Characters:*

At EcoFutures:
Nicky Dangerfield (Operations Manager)
Ian Duncan (Security Manager)
Robin Pryor (Head of the Parantos Coastal Development Unit)
Val Potter (Deputy Head of the Parantos Unit)
Bryony O'Neil (Office Manager of the Parantos Unit)
Justine Longford (Programmer in the Parantos Unit)

At the Parantos High Commission in London:
Carlos Martinez

In Whitehall:
Yauvani Anand (Home Secretary; YoYo to her close friends)

*To my good friend and fellow author Ruby Vitorino Moody*

# CHAPTER 1: CRASH

A dark and drizzly night. A lonely road, especially in these late hours, just before midnight. The tarmac surface wet and greasy, causing grip to be poor.

Was it usual for late May to have such poor weather as this? Or was it due to the vagaries of climate change? There were differing opinions. Bryony O'Neil remembered her grandfather telling her of the poor weather in early June 1944, an unexpected storm that had delayed the D-Day invasion of Normandy, and of the ensuing seasickness of the attacking troops, cooped up in their rolling ships for hours on end. Or had he mentioned days rather than hours?

Another flurry of rain hit the windscreen, causing the wiper blades to operate at double speed, squeaking their way across the glass. Maybe she should slow down. Driving near the speed limit was probably not the safest choice on a dark, stormy night like this, although she did know this road well, travelling along it this third Thursday evening every month to and from a Zumba session in Bridport. For many years she'd shared the journey with a friend, Mel Jones, but that had stopped when Mel and her husband had moved to Weymouth some two months earlier. None of the other Zumba members from Lyme Regis seemed to want to share the trip to Bridport and back with her. They were all older than her and a bit more conservative in their outlook. Maybe they disapproved of tattoos on a middle-aged woman, even though hers were small and tasteful. Well, the ones on public display, anyway.

A pale figure flashed by at the side of the road. Bryony blinked. She slammed on the brakes so hard that she came within a whisker of losing control of the car. She looked in her rearview mirror, trying to probe the darkness, her eyes wide in shock. Had she really seen that figure by the road, or had she somehow fallen asleep at the wheel and dreamt it into some kind of phantom existence? No, the person was still there, waving at her, but weakly. A distraught young woman, half-clothed, bedraggled and panic-stricken.

Bryony reversed the car, backing towards the solitary figure. She pressed the window button so the passenger-side window slid down. The girl lurched across. She was as dishevelled as Bryony had thought, her thin blouse torn and dirty, her short black hair looking grubby.

'Please help. Please,' she pleaded, leaning in the window. Her voice carried the trace of an accent. 'I've been attacked. But I got away. Can you get me away from here?'

Bryony could hear her trying to get the door open but failing to do so. The central locking was active, something that Bryony always engaged when she was alone in the car while travelling these quiet Dorset roads at night. She pressed the button that cancelled the system, allowing the fraught young woman to open the door and slide in. She turned to face Bryony.

'Thanks,' she gasped. 'Thanks so much.'

'Where to?' Bryony asked. 'The police? Hospital?'

The young woman seemed to have calmed down quickly, just in the space of a couple of seconds.

'Um, not sure.'

She seemed to be peering out into the gloom, but not in a particularly frightened way. Bryony, on the other hand, was feeling increasingly nervous. Something was wrong. She'd seen young women in the immediate aftermath of trauma before, but this one wasn't behaving at all as expected.

'Close the door,' she said to the woman.

Why wasn't she responding? She seemed to be holding the door open deliberately, peering back into the murk as if she was looking for something, or someone. Bryony was using the mirrors to glance behind, trying to spot anyone or anything approaching in the darkness.

'Close the door!' Bryony shouted. She'd just caught sight of a figure running towards them from the trees at the side of the road. It looked like a man, wielding something shiny in his hand.

'For God's sake, close it!' she screamed.

Still nothing. The girl was holding the door open deliberately. Bryony quickly swivelled and kicked her hard, forcing her half out of the door. She then engaged first gear and accelerated as fast as she could. By now the woman was out of the car, still trying to hold on to the door handle. The running figure behind had reached the rear door and was trying to grasp the handle but missed it by a fraction as the car shot forward. The young woman was pulled along a few yards, her feet trying to keep purchase with the road surface. Bryony wrenched the steering wheel hard, causing the car to veer sharply one way then the other. The man fell back and, finally, the woman let go of the door and dropped to the road surface. Bryony stopped the car some twenty yards away and glanced in the mirror. The man was helping the woman up.

'What the fuck held you up?' the woman screamed at him, her accent stronger this time. Bryony heard the revealing words clearly through the still open door.

She leaned across and pulled the door closed. All her limbs were shaking but she didn't intend to hang around here. They'd surely have a car of their own hidden somewhere nearby. She re-engaged the door and window locking systems then moved off quickly, glancing into the rearview mirror.

She was driving too fast, she knew it. Taking corners at a much greater rate than normal. Even so, it was only a few minutes before she caught sight of a set of headlights in the rearview mirror. They were catching up rapidly, even though she was over the speed limit herself. It must be them, that couple of weirdos. Why were they after her?

She approached the junction with the main road far too fast, leaving it as late as possible to brake. Luckily the road was devoid of traffic at that point, so she slewed around the corner with her wheels skidding. The pursuing car was almost on her. What would they try to do? Why were they so intent on catching her?

A slow-moving lorry loomed up in front of her, its red rear lights twinkling in the darkness. She pulled out to overtake and was halfway past when a vehicle appeared, coming in the opposite direction. She shot past with a split second to spare, lurching back onto her side of the road. But she hit a particularly wet patch and started to skid. Her car pirouetted into several terrifying spins before finally sliding off the road. It skidded across a grass verge before ploughing into a row of bushes. Bryony was vaguely aware of a bang as the airbag inflated, then everything went black.

# CHAPTER 2: BREAK-IN

*A week later*

Justine Longford shook her umbrella one last time before stepping inside the door of the flat she rented. She'd already given it a good shake downstairs in the main porch area before climbing the stairs, but Justine had an aversion to droplets of moisture on her floors, or anywhere else, come to that. She entered the bathroom, expanded the umbrella and placed it in the bath to dry off, intending to put it away later. She returned to the hall and hung her summer raincoat on its usual end hook on the rack. Only she couldn't. That hook was already occupied by her Hobbs black leather biker jacket, her all-time pride and joy. She popped the mac onto the next available peg and walked towards the kitchen, then stopped. Strange. She always kept the leather jacket on the second peg, not the first. She walked back to check the arrangement of her coats. It was just as she'd observed. Her jacket was in the wrong place. She frowned, then continued to the kitchen to make herself a mug of tea. Once she was ensconced in her favourite chair, sipping the hot drink, she wondered about the strange mix-up. She must have got the coat and jacket muddled this morning before she left, maybe in a moment of confusion over what the weather would be like. Not that she could remember such a slip-up happening. The weather forecast had always been perfectly clear. Today was to be a wet one. A day for raincoats and umbrellas. She'd even considered wearing knee boots, but that would have been a step too far for late May. She'd finally decided on dark trousers and ankle boots the evening before, when she'd watched the forecast on TV, given by a solemn-faced presenter who obviously felt personally responsible for the deluge that would ruin the day for so many holidaymakers here on the west Dorset coast.

Justine sighed and took another sip of tea. Maybe she had a poltergeist in the house. That crazy thought occurred a few seconds before she glanced at the vase of flowers on the low table set against the wall, a bouquet sent to her the previous week, on her birthday. It had come from Adam Yeoman, an ex-boyfriend who still pursued her relentlessly despite the numerous brush-offs. She'd topped up the vase that morning before setting off for work. Now it was half empty. She walked across to the vase, looking at the surface of the low table. Everything else seemed in order.

She crouched down and slid her hand across the surface of the carpet. Decidedly damp. Yet the vase showed no sign of a crack and was perfectly dry on its underside. What was going on? She felt the hairs on the back of her neck bristle. Something was badly wrong, she could feel it in her bones and in her racing heart. It was almost as if there was a slight fracture in her own personal universe, something menacing lurking just out of sight, just out of hearing, just beyond the range of her perceptions. A discord. A vague sense of unexpected unease that she'd never felt before.

Justine quietly slid into the kitchen and grabbed a carving knife from the cutlery drawer before peeking in the two bedrooms. No lurking, threatening shape in either of them. She even opened each cupboard, knife in hand, ready to stab it into the chest of any figure skulking in the shadows, but, to her intense relief, no shadowy figure was hiding in any dark corner.

She looked in her clothes drawers. They seemed untidier than usual. Had someone been through her clothes? The bottom drawer, the one that held her lingerie, caught her attention. Her best silk camisole, a present from her favourite great aunt, looked ruffled. Was it that creep of a maintenance officer cum cleaner, Billy Pitt? His eyes were all over her when she occasionally passed him in the corridor or on the stairs while he was doing his once a week clean. Eugh. She shuddered at the thought of him inside her flat, groping through her underwear. She'd always wondered if he'd retained copies of the keys to the flats, from the days when he worked for the builder who'd erected the small block of eight apartments. One of her elderly neighbours had voiced the self-same worry. What to do? If in doubt, call the police. That's what her parents had told her many years before. Better to be safe than sorry. She could exaggerate the vulnerable woman living alone aspect to ensure her concern was taken seriously. She phoned 999.

A young police officer, PC Kieran Mathieson, who visited later in the evening, was honest enough to admit that there was little he could do. There was no visible evidence of a break-in. Nothing had been damaged, nor had anything been stolen.

'Did you say you worked for a hi-tech company?' he said.

She nodded. 'Yes. EcoFutures. That's why I had to report it. We work in a very specialised area, though I'm a programmer, not a scientist. Even so, it's drilled into us to take stuff like this seriously. I'll have to report it at work tomorrow.'

'Okay. I'll log that. You ought to get the lock changed.'

'That's difficult. I'm only renting it while the owners are away. I just have this strange feeling that I'm being watched. I don't know why, though.'

'Well, keep that security chain engaged when you're at home. I'll log the incident.'

Kieran stayed just long enough to offer Justine some reassurance and the suggestion that she should reconsider her decision not to change the lock. Meanwhile, she was to be extra careful and remain vigilant. Justine could understand his position, and had half expected this response. She re-engaged the security chain. That should prevent anyone creeping into her flat during the night while she was asleep. Even so, her sleep was patchy that night. Shadowy figures slipping through insecure doorways haunted her dreams.

\* \* \*

Justine left for work the next morning feeling weary and tense. Her workplace, EcoFutures, offered high-level environmental modelling advice to businesses and governments across the world and were highly regarded for their expertise. Justine was no scientific expert, however. As she'd told the police officer the previous evening, her job was as a computer programmer, even though she worked in the international projects department. On arrival, she sought out one of her bosses and reported the events of the previous day. Better safe than sorry. She then headed for her desk and settled down to work. Her office colleagues were full of sympathy, though she didn't tell them of her suspicions as to possible culprits. After all, the two most likely suspects, Billy Pitt and Adam Yeoman, were local men, both fairly well known. She couldn't just go scattering names about, could she? It might well be one or the other of them, but not both. She'd be destroying social reputations if she gossiped about them. And maybe it was someone else entirely.

Late morning, Justine made a quick call to the company's security manager. His response surprised her. Could she pop into his office for a word? The phrase *pop in* was, of course, a misnomer. It was a summons, plain and simple. She called into the loo and checked her hair, then made her way to Ian Duncan's office. She'd only been inside once before, when she first joined the company three years before. Every new employee was summoned to his office for a short security lecture and given a leaflet of the protocols to be followed. It hadn't been the most pleasant of experiences. Ian was a taciturn man, not given to small talk. She'd made a joke about selling secrets on the industrial espionage market and he'd just stared at her as if she was from an alien species. She could still remember the feeling of wishing the floor would open up and swallow her.

On this occasion he seemed pleasant enough, though he was looking serious. He offered her a coffee, which she gratefully accepted before settling into the chair in front of his desk.

'Tell me about this incident,' he said. He still hadn't smiled. Did he still remember her faux pas from three years earlier?

She launched into a recap of both her suspicions that her flat had had an unwelcome visitor and her visit from the police constable. Ian Duncan seemed satisfied with what she said.

'Is there something I'm not aware of?' Justine asked. She'd never expected her work superiors to take the incident this seriously, but there was no doubt that this particular boss did.

'Well, I can't go into details. But there have been one or two other odd incidents involving staff. You did well to report it so quickly.'

It was Justine's turn to frown. 'Are we being targeted in some way?'

He shrugged. 'I wouldn't have thought so, but we can't allow a whisper to get out. That's why I needed to speak to you. Don't mention it outside these walls. You know what we do. The company's future depends on how customers see our own reliability and security. We can't let our reputation be put at risk. We might start to lose clients.'

Justine was thinking hard, allowing her brain to cycle through recent gossip about incidents involving her work colleagues. But nothing. Then it was as if a light flashed on in her mind.

'Not Bryony O'Neil?' she gasped.

The man's face said it all.

'Oh, goodness. And she's still in hospital, isn't she? But I thought it was just a normal accident. There was more to it?'

Ian shrugged. 'I can't say.'

'You must be worried. Is someone targeting us?'

'Unlikely, as I said earlier. But we can't afford to lose contracts, so let's not speculate. Or gossip. And you say you've already reported it to the police and had a visit?'

She nodded but his expression was hard to read.

'Keep me posted if they decide to follow it up further.'

'Is that likely?'

He shrugged. 'I can't say.' And with that, his attention returned to the documents on his desk.

Justine stood up and left.

\* \* \*

It was late in the afternoon when Justine received a phone call from the front desk, informing her that two detectives had arrived to see her. Could she collect them from reception and take them to a small meeting room?

She felt apprehensive, and for several reasons. She'd never been interviewed by detectives before. In fact, she'd only had close contact with a police officer on one previous occasion, as a sixteen-year-old when she'd managed to get herself drunk and had collapsed on a street corner with two friends, both of whom were in a similar state. She'd been ferried home by the young male officer and had felt so mortified the next day that she'd sent him a thank-you card, vowing never to repeat the experience. The other reason for her worry was caused by the feeling of now inhabiting a different world to the one that existed before yesterday. The natural assumption of safety and security had gone. Some shadowy person had been inside her home and had fingered their way through her clothes. What else had they looked at? Her report of the break-in had obviously triggered alarm bells, what with the meeting with Ian Duncan earlier and now this.

Two smartly dressed women were waiting in reception, police lanyards around their necks. One was middle-aged, with long, curly light-brown hair that was beginning to show flecks of grey, the other probably in her late twenties or early thirties. They stood up as she walked towards them. It was the younger one, tall and dark-haired, who stepped forward, hand outstretched. She had a firm grip.

'Detective Sergeant Rae Gregson. This is my colleague, Detective Constable Jackie Spring. I'm with Dorset Police. Jackie is from the Somerset force. We're both seconded to WeSCU, the Wessex serious crime unit. Is there somewhere we can go?'

Justine nodded and indicated an open door. 'In here. It's a meeting room.'

They followed her inside and closed the door. They sat at one end of the central table. Justine poured water for them. She felt dry-throated even if they didn't. It must be nerves.

'This shouldn't take long, Justine. Is it okay if I call you Justine? We can be more formal if you prefer.' Her voice was warm and slightly deep, her attitude business-like but friendly.

'Justine's fine,' she answered, taking a sip from her glass.

'This seems a nice place. Do you like working here?'

'Yes. I've been here for about three years. I had a couple of ropey jobs before then, but this one's the best so far.'

'How do you get on with the other staff? Are your colleagues good?'

Justine nodded, relaxing into her seat. 'We get on pretty well.'

'A positive and supportive atmosphere then?'

'Yes. But we're expected to put the effort in.'

'But with a focus on security? I don't just mean the nature of the work the company does, but the procedures you all follow.'

'Yes. We have a monthly staff meeting and that always gets emphasised.'

'You must be a bit puzzled why we're here,' the sergeant went on. She didn't elaborate.

'A bit, I suppose. But I wondered if there was a link to something that happened last week, to someone else from here. Bryony. She's still in hospital, I heard.'

'She's due out in a week or so if things go well, but will need some recuperation time. But someone tried to break in to her place a few days ago. They didn't succeed, luckily. She's now under protection. Can you see why we were concerned when your break-in came to our attention?'

Justine shivered. 'Why? What's going on?'

'We don't know. Nor do your bosses. But we need to follow it up.' The sergeant glanced at the older detective, the constable. She had a soft smile and attractive freckles. What was her name? Jackie? She took over the questioning.

'I have a few questions to ask you, Justine. We've seen the report that was filed by Kieran, the PC who visited you. But we need to take things a bit deeper, now it's possible the motives were not what they seemed.'

'So you think it was linked? My break-in and the incident with Bryony?'

'We don't know. You work in the same department?'

Justine nodded. 'She's the office manager. We were all surprised when we heard she was in a high-speed car crash. We thought, that's not like her. I was in her car a couple of times. She never drove too fast.'

'That's useful to know.' Jackie jotted a few words down in her notebook. 'Now, let's get back to the break-in at your flat. You gave two names to Kieran. Adam Yeoman and Billy Pitt. Why?'

Justine sighed. 'Adam has been chasing me non-stop for months. He just won't take no for an answer. It sometimes makes me frantic. I went out with him a few times a few months ago, but we just didn't click. Well, that's what I felt. He obviously felt differently. He just won't leave me alone. Sends me flowers and chocolates. He's never been nasty, though. It just gets a bit much.'

Jackie nodded. 'I know the feeling. Attractive single woman. Target for all kinds of stuff. What about the other man?'

Justine managed to stop herself from shuddering openly. 'Billy Pitt. He's the cleaner at the flats. Well, his official title is Maintenance Officer. I don't know what maintenance he does. As far as I can see, he just does the cleaning in the corridors and on the stairs. And not very well. Some of us have been trying to get him replaced.'

Jackie seemed to be studying some notes. 'He was part of the building team that put the flats up?'

'That's what we've been told. He gives me the creeps. It was something I couldn't really explain to your constable, Kieran. He's got a leer, Billy Pitt. It's how he looks at me. It gives me the shudders. The thing is, I've heard that when my landlords first moved in about ten years ago, they were only given a single key to the flat. They had to make a second copy themselves. That's not right, is it? All locks come with two keys, don't they? When they complained, Billy Pitt just shrugged it off and sidled away. That's what I heard. So my question is, what happened to that other key? Did he just keep it? He's always denied it, but he would, wouldn't he?'

'Is it your flat now or do you rent it?'

'I'm renting it. The owners are abroad for two years. I'm about halfway through. They're friends of my parents. It's a good deal from my point of view and they get someone to look after the place while they're away. I'm trying to save for a deposit and buy a place of my own. It's hard though.'

Jackie gave her a sympathetic look. 'Don't I know it!' She glanced at her notes. 'About Bryony. Do you know her well?'

'Not really. She's the overall office manager for the work group I'm with at the moment. That means she's in charge of all the admin. She's a bit of a stickler. I'm not complaining about that, though. I think it's right to have some clear boundaries. We all know where we are then. I like her but we don't socialise except at work events. She's quite a bit older than me, anyway.'

'What about office relations in general?'

Justine didn't seem fazed by this question. 'Pretty good, I'd say. I suppose that's why I'm still here. There was an undercurrent of nastiness in one of my previous places. It's fine here, though. Maybe that's down to our group manager, Robin. He's very efficient and really nice. People respect him. We're an odd mix, really. We all have a role to play and we're the experts in our particular specialism. I'm the group programmer.'

'What about your feelings for the company as a whole? Is it a good place to work?'

Justine shrugged, but in a positive way. 'Yeah. I haven't come across much animosity. They're good to work for. I think most of us feel valued. That makes a difference, doesn't it?'

'I'd agree with you on that, I guess. Have you ever picked up on negative feelings from anyone?'

'No. Not enough to target the company in this way, if you think that's the case and we are being got at. Why do it like this? What would be the point?' She shook her head. 'I just don't see it.'

The detective slipped a card across the tabletop. 'Get in touch if anything does occur to you.'

* * *

Rae led the way back to the car. 'What do you think?'

Jackie frowned and pursed her lips. 'Justine came across as a pleasant enough person. I don't think she's a fantasist, so I'd take her story of a break-in on trust. And she comes across as a pretty honest person. Ian Duncan's a worried man, no doubt about it. I think I'd feel the same way in his position. But I just had the feeling that he wasn't telling us everything. I wonder if he's got one or two suspicions but he's not willing to share them just yet.'

Rae smiled at her. 'Well spotted. We all thought you had the makings of a good detective, Jackie.'

'So have I passed the test?'

'Early days yet. So far so good, though. That's all I'm willing to say.'

'You cruel woman, you.'

This time Rae guffawed. 'Well spotted again. On both counts.'

14

## CHAPTER 3: LOOKING FOR LINKS

Barry Marsh listened closely to Rae and Jackie as they summarised their morning in Lyme. He was frowning, but that wasn't unusual for Barry, particularly given the current situation within WeSCU, with its charismatic commander laid up in hospital for the foreseeable future. Added to which, Polly Nelson, the unit's second in command, was heavily involved in a joint initiative between the Somerset and Bristol police forces in an attempt to take down a particularly vicious organised-crime group. She'd be unavailable for the next month at least. So, here he was, Barry Marsh, acting chief inspector, and running the region's top murder squad. Though there was no murder to investigate — not at the moment, anyway. Dorset seemed eerily quiet on that front, thank goodness. It meant that they could ease Jackie Spring, their newest recruit, into the somewhat quirky ways in which they worked while the pressure was off. Not that she needed much training. Jackie was a natural. They'd spotted that during their previous big case, one located in her hometown of Watchet in Somerset, where she'd been a special constable. Jackie had jumped at the chance of leaving her increasingly insecure part-time job in the town library in order to become a full-time police officer, in training to become a detective. Her past experience had stood her in good stead, and she'd demonstrated what an asset she might prove to be during that recent investigation.

Barry explained his thoughts. 'I wonder if something odd's going on. It's like a join-the-dots puzzle. Peculiar things happening here and there. Nothing looks particularly serious when the events are taken individually. But together? It could be a different story.'

'I can see that, boss. But the thing is, are they definitely connected? We don't know that, not for sure. We could go and ring a lot of alarm bells on high, get allocated a lot more resources, then end up with egg on our faces if it all turns out to be sheer coincidence. A push like that wouldn't work, anyway. The chief super has always said that if it isn't one hundred per cent watertight, it won't get past the powers that be. They scrutinise everything for cost-efficiency factors, don't they?'

By now even Rae was frowning. 'Is it just the four of us until something more definite turns up?'

'Afraid so. Polly said she might try to get down here in a couple of days if we need her input. At the moment I'm sure we can cope, particularly if I can call on Rose and George if we need them.'

Barry glanced across the table at Tommy Carter, the unit's junior officer until Jackie Spring appeared as a trainee. 'Anything to add, Tommy?'

'How many incidents do we actually have at the moment?' he asked.

'The two odd ones — the O'Neil woman's car crash and now this break-in at the other woman's home, even though nothing was taken. Both of them are staff at EcoFutures in Axminster, which is a bit worrying. Then there's that strange report from the neighbouring premises, Hewton Distribution, that might or might not be connected. Finally, there's this missing man we've only just learned about, the one who's a keen rambler. What's his name? Robin Pryor? He works at EcoFutures too. Could it all be linked? We don't know.'

'It all seems a bit much to be mere coincidence,' Rae said. 'Those three all work in the same department, not just the same company.'

'I don't know the details of that last one,' Jackie said. 'I'm new around here, remember.'

'We don't either,' Barry explained. 'It got reported by Hewton's security manager after someone was seen acting suspiciously outside the premises. One of their employees claimed they saw a couple of people in a car with binoculars and a camera. It looked as though they were keeping a watch on something. By the time a local squad car arrived, they'd gone. I only heard because Rose Simons is chummy with the local sergeant, and they gossip together occasionally. Rose was intrigued by it. The original assumption was that they were monitoring Hewton's place, for some reason. But it distributes reconditioned health equipment around the region. Nothing hi-tech. A bit odd, Rose thought. When she heard about the stuff involving the EcoFutures staff, she thought it might be connected. She phoned me about it just now, while you were out.'

'Should we check into the background?' Rae asked. 'On the quiet, of course? Tommy could do it. It might only take a couple of hours.'

Barry thought for a few moments. He was aware that his long-term boss, Sophie Allen, would sometimes decide to follow up seemingly pointless distractions only to find that they turned up trumps. 'It needs to be done. Let me think about how best to go about it.'

'What about this missing man?' Jackie asked.

Barry explained. 'Again, we know next to nothing. Apparently, Robin Pryor is a keen rambler who went missing at the weekend. He lives in Lyme. He's single and lives by himself. No one knows where he is. Someone who might be him was seen setting off west along the coast path last Saturday but that's all we know. The local cops are dealing with it too, and aren't making much progress according to my contact.

Pryor's a project manager at EcoFutures. You see why we're concerned?'

'Did that come via Rose Simons too?' Rae asked.

Barry nodded. 'I sanctioned a mobile phone trace, but nothing detailed so far. The last ping was Saturday morning leaving Lyme and heading west. Rose said it corresponded to Pryor reaching the start of the coast path. She's been really helpful with background stuff.'

Rae laughed. 'She's a one, isn't she? Knows all the gossip across Dorset Police, as far as I can tell. She's a one-woman intelligence unit.'

Barry's frown deepened. 'But she's another one who turns up trumps. Good judgement.'

'Oh, I know. Her and George. What is it they call themselves? The cream of the county?'

Barry's mood seemed to lighten. 'Rose does. I've never heard George refer to them that way. He's much too polite.'

'And still in a seriously dangerous relationship,' Rae said. She turned to Jackie. 'He's dating the chief super's daughter. Maybe dating is an understatement.'

Barry looked around at his team members. 'The point is, everyone, until we get more evidence from other people, we can't tell whether there's a link or not. And even if there is a link, we have no idea what it is. A lot of other detectives would just walk away from it and get stuck into something a bit more mainstream.'

'Like the DCI, you mean?' Jackie said. 'And she's our overall boss at the mo, isn't she, what with the chief super still in hospital. I got to know Polly quite well when she was in Watchet on that case. She thinks in a different way to you. Don't take it as a criticism, by the way. I like quirkiness. She's a bit more coldly logical.'

Barry felt even more unhappy, if such a thing was possible. Should he allow a junior officer to get away with making comments like that about a senior colleague?

Jackie must have spotted his unease. 'Sorry, sir. That didn't come out the way I meant it. She was like a breath of fresh air compared to the bosses I was used to. They were plodders in comparison.' She paused and held her hands to her face. 'I didn't quite mean that either, not the way it sounded. I'm just going to shut up before you find an excuse to sack me.'

Rae grinned before returning to the main point of the meeting. 'When you put everything together like that, boss, it's logical to look for a connection. It's a shame we didn't know about Pryor before. We could have asked about him while we were at EcoFutures this morning. As it is, we'll have to pay another visit, surely. He's a misper. Or is it still unofficial? Hasn't he been reported as missing by a family member yet?'

'No. It only surfaced a couple of hours ago. It takes time to gather all the info on a misper, as we all well know. And the report suggests he lives by himself.' Barry felt annoyed but tried not to show it. 'Maybe you and I should pay them a visit, Rae. We need to see what they think of all this stuff. Tommy and Jackie could make a visit to this Hewton place tomorrow morning. We need to find out the facts about this supposed shadowy surveillance that might or might not have happened.' He felt somewhat happier now a plan was beginning to form. 'Then the two of you visit where the missing man, Robin Pryor, lives. Talk to the neighbours. Find out about his family background. Talk to them too. You'll need to liaise with whoever's dealing with it from the local squad. Rae and I can visit Bryony O'Neil to see what she has to say. Then we can meet back here for a roundup tomorrow afternoon. It goes without saying that we need to tread delicately. I don't want the local cops upset in any way. We'll be going over some of the same ground they'll have covered. Be thoughtful.'

One of the reasons Barry was worried was because of an item of information he'd been told about a single possible sighting of the missing man, Robin Pryor, on the morning of his likely disappearance. A fellow Lyme resident had spotted someone of his description heading up the steps from Monmouth Beach, the start of the stretch of coast path at the western edge of Lyme. It was a notorious six-mile section of track heading towards the River Axe in Devon, crawling through dense undergrowth that was more like a jungle than the open walking that was common in Dorset. The whole section was formed by a series of gigantic landslips that had occurred in the distant past and had left the walking surface extremely uneven. Notices at either end of the track warned ramblers of the difficulties ahead, with no side paths that could be used to escape from the dingy and claustrophobic atmosphere. One of the most reliable walking maps of the region described it as arduous. Quite simply, people could get lost in its densely wooded interior if they strayed from the path. They might then struggle to find a way out of its tortuous undergrowth.

It would be a nightmare if he was forced to organise a search of the area. He'd once walked it with Gwen, expecting that the seven miles could easily be completed in a morning. They'd finally stumbled into Seaton, at the Devon end, in mid-afternoon, tired, hungry and feeling slightly disorientated. He really didn't want to pay the place another visit if he could help it. If it came to it, he'd offload that particular task onto the other squad members. Rae always seemed up for a ramble in the countryside. She'd probably volunteer like a shot.

Rae phoned EcoFutures and made an appointment for them the next morning. Two managers would be present at the meeting. Ian Duncan, the security manager, who Rae had briefly met earlier in the day, and Nicky Dangerfield, the operations manager. At the same time Tommy and Jackie would be visiting Hewton Distribution. It seemed rather too much of a coincidence that neighbouring premises had experienced unusual incidents, although, of course, the nature of the two events were entirely different. It needed checking, though.

# CHAPTER 4: LOYALTY

The EcoFutures complex had impressive security measures, something Barry hadn't expected, although he was unsure why. He came to the conclusion that he'd always connected ecology with slightly hippy individuals who wore faded denim or corduroy dungarees and had untidy hair. He realised that this was just a part of his inbuilt prejudices. He remembered that a local environmental enthusiast had plagued his parents farm when he was a youngster, urging them to take up a more ecological style of farming. Barry remembered his father becoming angry, saying that of course he'd like to farm in a more environmentally friendly way but that he couldn't make a complete switch in a single year. It would require several years of careful planning. After all, he had a living to make and a farm to keep in profit. That particular amateur ecologist had stormed off, clearly angry, his faded denim dungarees flapping in the breeze.

As far as Barry could see, no one on site at EcoFutures was wearing denim of any kind. The security staff were in dark uniforms and everyone else was either clad in smart-casual clothes or office-wear. although, in many cases, these were protected by pristine lab coats.

The first person to appear to greet them was a middle-aged woman, who was waiting at reception when the two detectives signed in. She walked purposefully towards them, hand outstretched. She was wearing a black business suit, an emerald-green blouse and matching green low-heeled court shoes. Barry could sense Rae's eyes focussed closely on the woman.

'Nicky Dangerfield, operations manager,' the woman said. 'You must be DI Marsh?'

Barry nodded in reply. 'Barry. And this is DS Rae Gregson.'

'Come into my office. We can have coffee, if you'd like some. It's a morning necessity for me, I'm afraid.'

They settled into comfortable chairs and Barry took a sip of coffee. It was good, something that Sophie Allen would approve of. They were soon joined by Ian Duncan, the security manager. Barry watched carefully as Rae explained the reason for this particular visit, one with a senior officer involved. She mentioned the series of worrying occurrences involving EcoFutures staff and the strange report of the possible monitoring of the neighbouring premises, reported to the local police. Barry watched carefully as Nicky responded to Rae's words. There was something vaguely familiar about the woman, but where might he have met her before? He forced himself to focus on the matter in hand. Rae had just mentioned the report from the neighbouring premises.

'Whoever it was, they didn't hang around long,' she explained. 'A local team made a brief visit to check but they'd gone. There were no signs of someone trying to gain entry. The security manager at Hewton wonders if they could have been thieves on the lookout for stuff that could be sold on easily. But Hewton don't have anything like that on site. They recondition health-based equipment and furniture for distribution across the NHS. There's always a possibility that the guy was mistaken in what he claimed he saw. But it's possible he was right and that it was your place being watched.'

Ian was leaning forward, frowning. 'So it could fit with our own incidents? Is that what you're saying? It could be part of the same pattern?'

Barry took over, picking his words carefully. He didn't want to worry these people unnecessarily.

'We'll make a judgement on that when we see the outcome of our colleagues' visit there. And, of course, we'll let you know immediately if we think it is connected. Meanwhile, Rae and I need to find out more about your own background here. The bigger picture helps. Rae has some questions to help us get a feel for the context.'

He glanced across at Rae. She was looking at him with a slight smile on her lips. She obviously thought that well-rehearsed set of phrases had worked well.

'What exactly do you do here?' Rae asked.

'We research and design advanced ecological developments and monitoring systems. It's all very hi-tech.'

'Is it very cut-throat, this area of work? Is it possible that you have competitors trying to find out what you're doing?'

Nicky looked at Rae carefully before replying. 'It's something we're always aware of. Our production side develops high-end bespoke equipment. It isn't cheap and our systems are very costly to develop. We don't have any direct competitors in the UK, not that we know of, but there are foreign alternatives to our stuff. Some of it's a bit ropey, some is pretty good. We think we're the best. So do many of our customers.'

'So you could be a possible target for industrial espionage?' Barry broke in. 'You said *our production side* as if there's some other side to your operations. Is there more?'

'Yes. In fact, it's become the larger of the two divisions. We offer tailor-made ecological modelling to all kinds of organisations, including government departments, both here and abroad.'

Barry was puzzled. 'What does it involve?'

Nicky took a sip of coffee and sat back in her chair. 'I can only give you generalities because much of it is sensitive. We look at possible ecological outcomes of developments and building projects. We do it by modelling various scenarios. Then we either suggest modifications to the plans to minimise environmental impact or suggest changes that will be positive to local eco-systems. It's a growth area. The UN encourages developing nations to follow good eco-practice by thinking more environmentally. We offer that service to our clients. They don't always have local expertise to draw on.'

Barry felt his stomach tighten. Here was something. Some of the work was clearly sensitive, as Nicky had described. Surely that meant *secret* in everyday parlance? And where there were secrets, there were bound to be opportunities for unscrupulous people to make a fast buck. He looked at Rae. She was looking back, and momentarily widened her eyes. Her thoughts were in tune with his.

'What projects are you working on at the moment?' he asked. 'Anything contentious?'

Nicky shook her head. 'I can't really talk about them, for obvious reasons. But I don't think any should generate problems.' She paused. 'Look, if some evidence arises that tells me I'm wrong in that judgement, we'll act on it quickly. But we're in the ecology business. Our aim is to improve things for local people and the local environment. I really can't see how it would link to what I think you might be suggesting.'

Barry looked at her grimly. 'Because the real world has criminal thugs in it. Believe me, they don't give a toss for either local people or the local environment. They follow a completely different set of rules.'

Rae broke in. 'You've got a missing worker, Robin Pryor. What can you tell us about him? His role? What he's working on?'

Nicky was looking at Rae. 'We weren't worried until yesterday, after your short visit to see Justine. Reception staff alerted me to it. I was sufficiently concerned to pay Ian a visit. We did a staff check, looking for other oddities, and Robin's absence cropped up. He goes off on trekking breaks. It's his favourite pastime. He was probably on one at the weekend and, with the bad weather in the Lake District, he's possibly had to hole up somewhere. It's happened before and it'll happen again, I expect.'

'What's his role here?'

'Development. He's a project manager.' There was an edge to her voice.

'Did he ever talk of family? Friends? Favourite places that might be possible boltholes?'

'Not much. He wasn't married and I don't think he was in any long-term relationship. His parents live in the north-east of the county, in Blandford Forum. He grew up there, as I recall. I think he has one or two friends still there, but I can't be sure.'

'And if he isn't in the Lake District? Does he have anywhere more local he likes to walk at weekends?'

'He's a keen birdwatcher. He likes the undercliff area, west of Lyme Regis.'

'What's he currently working on here?' Barry could sense that Nicky was worried.

She glanced across at Ian, the security chief, as if checking for his opinion on opening up a little, but he was looking at the tabletop. Her gaze returned to Barry.

'A coastal development for the government of Parantos. It's a Commonwealth country in South America. But it shouldn't be a problem in any way.'

Rae broke in again. 'What about Bryony O'Neil and Justine Longford? They have a work connection, don't they?'

There was a tense pause. 'Justine is the programmer assigned to Robin's group. Bryony is the group's admin manager.'

A short silence fell on the room, finally broken by Barry.

'And you didn't twig?'

Nicky shook her head. 'No, because everything only came together late yesterday, when it became obvious that Robin was nowhere to be found. Bryony's incident was last week. Justine's, just the day before yesterday. Your detectives who called yesterday mentioned the possibility of a connection but that was before we were so concerned about Robin. It's not something that would cross our minds. You may think we're naïve but as police officers you inhabit a world of criminality.

We don't. We're ecologists, for God's sake. We just don't think along those lines. Ian realised late yesterday and came to see me with his concern. If you hadn't phoned to fix this meeting, we'd have called you.'

Barry thought she looked extremely troubled. It was as if a cloud had passed over her eyes. They finished the meeting at that point and walked into the corridor. By the time they were halfway across the spacious reception area, a little of Nicky's previously positive manner had returned. Outwardly, at least.

'We need to check up on what our colleagues have discovered. We have another visit to make. But we'll be back in touch very soon,' Barry said.

Nicky faced him as they shook hands again. 'You don't remember me, do you?' she said.

In fact, Barry had been thinking hard throughout their conversation as to why she seemed vaguely familiar, but he'd got nowhere. 'In a way, I do. But I can't remember the details of where we've met before.'

Nicky smiled. 'We were at primary school together. I was Nicky Turner back then. My family moved away before our class moved up to secondary school. I hope you don't mind me saying, but I recognised you from your hair.'

'And my name hasn't changed, which gives you an advantage,' Barry said. He was trying desperately to remember what she'd looked like back then, but there were just too many school memories to trawl through. 'How did you get into this line of work?'

'I did a degree in environmental science. I was always interested in wildlife, even in my younger years in Swanage. I ran the university ecology group when I was at Exeter and then got a job here when it was just a fledgling concern. I've never looked back. I love it.'

'Well, good for you.' He gave her a polite smile.

The two detectives remained silent until they were in their car.

'They're worried, and I'm not surprised,' Rae said.

26

Barry's thoughts were following similar lines. 'Were they being totally honest, though? It's possible that they didn't realise what was going on until late yesterday, as they claimed. But isn't it the job of a security chief to be on top of these things? The thing is, Rae, there's a narrative here that makes that claim seem plausible. They were very convincing. But there might have been other odd incidents happening that they haven't told us about, stuff that might throw a different slant on things.'

It was time to move on to their second visit, to interview Bryony O'Neil, the car accident victim. While Rae drove to the hospital, Barry called Greg Buller in order to set the ball rolling for a detailed search of the jungle-like undercliff area west of Lyme. Six miles of densely tangled undergrowth to search, looking for traces of the missing Robin Pryor.

'It won't be as easy to get organised as you think, Barry,' came the reply. 'Dorset's county boundary lies just on the west side of Lyme Regis. That area you want searched? It's all in Devon. We'll have to liaise with them. Leave it with me.'

Barry felt like swearing in frustration. Yet another hurdle erected in his path. His irritation must have been obvious.

'Problems, boss?' Rae asked.

'That area we need to search. It's all in bloody Devon. I thought the county boundary was the line of the River Axe, along at the end of the search zone. Greg corrected my ignorance. I feel a bit stupid.'

She laughed. 'You're no fool, boss. We all know it. You're just feeling the pressure of the absent ones, that's my guess.'

'The absent ones?' Barry was puzzled.

'The chief super and Polly. Without them here, you'll be feeling it all rests on you.'

'You're a real psychologist substitute, aren't you?' He paused. 'But you may be right. I hadn't really thought about it that way.'

'If you need to offload, you can trust me, boss. I owe you and the chief super everything. I'll never let you down. I know I've said it before, but now seems a good time to remind you.'

She reached across and momentarily patted his arm. Barry smiled but remained silent. He was still trying to spot if a connection might exist between these varied occurrences. Or were they just odd coincidences?

## CHAPTER 5: WEAK SPOT

In Jackie Spring's eyes, Tommy Carter came across as a slightly bemused individual, half a step out of alignment with the real world. He seemed to be a quiet and diffident young man, something rare in Jackie's experience, and even rarer in her assessment of male police officers. He rarely spoke up when the WeSCU members were gathered around a table or incident board, discussing a case. Yet he was clearly valued, and his opinion deliberately sought out. She'd never had the opportunity to work closely with him before, and Barry's decision to put the two most junior team members together for the day had come as a surprise. Unless, of course, the action was part of a deliberate plan of assessment of her capabilities, as the unit's newest recruit, still on probation. They'd then be able to ask for feedback from everybody, helping Polly and Barry to make a decision about her long-term future. Yes, that would be it. Time to be careful, Jackie, she told herself. Steer clear of those aggressive confrontations with people who'd upset her, even if the culprits did deserve it.

They were on their way to interview the security chief at Hewton Distribution to find out the details of the recent incident, the report that someone was carrying out an observation of either Hewton or EcoFutures. Could it just be down to someone's over-active imagination? Part two of their morning would be a visit to the neighbours of the missing man from EcoFutures, Robin Pryor.

'Have you been with the team long?' she asked Tommy as he steered the car out onto the main road heading west.

'A couple of years. I'm the unit dogsbody, I guess. But I don't mind. It's a lot better than my first placement, with Weymouth CID. For some reason the chief super picked me to help the unit out with local information when they were there to investigate two murders. I liked what I was doing, so when I heard that a vacancy had opened up, I applied. I didn't think I stood a chance, so I was surprised when she took me on. I was on probation, just like you are now. It's worked out so well, though. I'm always worried I'm not up to it, but Rae tells me I ought to have a bit more confidence in my abilities.' He paused. 'The two of them saved my life last year, Rae and Barry, the DI. I was unconscious in a ditch, knocked off my bike by a speeding car. They were worried and came looking for me, the two of them. I'd have died of exposure if they hadn't found me.'

This was something else that Jackie had picked up on, even though she wasn't aware of any details or reasons. She'd noted the emotional closeness of the Dorset-based members of WeSCU. Rae, Tommy, Barry and, of course, the overall boss, Sophie Allen. And the other Dorset detective she'd seen at the hospital. What was her name? Lydia? She acted as if she was one of them too, even though she wasn't in WeSCU. Interesting. So where did Polly Nelson fit into all this? She was WeSCU's official second in command, but Jackie had sometimes sensed a possible disconnect between her and the others. All this life and death stuff might explain it. But then, Ade Ahmed, the other Somerset-based detective in WeSCU, seemed to fit in well. Maybe it was also a question of person-ality types. Polly Nelson could be prickly. Jackie sighed. It was all a bit complex.

'Something wrong?' Tommy asked.

'Not really. I suppose it's because I'm joining a unit that's fairly new. So, as well as me getting used to the way it all works, you're all still getting used to each other. Although you seem quite relaxed, Tommy.'

He shrugged and pulled a face. 'I may look as if I'm a bit distant, but it isn't true. Underneath, I'm a bit of a worrier. We're not really new to each other though. The Dorset lot have worked together for a few years now. And Barry and the chief super have known Polly for some time, before WeSCU was formed. They were all involved on a big case in the Quantocks a couple of years ago, even Ade. Maybe that case was what gave the chief super the idea. We base ourselves in the county where the murder's happened and pull people in from the other counties as they're needed.' He paused. 'The thing is, things are tricky at the moment. With the chief super still being in hospital, I mean.'

Jackie frowned. 'That's what I mean. You'd think the DCI, Polly, would be down here taking charge. Where is she?'

Tommy shook his head. 'I don't know. But there hasn't been a murder, has there? Not as far as we know. Maybe that's the reason. I don't ask those types of questions, Jackie. I prefer to stay out of the politics.'

Jackie shrugged. 'Point taken. I just find everything a bit odd, to be honest. We're a murder squad who aren't investigating a murder, with the two most senior people not here. Have I done the right thing in joining WeSCU? That's what I ask myself.'

'Course you have. It's a great team, honestly. And you must have really impressed the bosses in that last case, in Watchet.'

'Luck, I expect. I still worry whether I'm cut out for this. Have I made a blunder? Maybe I'm just missing my home in Watchet. And my partner, Tony.' She looked out of the car window. 'This is us, isn't it? Is that the Hewton building ahead?'

Tommy steered the car into a visitor's parking space. The two detectives climbed out and made their way into reception.

The security chief, Glen Blackford, was waiting for them and led them to his office. 'You've come about that possible incident,' he said. 'But we're not really worried about it. We're not sure what they were up to, the culprits. A bit odd really.'

'What do you mean?' Tommy asked.

'Nothing's gone missing, and no damage was done.'

'Why did you decide to cancel the local police's visit, after calling it in?'

'There were no signs of an attempted break-in, and we've looked at the whole site thoroughly. No obvious damage. We're pretty secure here. Nothing left out and all buildings kept locked overnight. I just didn't want to waste your time.'

'So you didn't want it to be formally logged?' Tommy asked.

'I guess it was a matter of crossed wires,' Blackford replied. 'I just wanted the visit cancelled, but the receptionist who made the call thought we wanted to cancel our whole report about it. A mix-up, plain and simple.'

Jackie took over and changed track. 'Who spotted them?'

'One of our mechanics. He left work earlier than usual for a medical.'

'It would be useful to speak to him.'

'Okay. If you can wait a few minutes, I'll try to find him. Josh Benton. He's pretty reliable. Never given us any cause for concern.'

'Any CCTV?'

'It didn't pick much up. I've had a look at the footage from the only camera we have facing that way. There's a car parked there, out on the street, but no real details.'

'We'll take a copy. We've got access to tech forensics who might be able to get something from it.'

The man who'd spotted the suspect car arrived sooner than the two detectives expected. He was wiping his hands on a paper towel. Josh was in his late twenties and seemed an amiable sort of man. He was of middling height, had fair hair and looked at them steadily through his light-brown eyes.

'Hi. I'm Josh. You wanted to see me?'

'Good of you to give us a few moments,' Tommy said. 'Maybe we could go outside, and you could show us where this happened.'

'Of course.'

He led the way out to the front of the building, past the parked cars, through the open gate and stopped on the pavement.

'I was on foot,' he said. 'I wouldn't have spotted them if I'd been in a car.'

'Why were you walking, out of interest?'

'I'd arranged to get a lift to the hospital from my partner. She works just a few hundred yards down the road. We had an appointment at the antenatal clinic. After the appointment she dropped me off and then went straight home. The car I saw was gone by then.'

He walked a few yards and showed them where he'd spotted the vehicle.

'I couldn't understand what they were watching. I wondered if it might have been birds of some type but there were none in sight. And there was something a bit secretive about the way they were doing it. Sort of like you'd imagine a spy or undercover cop would. But they weren't very good, to be honest. They were looking that way.' He pointed to the neighbouring premises, EcoFutures.

'Could you describe them? And the car?' Jackie asked.

He frowned. 'I'll try. The car was a dark-coloured SUV of some type. A woman was behind the driving wheel, though the engine was off. She had short, dark hair. The guy was bearded. That's all I remember. We don't do anything at our place that's worth watching like that. But I've heard they do at that other place.'

Jackie finished making notes. 'That's helpful, Josh. Thanks.'

He went back inside, leaving the two detectives with Blackford, the security manager.

'Did you tell anyone at EcoFutures?' Tommy asked.

Blackford nodded. 'I had a message sent to their security chief.'

Tommy took several photos before they set off to their second point of call, the missing man's neighbours.

* * *

Robin Pryor lived in a house in a relatively new development situated on the north side of Lyme Regis. This gave easy access to the main road heading north to his workplace at EcoFutures in Axminster. Maybe a fifteen-minute drive, on average? Jackie didn't think the area, although very attractive, had quite the charm of Watchet, but she was aware of her own inbuilt bias towards her hometown. Maybe she was being a little unfair on this area of the south coast. It was world famous, after all. And not only because of the Jurassic Coast's designation as a World Heritage Site. After all, there was the area's connections with literature, stretching back for two centuries. Several mentions in Jane Austen novels; the fact that it formed the core of Thomas Hardy country, with many connections to the great man. Watchet couldn't really compete with that level of public exposure, even with its link to the Ancient Mariner, but Jackie realised that she probably wouldn't want her hometown to get the same ridiculously high number of tourists and visitors as here. Its quiet quaintness was part of Watchet's charm. She missed it when she wasn't there.

Tommy parked the car on the street outside Pryor's house. The driveway was already occupied by a CSI van, with the unit combing through the house interior. The property was in a cul-de-sac, with neat semi-detached homes side by side along the tree-lined road, all with small front gardens displaying various levels of horticultural attention. The missing man must have had some level of gardening ability. A small circular rose-bed occupied a spot in the middle of the lawn, with a few bedding plants beginning to display their summer colours. It was one of the neater gardens on the estate.

'Do we need to go inside?' Jackie asked.

Tommy shook his head. 'Just check with the neighbours. Everyone in the road. We ask about Pryor himself and what he's like as a person. Then if anyone has any ideas of where he could be. Then any general gossip. You know the kind of stuff. Relationships, friendships, where he did his shopping, if he had a favourite pub. The boss suggests that we stick together, even though we'll make slower progress.'

Jackie grimaced. 'It's really to help me learn the ropes, Tommy. I can understand it, though. I'm on probation. I expect you've been asked to assess me.'

Tommy looked away without answering.

In fact, little came out of the two hours they spent questioning the occupants of the nearby homes, until they reached the occupant of the last house in the cul-de-sac, next to a footpath that led downhill towards the town centre and seafront. She'd spotted Robin Pryor on the morning of his walk, heading off in outdoor gear with a small backpack slung across his shoulders. Possibly the last sighting of the missing man by someone who could identify him reliably. They did gain background information of a more general nature from other neighbours, though. Robin Pryor occasionally shopped in the town centre but tended to buy most of his groceries from the large superstore in Axminster, just like everyone else. It had a convenient car park, unlike the shops in the narrow streets of Lyme, and was easy to reach from his workplace, EcoFutures. His favourite Lyme Regis pubs were on the peculiarly named Broad Street, an extremely narrow thoroughfare winding down the hill towards the town's small theatre, set back a few yards from the seafront. His neighbours described him as being rather solitary, but friendly enough. He rarely talked about his work and, when he did, it was in generalities. He did talk to them, though, about his love of the outdoors. Birds, deer, reptiles. Even trees. No wonder he worked in ecology, Jackie thought.

'No mention of any partner,' she said as they walked back to the car from the last house.

Tommy seemed disinterested. 'Well, maybe he didn't have one, not since his marriage broke up. Or maybe he was secretive about it. There could be any number of reasons, couldn't there?'

'Everyone I know either has one or is looking for one,' she replied. 'Isn't the search for a soulmate one of the accepted driving forces of human behaviour?'

He shrugged. 'Don't know. What about monks and nuns and those sorts of people? Not everyone is seeking love all the time, surely?'

'Suppose not. It's sometimes easier not to bother. Too many relationships come to grief, sooner or later.'

## CHAPTER 6: BIZARRE

Barry looked out of the car window as Rae steered the vehicle into a visitor's parking space at the Dorset County Hospital. Was it really only two years since that case with the boat wreck survivors, the overturned dinghy packed with half-starved migrants from Iran seeking asylum? It was all he could do to stop himself from shuddering at the thought of that murderously evil woman who'd manipulated the ongoing tragedy of migration for her own gain. What was her name? Corinne Lanston? He wondered how she was coping, locked up in prison for the rest of her life. She'd been watching the comings and goings at this very hospital, sitting inside a van with darkened windows, planning when to strike.

'How much longer will she be in for, boss?' Rae said.

Barry was instantly alert. Had she been reading his mind? Of course not. Rae was thinking about the woman in the hospital, not the prison inmate. 'Maybe another week or so? We can ask. We need to know because we'll have to keep an eye on her for a while, keep her safe.'

They used the stairs to climb to the upper level where Bryony's ward was situated. Exercise was good, Barry told himself. Even when it didn't feel like it.

Bryony was sharing a small room with three other women, which surprised Barry. He had expected her to be in a room by herself, something that had been suggested to the hospital managers by the police for security reasons. Why had that request been ignored?

They guessed who Bryony was the moment they entered the room. One of the women was sitting on a chair, elbow crutches leaning against the armrests, looking expectantly at the detective duo as they appeared. She even gave them a small wave as if to say, here I am. Her left arm was bandaged, and her right foot was in a plaster cast. Her forehead was partially covered by a dressing and her face still showed some residual bruising. What was the colour of her hair? Difficult to be sure given that only a few loose strands peeped out from beneath the bandages. But she looked alert. Barry did the introductions.

'We can go into the small visitors' room,' Bryony said. 'I asked for it to be kept free for us when the nurse told me you were coming.'

'I expected you to be in your own room, not sharing,' Barry replied. 'Why the change?'

'My choice,' came the reply. 'I was going mad by myself. I like the company. Well, once the first couple of days passed and I was off the really strong painkillers. I'm a bit of a chatty person, I'm afraid. I insisted on it. It was only yesterday. I think the staff are still being extra cautious at the ward entrance, checking visitors and the like. Anyway, I hope to be out in a couple of days.' She paused as they made themselves comfortable. 'I'd like to offer you tea and biscuits, but that's not possible. There is water, though.'

'Don't worry,' Rae said. 'We're fine.'

'I'm not sure what it is you want. I've already been interviewed twice, first by a uniformed PC, then by a sergeant. Rose Simons? Was that her name? I haven't really remembered anything else, so I've got nothing to add. I hope that doesn't mean you've had a wasted journey.'

'We have those statements and Sergeant Simons has been to see me. We're here with a different slant. Are you aware that your colleague Robin Pryor is missing?'

Bryony looked shocked. 'No. What do you mean, missing? Has he done a disappearing act again on one of his weekend trekking breaks?'

Barry shook his head. 'We don't think so. He was seen leaving his house on Saturday morning in walking gear. We think he was heading west, along the coast path towards Axmouth and Seaton. As far as we know, he never arrived. We're starting a full scale search this afternoon. Nothing's been spotted by preliminary checks along the path.'

She looked puzzled. 'I don't see how I can help. It's not as though we were close, other than being work colleagues. Well, colleagues is maybe stretching things. He was my boss.'

'Also, someone may have broken into Justine Longford's flat a couple of days ago.'

'Well, that is weird. That's quite a set of coincidences, isn't it? Worrying. Anyone would think that . . .'

Her voice trailed off as the implications sank in.

'God. You think it's connected?'

'We have to consider that possibility,' Barry replied.

Bryony's face paled. 'So you think I was targeted? It wasn't random, what happened to me?'

'As I said, we have to consider it. So what connects you? Apart from working for EcoFutures, that is?' He poured a tumbler of water for her and pushed it forward. She reached out with her good hand and took a sip.

'This is a shock. I'm finding it hard to think straight. We're currently all on the same project. Did you know that?'

'We did. It came to light yesterday.'

'Robin's the overall project manager and team leader. He does the science. Val is Robin's deputy. Justine's the programmer. I'm the office manager. There are ten of us all together.'

'What's the project you're currently working on?'

'I'm not allowed to talk about it. Company policy.'

Barry looked her in the eye. 'Bryony, we're treating your case as attempted murder. Your boss has gone missing in suspicious circumstances. One of your colleagues has had her home broken into. We need your help if we're to make sense of it all, and we might not have much time in Robin's case. Would it help if I got Nicky Dangerfield on the phone?'

Bryony nodded.

Barry called the EcoFutures operations manager, had a few words and passed the phone to Bryony. She listened carefully then sat thinking for a while.

'We're in the early stages of a coastal development project in Parantos. I don't see how it could possibly create these kinds of problems. I mean, abductions, intimidation, breaking in? It's all a bit fanciful, isn't it? We're just working on ecology projects.'

Barry felt Rae stir in her seat beside him, so he turned to face her.

'Parantos is one of the routes out of South America for the Colombian drug gangs,' Rae said quietly.

'Oh, God. I didn't know that. But how can that possibly affect us and this work? I mean, it's bizarre.' But Bryony's facial expression turned to one of shock as the implications sank in. 'They're killers, aren't they?' she whispered.

Was she seeking confirmation of that last remark?

'We can keep you safe,' Barry said. 'You're not in danger now we know.'

'Christ. This is awful. So that man who ran out of the bushes with the knife? Was he going to kill me? I've convinced myself not, in the days since it happened. That he was just trying to scare me.'

'We don't know what they were planning. We're putting a lot of effort into searching for them.'

She looked at him. 'No sign of them yet?'

He shook his head. 'We're working on the assumption they were local. Or at least from Britain. We've got to start somewhere.'

She shook her head gently from side to side as if trying to clear a bad memory. 'It's all too . . . bizarre,' she repeated. 'I can't quite believe it.' She looked around her. 'Are you sure I'm safe?'

'We'll have someone outside the ward entrance. And we'll plan ahead, ready for when you go home. No need to worry.'

Bryony took another sip of water. 'I wish this had some gin in it. This is all a bit of a shock.' She paused momentarily. 'I thought they were British, those two who tried to ambush me. I suppose it's difficult to tell, though, isn't it? It was dark.'

'Our guess is that they were trying to intimidate you,' Rae said.

'Well, they succeeded, totally. I was scared witless.'

'No, I mean a bit more than that. If they'd have got hold of you, they'd probably have tried to get some key information out of you. Possibly something about the project. It's all just conjecture, though. There could be other explanations.'

'And you think they might have Robin?'

Rae shrugged. 'It's possible. We're planning a big search for this afternoon. Several teams are assembling as we speak.'

'What did you think, Rae?' Barry asked as they left the main part of the ward.

'Not sure, boss. She's clearly scared. Who wouldn't be, after an event like that? But I've got the uneasy feeling that she knows more than she's letting on. There was just something about the way she was watching us. I don't think she's given us the full story. Not yet. It might just be my imagination, though.'

Barry shook his head. 'No. I sensed something too. I haven't a clue what, though.'

The two detectives didn't head directly to their car after leaving Bryony's ward. Their boss, Sophie Allen, was still in a specialist unit in the same hospital and always appreciated a visit, however short.

## CHAPTER 7: SEARCH

The search for the missing man would involve two teams, one from Dorset, heading west from Lyme Regis, and one from Devon, taking the route east from Axmouth. The stretch of coast path to be explored was only seven miles but the search leader, Greg Buller, had no illusions about the difficulty that faced his people. It wasn't a normal, benign stretch of track that the teams were investigating. This was a long section that had experienced a major slippage in Victorian times, creating weirdly shaped land islands that rose up from near sea level. The tortuous path rose and fell, simultaneously twisting and turning through dense woodland. The surface was wet and slimy. The cliffs on the landward side were composed of soft crumbly rock, extremely insubstantial, and dangerous even to approach without a hard-hat and someone on standby. Added to which, the missing man could have wandered off the path, entered the quarter-mile wide jungle region and had some kind of accident.

Greg was convinced that Pryor would be somewhere away from the path, if he was there at all. After all, it was spring. Plenty of walkers would have made their way along the stretch every day, attacking this section of the south-west coast path. He would have been spotted if he was close to the track. Maybe even if he was hidden in the undergrowth nearby. After all, many walkers had dogs with them, and they loved exploring the acres of tangled greenery. Surely one of them would have sniffed out a body if it was hidden in undergrowth near the path?

He talked these points through with Barry Marsh before the search started at noon. Barry had made the decision to set the ball rolling after discussing the morning's interviews with the rest of the team. He then called Greg who was ready and waiting.

'You miss Sophie Allen, don't you?' was the comment Greg said to the detective when he arrived on the scene. Greg had noticed the worry on Barry's face.

'Don't we all?' was Barry's reply.

'How is she?'

Barry grimaced. 'It's taking longer than she thought. You know what she's like. Impatient to get things done. She seriously thought she'd be out of hospital and back to work within a few weeks. No one else did, but we weren't brave enough to tell her so directly. We just dropped hints. The medics told her, but her view was that they were just being unduly pessimistic. It's better for her to be kept in, to be honest. She'd just drive everyone barmy if she was out, staying at home. The doctors would be trusting her to be sensible. Fat chance. Martin agrees with me on that.'

'Well, let me know when she's out. I'll pop round with a lasagne and some red wine.'

Greg looked around at the various teams, each with a set of instructions about their own search zone priorities. The teams would be spread out along an axis roughly perpendicular to the path, but remaining parallel to it as they progressed westward. Some would be close to the shoreline, and others, at the inland end of the sweep line, close to the cliffs. He blew a whistle and the teams moved off, probing the undergrowth with poles. The same thing should be happening at the other end, where the search teams would be setting off from the River Axe and moving eastwards. With luck they might be finished before nightfall. Thank goodness it was late May, and it didn't get dark until late.

\* \* \*

The search proved to be one of the most arduous the team had ever attempted, but at least they made steady progress, even if it was a bit slow. Jackie Spring was teamed up with her two WeSCU colleagues, Rae Gregson and Tommy Carter, and she was finding the task much harder than she'd expected. She was used to taking part in searches like this, but her previous experiences had always been on the more open areas around Exmoor and the North Somerset coastal strip. She was glad of the brief pause at the first rest point, only a third of the way along their allocated zone. She took another sip of water and looked around her. Her previous searches had involved wooded areas, but none of them had been like this tortuously tangled land-scape. What forces of nature had created this six-mile strip of land? She glanced again at the map she held. It was the same for almost the entire distance to the river, miles ahead. Maybe huge slippages had been going on for thousands of years. She told herself that she must read more about the causes and the history of the most famous slippage event, back in Victorian times. Of course, it was still ongoing in other nearby parts of the coast. The famous Mary Anning had made use of cliff falls to hunt for fossils at a time when such activities were deemed inappropriate for a woman. Jackie knew little of the details of Anning's life, but she had learned about the constant opposition the now-famous palaeontologist had received from her male counterparts. And that was supplemented by the constant niggling opposition that her family had experienced from the established Church because of their nonconformist views. Little change there then, Jackie thought. Some male-dominated organisations, including religious ones, were little altered in their largely misogynistic approach to change. Men always seemed to grab the attention and historically had paid little regard to fair play, steadfastly refusing to acknowledge the contribution women had made. And it wasn't just prior to the twentieth century. What about that famous woman scientist who made a major contribution to the structure of DNA and wasn't acknowledged? Who was she? Rae might know. She asked her boss.

'I guess you mean Rosalind Franklin,' came the reply. 'But I really remember her because of something else she said, as a girl, to her mother, during an argument about God and religion. *Well, anyhow, how do you know He isn't She?* I mean, that's a pretty revolutionary thing to say for a kid in those days, nearly a hundred years ago.' Rae paused. 'What brought that on?'

'Mary Anning. I was thinking about her.'

'We ought to take a look in the local museum while we're in Lyme,' Rae replied. 'Those two women are important culturally, not just because of their scientific discoveries. Girl Power started a long time before the Spice Girls. Isn't that right, Rose?'

Rose Simons was also involved in the search. She was leaning against a fallen tree trunk, rubbing her knee.

'Bloody hell, yes. What do people think I was doing in my teen years? Being prim and well behaved until Scary Spice gave me permission to be myself? Hah!'

'If we do a visit to the Mary Anning place in Lyme, do you want to come along?'

Rose narrowed her eyes. 'What? Rocks and stuff? Me?'

'It's fossils, Rose. And things related to her life.'

'If there's a pub visit at the end of it, count me in. God, I could murder a beer right now. And fish and chips. Maybe I could make do with a thick ham sandwich if pushed. Mustard. Fresh wholemeal bread.'

Rae laughed. 'You're torturing yourself, Rose.' She glanced across at Greg, waving for everybody to start moving. 'We're off. Eyes peeled, everyone.'

\* \* \*

The afternoon turned into early evening. Everyone was beginning to feel tired and disheartened as the search squads entered the darkest and most tangled area of woodland they'd yet come across. Every thicket had to be checked, but the gaps between them were often blocked by branches hanging across possible paths. Rose and Rae were trying to push through a particularly dense clump, poking the ground with rods, when Rose suddenly stopped.

'Something here,' she called.

Greg blew his whistle and signalled for the team to stop moving. He joined the two officers as they cleared some more foliage.

'It's a body,' Rose said. 'Hidden really well. It might be our man.'

# CHAPTER 8: CORPSE

The body was that of their man, as Rose had put it. Several experienced forensic officers had been included in the search team, in preparation for possible discoveries, and they took over immediately, moving personnel out of the way and beginning their task of probing and recording the immediate area around the body. Barry arrived, having chosen to remain with the mobile communications unit, close to the nearest road. Benny Gooding, Dorset's senior county pathologist, arrived within the hour, having been collected from the closest road by a police Land Rover. The driver had managed to find a way to get within four hundred yards of the crime scene, from which point Benny had had to don boots and splash his way through the mud.

'Afternoon, everyone,' he said as he arrived. 'You have a body for me, Barry?' After being given the go-ahead by the forensic photographer, the body was turned over.

'That's him, Robin Pryor,' Rae said. 'No doubt about it.'

Benny masked up and carried out the usual checks on body temperature and muscle flexibility.

'Several days,' was his first comment. 'But you knew that anyway from the level of decomposition.' He turned to the forensic people. 'Ready to move.'

'Any clues as to how he died?' Barry asked as they watched them slide the body onto a stretcher.

'There's blunt force trauma to the front left side of his skull. Quite severe. It may not have killed him immediately, though. There may be other injuries that will show up at the PM. I can push it through as a priority, if you want, Barry. Tomorrow afternoon any good?' Benny's voice was sharper than usual.

'Please.' Barry felt awkward. He'd always had a good working relationship with Benny. This unease was something new, and he realised what was causing it. The fact that Sophie Allen, a close personal friend of Benny's, had been so badly injured a month or so earlier and was still in hospital. Hadn't he, Barry, felt that same sense of anger when he'd arrived back from his honeymoon and learned of the murder attempt on his boss? Of course, he'd been able to trawl through the event logs and soon realised that there had been no negligence on the part of any of the detective team. But he knew he'd been looking for a scapegoat, someone to blame. That sense of intense frustration and fury was hard to deal with. He could guess how Benny felt. If he, Barry, hadn't been away on his luxury post-wedding break he would have been at the scene and might have prevented the catastrophe from happening. But such conjectures were pointless, a nonsensical sequence of what-ifs.

He followed Benny back to the Land Rover. 'You're still sore about Sophie, aren't you?'

The pathologist turned. 'Yes, if I'm honest about it. It's shaken me to my core. We nearly lost her. I never knew quite how much she meant to me until it happened. I don't think she'll ever recover fully. Her leg injuries were awful. I just feel a sense of rage when I think about it. Such a force for good and she's likely to be crippled for the rest of her life. I mean, where's the justice?'

'When it comes down to it, much of life isn't about justice, is it? You're a doctor. You know that. If you must know, I had a discussion with Sophie about it just last week, when I was visiting. She's prepared for the worst. In a way, she always has been. This standby plan of hers may come into play a bit earlier than she'd anticipated, but she's actively considering it.'

'The academic option?' Benny curled his lip. 'I just don't see it. I mean, I can in theory, but the thought of such a free spirit doing fusty tutoring work just doesn't ring true.'

Barry could see Benny's point. But if the worst happened, it would give the boss a focus. And surely Benny was being unduly pessimistic? Sophie Allen was a people person. She'd probably thrive in the company of intelligent young people at university.

'It might not come to that, Benny. She told me a couple of days ago that one of the country's best bone doctors has been to see her. She's the one who did some of the initial operations, trying to pin Sophie's leg back together. I prefer to stay focussed on the positives.'

Benny sighed. 'You're right, of course. I just never realised how much she meant to me on a personal level until this happened. I love her, really. I think I always have done. She's the sister I never had.' He looked at his watch. 'Time to get back and prepare for this guy. See you tomorrow?'

Barry shook his head. 'Not me. I'll send Rae. There's only so many PMs we can cope with in our lives, and I reached my limit some time ago. Benny, I hope there won't be a problem but, technically, we're in Devon here. Are you happy to proceed? The Devon mob seem okay with it.'

'Hah! Now you tell me. You've learned too well from your boss. That's the kind of thing she's always been very skilled at, gently manipulating people so they don't even know it.' Benny smiled at last. 'It'll be fine. In fact, it'll be a pleasure. I must be some kind of masochist, though. Extra work? And the extra bureaucracy that goes with it? Maybe it's time I considered chucking all this in and starting a new life as a travelling troubadour.'

Barry waved him off. He hadn't been looking forward to his first meeting with Benny since the assault on Sophie. It had been good to finish on a cheerful note.

\* \* \*

The meticulous search of the immediate area now began. The detectives needed to work out the sequence of events leading up to Pryor's death. Had he been killed at the spot or despatched elsewhere, with his body subsequently dumped there? Could he have been injured but somehow escaped, to crawl away and then die from his injuries, cold and alone? Whatever had happened, there ought to be clues left in the immediate vicinity. Footprints, broken twigs, bruised leaves, flattened grass.

Rose Simons had been careful to retrace her own steps when she'd retreated to a point some yards away after finding the body. Others had done the same, keeping the immediate vicinity largely unspoiled in terms of its ability to yield reliable forensic evidence. The most important single discovery was a trail of blood spots that stretched some two hundred metres from a small clearing. It showed signs of a scuffle in the way some of the ground cover was disturbed. In turn, the clearing was about three hundred metres off the main path.

Greg Buller consulted some of his more experienced search personnel, then had a quick chat with the forensic experts, with Barry, Rae and Rose listening in. It looked as though Pryor might have been in a struggle with three others. Some kind of altercation had taken place, then it looked as though the fracas had moved about twenty metres to a more heavily wooded area, where a more serious assault had occurred. Had Pryor been killed here? It was difficult to come to any firm conclusion. All they could see was a trail of regularly spaced blood spots that led to the dense area where his body had been found.

It was no surprise that Rose Simons was the first to venture an opinion. 'My guess is that he was caught near the path and dragged off into the woods. They started to beat him up, and he managed to get away but only a short distance. They finished him off and dumped his body where it was unlikely to be found. Maybe they were after something?'

Barry gave his usual frown. 'Better not speculate too much, not until we get all the evidence collected.' He looked across at Rae. 'We'll need a local incident room set up. Find out if the station at Lyme has a suitable room, then get the ball rolling.'

# CHAPTER 9: BOREDOM

Sophie Allen felt that she was in grave danger of losing her mind through boredom. Weeks of bed rest, therapy and low-level chit-chat with fellow patients had made her feel that her brain matter was in danger of turning into marshmallow. She was itching to get stuck into a realistic and substantial problem of some kind, but what chance was there of that happening? The world seemed to be split into two. Real life going on as usual outside the hospital walls, and her new sphere of influence inside. Even that term was a total misnomer, not that anyone else used it, just her. Realistically, she had zero influence in here. But, as her husband Martin had pointed out, following the rules might mean she would recover more quickly and get herself discharged sooner. That piece of advice certainly resonated with her, so she stopped complaining and concentrated fully on being the perfect patient. Inside, though, she seethed. At least she now had access to a wheelchair, although she needed help to clamber in and out of it. Yet what a difference it made to her life. She could go rideabout, explore the corridors and lounge areas, visit the shop, call in to the café for a coffee.

She looked out of the window beside her bed. What a lovely day. She might well visit that sheltered outdoor area, the pretty one with the small pond and raised flower bed. Get some fresh air, listen to the birdsong. She swung out of her room into the corridor towards the nursing station, where she explained her plan. The moody nurse was on duty, the one she always felt was in sore need of a happiness injection.

Sophie smiled at her sweetly. 'Just popping out for some fresh air in the patients' garden. I've got my book to read.'

The nurse glanced at the cover and narrowed her eyes. 'Most people would read a crime novel.'

'I'm a police officer. I'm allergic to detective novels.'

'Romance?'

'Too gushy for me. I wondered about porn, but I've been advised not to get over-excited.'

At last she had the nurse's attention.

'So I settled on this biography of Eleanor of Aquitaine. It was on the charity shelf yesterday. Fascinating woman. Hugely rich and influential. Reputedly extremely beautiful too. I feel a lot of empathy.' She was trying to keep a straight face.

The nurse snorted. 'Good luck with that.'

'Well, we can but dream.'

Sophie headed off before the nurse could raise an objection to her planned expedition through the hospital and down to the outside world. She'd really like to have been zooming along at top speed, as if she was Tanni Grey-Thompson, but thought this might result in her losing access to the ward's only non-motorised wheelchair, always available when she wanted it for the simple reason that all the other patients opted for the motorised alternatives. Anyway, her injured shoulder was still sore, and she didn't want to put her recovery at risk.

She reached the small courtyard and managed to get through the doors into the open air beyond, seeking a sunny, sheltered spot. It was thrilling to be outside after countless weeks of being cooped up, first in a bed and then, more recently, in a chair. Beautiful. Maybe life was good after all.

She settled down to read, occasionally putting her book down in order to close her eyes and savour the joy of temporary escape. The spot she was in was in dappled shade, ideal now that the sun was getting hotter.

She came to with a start, caused by the entry door banging. Goodness, she'd dozed off. She yawned and looked around. She could hear low voices behind her. Another couple of people must have come out and settled onto one of the nearby bench seats. Possibly they hadn't noticed her. Within a few minutes, Sophie realised that the possibility was a certainty.

'And he never let on that he was married? No clues?' said the first voice.

'No. He didn't wear a ring. I feel so stupid. He's even got children. The eldest is nearly in her teens.'

'What a bastard! So typical.'

Sophie could sense the outrage in the first woman's voice.

'Though he never actually said he *wasn't* married. I don't think I got around to asking him, not directly.' The second voice trailed off a little as the final sentence came to an end. There was regret in the way the woman spoke.

Sophie lowered her book. No matter how fascinating its subject matter, it couldn't really compete.

'Trickery of the first order!' the first voice barked.

There was no reply. Sophie could guess why. The victim of the duplicity knew deep down that she was complicit in the subterfuge, that she hadn't really tried to find out, that she'd probably ignored signs that she could have latched onto. Was she married herself?

'You're right to stay single, Bryony. Don't trust any of them, that's my motto.'

Two things. First, that the woman was single, might be lonely and looking for some love and affection. Second, that her name was Bryony. Could she be the same person Barry had talked of the previous day? He'd said she was in the hospital recovering from injuries sustained in an extremely peculiar car crash.

Sophie leaned back, her senses finely tuned.

'No wonder you're looking worried, Bry. And he works at your place, too? What a worm. Deserves to be stamped on.'

'I don't know about stamping on him. He's the security manager. But, actually, he comes across as a nice guy. I wouldn't have fallen for him otherwise. The other thing is, I'm not single. My husband's in the navy. He's away for months at a time. I suppose I just felt neglected. But what really worries me is something very different. It's something that I remembered last night. You see, what happened to me, that guy running out of some bushes at me, carrying a big knife, that's been my worst nightmare for ages. Ever since I saw a film with it in, a few years ago.'

'Right.' The first voice sounded more uncertain now. Possibly she was having to reassess her friend. 'Hasn't your husband managed to get some leave to visit you, considering your experiences? Your injuries were rather serious, weren't they? That would be so typical. Out of sight, out of mind.'

'Actually, he got emergency leave really quickly and was across here within a couple of days. He's really thoughtful, to be honest.' She sounded wistful. There was no response from her friend, so Bryony's voice continued. 'The thing is, I told Ian, the guy I was having a fling with, about that fear of mine. It was one of those times when you feel really close to some-one and talk about ridiculous stuff. You know, lying in bed just after sex, sipping tea and opening up about your deepest thoughts. So I told him. I'd forgotten about it.'

'Don't you think the police need to know? It sounds really suspicious to me.' The second voice was still guarded, as if she was struggling with her friend's duplicity.

'I just couldn't. What if it got out? That I'd had an affair? It would finish things. Joe would never forgive me, I know he wouldn't. What a mess. And he's such a thoughtful man. I just don't really love him. I realised that within a month of getting married.' Bryony was beginning to sound tearful.

There was a long pause before the first voice said, 'Well, I'd better be off. Things to do. Do you need help back to the ward?'

Sophie could sense the disapproval in her tone.

'Maybe just get me through the doors. Look, I'm not proud of what I did, Virginia. I can see it's bothered you. But please can we stay friends? I'm not bad, not really.'

'Yes, I know. Okay. But I need to think things through.'

Sophie heard the sound of footsteps fade, then the doors squeak as they closed. The name Bryony. A security manager. An affair. Most of all, the fact that she'd told him of that particular nightmare, the one of a man running at her on a dark night, wielding a large knife. She picked her phone out of her bag.

'Barry? Something interesting for you.'

# CHAPTER 10: HYPODERMIC

Barry looked across the table at the tired-looking WeSCU team of Rae, Tommy and Jackie. Did they need to bolster their numbers somehow? Try as he might, the loss of Sophie Allen was a heavy blow, particularly at a time when her deputy, Polly Nelson, was busy in Bristol. How important was this Major Crime initiative Polly was engaged in? They'd had several chats on the phone, but he was starting to wonder about her personal commitment to WeSCU. Surely the discovery of Pryor's body should have been enough to tip the balance in her deliberations and bring her hotfooting it down to Dorset. Not so, apparently. He really needed someone with whom he could talk over the latest troubling news.

'The boss has been on the phone.'

Rae looked at him blankly. 'Who, Polly?'

'No.' He sounded exasperated. 'The chief super.'

'What does she want?'

'She doesn't want anything. She's just thrown a spanner into our works.'

He explained the crux of what she'd told him. A short, stunned silence followed.

'Well, that's a bit of a turn up, isn't it,' Rae finally said. 'In hospital, a leg broken in several places, a seriously injured shoulder, continued worry about the after-effects of concussion, and she still manages to turn up stuff like this. Unbelievable. But so true to form.'

Barry decided to ignore Rae's comment. 'Did anyone pick up on a hint of anything like this when we interviewed that pair?' They all shook their heads. 'No. Neither did I. The decision now is whether we tackle it head on and interview them both again, or be a bit more subtle and keep them under scrutiny. Particularly Ian Duncan. If what the boss overheard is true, he might have spilled the beans about the woman's fears to someone pretty nasty.'

'Could it all have been some kind of elaborate joke?' Jackie asked.

Barry shook his head. 'I don't think so. The evidence from the witnesses to Bryony O'Neil's car crash don't support that at all. The lorry driver she'd just overtaken, and the occupants of the car going the other way, the vehicle she only just missed. Their statements are all consistent. A terrified-looking woman driver. A car following at high speed with a bearded male driver and a young woman passenger with crazy eyes. It also corresponds to the dashcam footage we've managed to collect.'

'And the vehicle they used has disappeared completely. No trace of it, nor of its occupants,' Rae added. 'It's a dead end. How do we go about using this new information that the boss discovered? It's a bit of a tricky one, isn't it?'

Barry nodded. 'It's background only. We can't afford for it to slip out. The boss might well have overheard it accidentally, but that won't make any difference. It would be declared inadmissible in any court case, as would anything that hinged on it. So we have to rediscover it ourselves, by routine investigation. It won't be a problem if we probe the details as part of our background check on Bryony and the possible motives for the attack on her.'

'I would never have guessed the two of them had a thing going, her and Ian Duncan,' Rae said. 'Neither of them seems the type. Shows my poor sense of judgement, doesn't it?'

'Well, it needs to be checked out and as a matter of urgency. That'll be you, Rae, and Jackie. The usual stuff. When did it start? How long for? Who else knew? Don't people claim that it's impossible to keep a workplace affair secret? Is that true? Tommy, you're going back to EcoFutures to do a bit more gentle probing. And you say Ian Duncan's counterpart at Hewton was adamant about passing on his concerns about the place being watched?'

'Yes. He was pretty definite about it.'

'Keep it low-level at this stage. Then you're off to Robin Pryor's post-mortem this afternoon with Rae. At that point we'll shift the focus to him. I'm heading back to the crime scene just now. Greg Buller's squad have been searching the area, along with the forensic team. I'll be having a chat with him, our forensic chief, Dave Nash, and Rose Simons. With a bit of luck, more evidence will have turned up. The thing is, we still can't be sure all these different strands are connected. It makes sense if they are, all neatly intertwined with each other. But in real life? People can be so erratic, even chaotic. They can act in odd ways for strange reasons.'

'Maybe we should be looking for the lowdown on Justine Longford's life,' Rae said, somewhat conspiratorially. 'She might have similar secrets.'

'You're just being provocative now, Rae,' Barry said. 'We're struggling with the enquiries we have going at the moment. Let's get busy.'

Rae waited until the others had settled to their tasks.

'Why don't we bring Rose and George on board again, boss? They learned the ropes last year in that case near Poole. It would ease the load a bit.'

'Good idea. I'll see what Rose says, then approach HQ. It would help to solve our manpower problem.'

* * *

Barry felt more positive about his visit to the coast path on this occasion. The police had negotiated access to the area via tracks across a farm whose land adjoined the top of the cliffs. A single steep track wound its way down to the wooded enclave, although it was rarely used and was barred by locked gates at the upper end. Its lower end seemed to peter out in a mass of brambles and nettles, such that walkers on the coast path would be unaware of its existence. Not now, of course, with the track being used by police and forensic vehicles.

'We checked its surface before we started using it,' Greg told Barry. 'The farm people haven't used it for more than a month but there were tyre tracks. Something has been up and down it, and probably within the past week.'

'How did they manage that if the gate was locked?' Barry asked.

'Someone jemmied the lock off the upright,' Greg explained. 'The problem with timber gates and posts. It's too easy really.'

They climbed out of the Land Rover that Greg had used to drive down the track. Barry looked around him, once again taking in the dense undergrowth and the location of the crime scene, almost halfway along this stretch of the coast path. Why here? Surely there were more convenient locations, closer to possible escape routes? Why choose an obscure spot like this? And how could the killers have been certain that Pryor would come along here?

'I wonder if he was with someone,' he mused out loud. 'Someone bought him along here, led him into a trap. That way they could be sure.'

'Is there any evidence?' Greg asked.

Barry shook his head. 'We've got a positive sighting for Pryor himself, but the report said he was alone when he climbed the steps up from the beach area back at Lyme. But he could have met someone at the junction at the top of the first slope. A path comes in at a higher level, from the top end of the town.'

'You think he could have met someone there?'

'It's possible. Planned or by accident. Pre-arranged would make more sense.'

'Or maybe he was just followed. Someone shadowing him and messaging the group ahead.'

'I'm not sure how reliable that would be, Greg. Mobile phone signals are unreliable once you're down in this jungle.'

'You really don't like it down here, do you.'

'No. Too claustrophobic for me.'

'I can see your point. In a way, I'm glad it's in Devon. I don't feel any responsibility for it. I like to stick with my own patch, if truth be told.'

'Well, it seemed sensible to call you in to head up the search. But once you and Dave are finished here, you can pack up and go home. I know we're technically in Devon, but it's even more of a pig trying to get equipment in from that side. The Devon force are happy for us to handle everything. I have to keep them informed though. Axminster, where Robin worked, is in Devon. But he lived in Lyme, as do the other people we're checking on. That's how we got landed with it, originally.'

Rose Simons walked towards them. 'Dave's team have found something but he's staying tight-lipped, as usual. Won't tell me. Does he think I'm that much of a blabbermouth? Really. That man. Just because I'm not blonde.'

They walked off in the direction she pointed, where the forensic chief was talking to two of his personnel.

'Hi, Dave. I heard you've found something significant,' Barry said.

He gave his usual non-committal shrug and picked a sealed evidence bag out of a plastic crate that was in a neatly stacked row of equipment ready to be loaded up and taken away. 'Its significance is something only you can decide.'

Barry examined it and scratched his head.

'A hypodermic needle? Well, that's interesting.'

'It was in the undergrowth close to where we think the scuffle took place. I'll get it shipped back to the lab as soon as I can. There'll still be traces of its contents left, with a bit of luck.'

'I'd better warn Benny Goodall. Ask him to look out for skin punctures and something unusual in the blood. Great stuff, everyone.'

'How's Sophie?' Dave asked.

'Pretty good, all things considered. Getting bored, I expect. She's likely to be kept in for a couple more weeks, we think. Why don't you go and visit?'

'Maybe I will. Come with me, Greg?'

'Yeah, why not? We could tease her. You know, two good-looking younger men.'

Barry broke in. 'Well, warn her first. She made that pretty clear about me visiting, that she needs a half hour warning. You know what she's like. Needs to have the right shade of lipstick to match whatever she's wearing.'

Greg looked at him incredulously. 'What, even in hospital?'

'Even more so. She's got nothing else to occupy her time, so she's spending it planning alternative looks. That's what Rae told me last week. Apparently, she asked Rae what it was like being a brunette. Rae told her it meant she could wear more vibrant colours. Then she said a dreamy, faraway look came into Sophie's eyes.'

'Might have just been a spot of indigestion,' Greg suggested. 'Hospital food can sometimes do that.'

'Seriously, Barry, how is she really? The injuries, I mean. Will she recover completely? This is between friends. Don't bullshit us.' There was real concern in Dave Nash's voice.

Barry looked troubled. 'Her leg's pretty bad. One of the breaks wasn't clean. It had several sub-fractures. That's what Martin told me. They're pinning all their hopes on some super-surgeon who's coming to see her next week. Rumour has it she's got a magic touch.'

'What happens if it doesn't work, and Sophie doesn't recover fully?'

Barry shook his head and frowned. 'It doesn't really bear thinking about so let's not go there.'

## CHAPTER 11: WORKPLACE FLINGS

Rae and Tommy were observing the post-mortem examination that Benny Goodall was carrying out on the body of Robin Pryor. Tommy seemed unfazed by the procedure whereas Rae always felt queasy at autopsies. She'd refrained from eating any lunch, instead earmarking a mid-afternoon slot for some food and coffee. The obvious signs of the beating that Pryor had sustained were there on the body. Bruising and lacerations to the head, face, shoulders and arms.

'Maybe a heavy stick of some kind?' Tommy mused. 'How about a baseball bat? Would that fit the wound shapes?'

'Could well do. I'll do some measurements and you can compare sizing.' Benny turned his attention to the legs. 'More bruising, especially on the knees. I wonder if he was tripped and fell forward onto his face? That would explain the lacerations on his cheeks and the bruising on his nose.'

He continued the close examination of Pryor's skin. 'There are a couple of points that might be the result of a hypodermic needle. On the rear of his right shoulder. We'll look more closely because, if the needle went through his clothes, there should be fibre fragments embedded into the skin.'

'When will we know what he was injected with?' Rae asked.

'Maybe tomorrow? I took a blood sample as soon as the body arrived late yesterday, then sent it for analysis as a priority.'

'Some kind of incapacitating drug, probably,' Tommy said.

Benny shrugged. 'I'm not going to speculate. That's not in my remit and would be wrong anyway. Wait for the results, that's my tip. Too many over-zealous coppers have come a cropper when they've followed their instinct rather than waiting for the science.'

He got on with his unpleasant task, watched by an eager Tommy Carter and a pale-faced Rae Gregson.

* * *

Jackie Spring looked up as Rae and Tommy returned to the incident room.

'You both look okay,' she said. 'People have told me that watching an autopsy leaves them feeling nauseous for hours. What's your secret?'

Rae grimaced. 'Tommy seems to be immune, one of the lucky ones. I just don't eat beforehand, then have a bit of toast and some peppermint tea afterwards. Works a treat. Attending a PM is on the list for you, Jackie. Just be prepared, that's my advice.' She paused. 'How have you been getting on?'

'Bryony has a close friend, Mel Jones, who's a fellow member of the Zumba group she's in. They used to share a lift until Mel moved to Weymouth. I've fixed up for us to speak to her late this afternoon. Is that okay?'

'Of course. Anyone else we can talk to about Bryony?'

'I wondered about Justine Longford. She works in the same team and knows something's up because of her own suspicions about that possible break-in at her flat. By now, she's used to talking to us so may be more open.'

'Sounds good. Fix up a time. After Mel Jones, if possible.'

'The other idea I had was to speak to Nicky Dangerfield, the person you and the boss saw at EcoFutures.'

'The operations manager?'

'Yes. She might know more than she's let on. And according to the DI, he knew her from school. So is he the best person to try to get her to open up about Bryony's personal life? That's if she knows anything and is willing to tell us.'

Rae frowned. 'That's a tricky one. She's one of the company bosses really, probably senior to them all, including Ian Duncan, although she looks for agreement from him on security matters, judging from their interactions a couple of days ago. I'm not sure Barry is the right person. I'll speak to him and get his take on it. I can see your reasons for suggesting that we talk to her. She might well have a handle on staff relations in her management role. Leave that one with me.'

'There's something else been niggling me, boss. It's Bryony herself. Clearly, she realises the implications of what happened to her, from what the chief super overheard at the hospital. She now realises that Ian Duncan might be somehow involved. So why didn't she tell us when she had the chance? It doesn't really make sense. She must be scared stiff, but she still kept quiet about her fling with him, and the fact he knew about her terror of being chased by a guy with a knife. Does that make any sense to you?'

'Well, it's worth thinking about. But to be honest, so many people caught up in criminal activity don't follow normal behaviour patterns. In her case, it might just be panic creeping in. She's probably trying to keep a lid on a fling she's not proud of. It could be as simple as that.' Rae glanced at her watch. 'Barry should be back from his meeting at HQ by now. Let's put your ideas to him.'

Barry instantly saw the sense in Jackie's suggestions and made his decisions quickly. 'Jackie, you and I can see Nicky Dangerfield together. Rae, take Tommy with you and speak to Justine. And Ian Duncan, if Tommy hasn't managed to speak to him yet. All of us try to keep it low key. Take the line that we're just trying to build up a picture of the way the group works. Try not to concentrate on Bryony too much.

Don't give a hint that she's under suspicion in any way. We can confirm that we're now involved in a murder investigation, looking for whoever killed Robin Pryor. That might help to open them up a bit.'

They drove to the EcoFutures premises in two separate teams, with a ten-minute gap between them. Barry guessed that the arrival of four detectives at the same time would create waves within the company's senior management. He wanted it more low key. Jackie phoned ahead to fix up their appointment with Nicky Dangerfield. Rae and Tommy would arrive unannounced a little later to see Justine Longford.

\* \* \*

Nicky welcomed Barry and Jackie into her office. Jackie thought she looked deeply troubled, no surprise after finding out about Pryor's murder.

'It's terrible news, Barry. We're all bewildered by it. You said you want to see me about workplace relations within Robin's team? How can that help? Surely you don't think it was one of them. The idea is inconceivable.'

Barry spoke quietly. 'It's standard procedure, Nicky. All murder investigations work this way. Build up a picture by looking into family, friends, work colleagues. Ask questions about who knew who, how they all got on, whether anyone had a glimmer of something suspect. The process has its own momentum. As the SIO, I can direct that momentum, switch its direction as facts accumulate. Don't take it personally. No one should at this stage.'

'He was definitely murdered then? There's no room for doubt?'

'That's right. We have to find out if there's anything behind this strange set of occurrences that your staff have experienced recently. Are they linked or is it just a series of coincidences? Jackie's going to take over the questioning at this point. She's been working on this angle. Two other members of the team will be speaking to Justine Longford again shortly, just to double check what she's already told us.'

Jackie looked across the low table at Nicky, sitting on a chair opposite her. She was wearing a very smart burgundy trouser suit with a black silky top and black shoes. She obviously knew what looked good on her. Rae had already given Jackie the tip-off about that.

'We can understand that this has shaken everybody, Mrs Dangerfield. What I'm looking for is how the team got on with each other on a personal level, and how they got on with more senior staff. With you, for example, or Ian Duncan, the security manager. Even the company personnel manager. It seemed obvious for us to come to you because the DI and DS Gregson have already spoken to you. Does that make sense?'

Nicky nodded. 'Yes. I can see what you're getting at.'

'The thing is, we know coincidences happen. That's obvious to anyone involved in police work. But we can't ignore the events that have happened to Bryony O'Neil. Who was she close to here at work?'

Nicky seemed puzzled. 'Well, the team she worked with, obviously.'

'How many people on it?'

'Six. Robin, the team leader. Then Bryony as the admin manager and Justine as the programmer. Val Potter, Robin's deputy. She's now heading up the project. Three technicians, Simon, Nina and Nabila.'

'Was there any friction that you were aware of?'

'No. They all seemed to get on well together, more so than many of our teams. No problems, as far as I know.'

Barry took over again. 'Did any of them get closer than a working relationship? Any deeper entanglements?'

Nicky drew back in her seat. 'I wouldn't really know. Anyway, should I be interested in things like that? I don't see it as being relevant to the work we do if people form attachments. That's as long as the work doesn't suffer.'

'Chat and gossip, Nicky. It goes on in all workplaces. People gossip over coffee and lunch. Don't tell me it doesn't happen here, because that really would make me suspicious. And workplace relationships can create jealousies and friction.'

Nicky frowned and pursed her lips. 'I don't see how it's relevant but there was talk about Simon and Nina having a fling six months ago.'

'What about with someone outside the group but in the company? Any potential connections there with Robin? Was he close to anyone at social events?'

Nicky shook her head. 'Not that I'm aware of. There was recent talk of him having a girlfriend in Lyme, but I don't know any details.'

'We've got that covered, thanks. What about the other two? Any talk about them? Bryony?'

There was an almost imperceptible change in Nicky's demeanour. It lasted a mere second, a slight stiffening of her shoulders and a flicker in her eyes, but Jackie spotted it. She knew that Barry would have observed it too. Interesting.

'None that I'm aware of.'

There was a slight change in her voice timbre too. Nicky definitely knew something but was choosing not to let on.

'What about Justine?' Barry asked.

'I think there was talk back in the winter about Justine and Pete, one of our maintenance guys. But I guess it fizzled out.'

That's interesting, Jackie thought. She was happy to pass on gossip about Justine but not Bryony. There could be a number of reasons, but the obvious one was that Bryony could have been linked with someone in a sensitive position. Ian Duncan, maybe? Would Barry choose to follow it up?

'Nicky, you need to tell me if you're aware of any rumours about Bryony being involved with someone in the company, even if it was in the past. This is an official murder inquiry. If we uncover something further down the line and you could have told us now, saving us time, we could charge you with wasting police time. In fact, it wouldn't even be my choice. My boss is pretty ruthless in that regard. She'd spot it.'

Silence. Nicky fidgeted, rotating her wedding ring.

'There was a rumour that Bryony had a brief fling with Ian Duncan some time ago. I don't for a moment think it could be connected.'

'You were right to tell us.' Barry paused for a few seconds, as if he was thinking things through. In fact, the two detectives had already planned how they'd appear to react during the drive across to EcoFutures. This was mere play-acting. 'It ties in with something we already know. Be cautious, Nicky. Do you get my drift?'

'But Ian's one hundred per cent reliable,' she protested.

'I've said what I've said,' was all Barry replied.

## CHAPTER 12: FINGERS AND CURLS

Rae thought that Justine Longford seemed even more tense than on her previous visit to talk to the work group's programmer. She was winding her long hair through her fingers as she listened to what the detectives had to say. Of course, she'd have learned about the discovery of Robin Pryor's body the previous day. It had been the lead story in local news reports, although few details had been released to the media by the police press office. Even so, the shock waves passing through Pryor's small team would have been immense. Justine would still be worrying about the possible break-in at her home and fretting over her own safety. If she'd had the locks on her door changed, as advised, the extra security should have given her some reassurance for a couple of days, but the latest news about her boss had probably filled her with dread again.

'Nothing has shown up in the checks we've made about the two men you were worried about,' Rae told her. 'There's absolutely no evidence that either of them was involved. That doesn't mean they weren't, of course. But nothing else has surfaced. As you can imagine, we've shifted priority since it became clear that Robin Pryor's fate was more than an abduction. It's now a murder investigation, so it's been ramped up to top level. That doesn't mean we've forgotten you. Far from it.'

'So why are you here?'

'Background. We need a clear idea of working relationships within the group. Also, any other possible causes of tensions. Friendships, enmities. That kind of thing. Workplace romances. You get the idea?'

Justine gave her a suspicious look. 'Is all that really necessary? It sounds a bit like muckraking to me.'

'We have to cover all possible motives when we're investigating a murder, Justine. And we need to build up a picture of all the relationships the victim had, work-based and personal. Sometimes the two are linked.'

'I'm probably not the person to ask. I'm a bit clueless when it comes to knowing what's going on around me at a personal level. Robin was the boss. That's how I viewed him. I was a bit in awe of him, actually.'

'Why was that? Wasn't he very approachable?'

'It's not that. It's the way I always relate to someone senior, at work or anywhere else. I feel that I should always do what they expect of me. Maybe it's the way I was brought up. I didn't question things very much. I guess I have this inbuilt need to please people. My approach here is to work at things in a way that would please Robin. I never joined in any gossip about him. It would have seemed wrong, to be honest.'

'Could you explain?'

'He was really good as a project manager. He knew his stuff.'

'What made you take up a job here?' Rae asked.

'I might be a programmer, but I've always been interested in ecology and the environment. When the vacancy came up, I could see it was right up my street. In a way, it's my dream job. And Robin was a great boss, as far as I'm concerned. We'll all miss him.'

'Did you know anything about his private life?'

'I preferred to shut my ears if that kind of gossip came up. Not that it did, not very often, anyway. Robin was a private person. He kept his personal life to himself. That's the way it should be, in my mind.'

'He's been murdered, Justine. That's why we need to probe a bit,' came Rae's response. 'There's got to be a reason. We need to find that reason. It might not be anything linked to his work. It could be because of something in his private life. That's why we need to know.'

Justine sat silently for a few moments, as if pondering.

'He did mention a possible girlfriend recently, but she wasn't anything to do with the company.' She paused. 'Someone suggested he might like darts, so he decided to give it a try. Anyway, this woman was in the pub one night when Robin was there playing darts. They got chatting and must have hit it off. He was talking about her over coffee one morning recently.'

'Did he mention a name?'

'Bella? Belle? Something like that, I think.'

'This is all very helpful, Justine. Do you remember who suggested the darts idea to Robin?'

She shook her head. 'It might have been Ian Duncan. Can't be sure though.'

'Do you currently have a boyfriend or partner? You implied in your recent interview about the possible break-in at your flat that you didn't, but I'm not sure it was explicit.'

'I've been seeing someone for a couple of weeks, yes. Pete Bennett, one of the maintenance guys here. We went out a few months ago on a couple of dates but it didn't seem to work. He asked me out again last month, so I thought I'd give it another go. He seems more focussed on me this time, so I'm a bit happier with the way it's going.'

'You didn't tell me this when we spoke a few days ago about the person who might have got into your flat.'

'It couldn't have been him. He was away on a break in Spain with his local football club. I got a postcard from him.'

Tommy spoke up. 'Do people still send postcards? I thought that stopped years ago, when I was a kid.'

'I do,' Rae said. 'You should know that, Tommy. I sent one to you and Olivia back in the autumn. Are you telling me I wasted my hard-earned money?'

Tommy squirmed slightly. 'Sorry, boss. Come to think of it, Olivia did stick some to the fridge. Is yours the sunset view in North Wales?'

'Yes. The Menai Strait.' Rae turned her attention back to Justine. 'Excuse my slightly thoughtless colleague. He's demoted to tea boy for the next week. We were talking about relationships at your work. Are there any others that we should know about? Particularly ones involving members of your work group.'

Justine shrugged. 'I don't think so. Almost everyone else is married or in a long-term relationship. Robin and I were the only ones single in that respect.'

'That's useful. Thanks.' She paused. 'What about Bryony?'

'Ah.' Justine fidgeted and turned slightly pink-cheeked. 'Um, she's married, isn't she? Her husband's in the navy.'

'Yes, that's what we believe. Why, Justine? Are there rumours?'

'Well, I shouldn't really say.'

'Yes, you should. Tell us what's on your mind.'

'Well, I did overhear something about Bryony being seen out with Ian Duncan, the security manager. It's probably completely untrue. Either that or there's an innocent explanation. I feel awful for mentioning it.'

'No, you did the right thing. Absolutely so.'

As they left, Rae turned to Tommy. 'That worked well. See what I mean, Tommy? Showing a bit of a human face can win people over and get them to open up a bit. The postcard comment was a good twist.'

'Yeah, but I meant it, boss. I wasn't acting.'

Rae frowned at him. 'I don't want to know that. You shouldn't have told me.'

72

# CHAPTER 13: COOL MORNING AIR

Sophie Allen was out and about in her wheelchair again. From her ward to the hospital shop to buy a newspaper. From there to the café for a takeaway coffee. Then out to the secluded garden area to sit in the cool morning air, sip her drink, scan the paper, continue reading the book about Eleanor of Aquitaine and, occasionally, listen to the birdsong. This should form the basis of an idyllic existence, she thought. Just whiling away the time, not doing much at all. In reality, she felt the exact opposite, an intense feeling of frustration and impatience, a sense that the world was hurrying on and leaving her behind, that she might never catch up with it.

Just as on the previous day, no one else was in the garden so Sophie had the pick of the seating areas. This time she didn't doze off so heard the door open as another patient came out to enjoy the fresh air.

'Good morning.' It was a woman's voice. 'May I join you? I think I've spotted you zooming around the corridors over the past couple of days. You seem to know many of the staff quite well.'

It was the same voice as the previous day. Bryony O'Neil. Sophie squinted into the sun, trying to shade her eyes. Bryony was alone today. Sophie pointed to the nearby bench seat.

'Of course. Be my guest. It's always nice to chat to someone. I get rather bored in here, day after day. And it's true, I've been in long enough to be recognised by a lot of people. Shattered leg, broken shoulder. Skull fracture. It's all getting better though, hopefully. You?'

'Car crash. Ankle, arm and head. It looks worse than it is. I should be out in another couple of days.'

'Lucky you. I'm envious.'

'Do you mind if I smoke? I gave up several years ago but once I came round in here, just last week, I was gasping for a fag. No idea why. A friend brought a packet in for me. Just two a day, though. One in the morning, one in the afternoon.'

'That's a bit odd, isn't it?' Sophie said. 'I mean, if you'd given up.'

Bryony lit her cigarette and took a puff, closing her eyes momentarily as if in some strange kind of ecstatic state.

'It's a strange thing, the human brain. But I'll stop when I'm out and life gets back to normal. You don't indulge then?'

Sophie shook her head. 'Tried it once when I was young. It made me sick, so I've never touched them since. Now beer, that's an entirely different story.'

'Really? Tell me more. I've got no pressing engagements to worry about.' She laughed.

'When I was about thirteen my Uncle Reggie lived close by, and he was a keen home brewer. I used to help him one Saturday a month, when he made the stuff, and the next week when he racked it into a small keg. When he became disabled, I took over and did most of the work, leaving him to drink it. I've never lost the taste for a good pint. Wonderful stuff. Life-enhancing.'

Bryony laughed. 'I'll take your word for it. How did you get your injuries?'

'Assaulted by a thug with an iron bar. Smashed my leg and tipped me into a river.'

Bryony's eyes widened. 'God, that's terrible. Why are some men so bloody violent?'

Sophie smiled grimly. 'It was a woman. She had the iron bar. The bloke only had a wooden stick. That caused my shoulder injuries. But it was the woman who smashed my leg up. Far worse.'

'God. Why on earth did they pick on you?'

'I'm a police officer. It goes with the job.'

'Unbelievable, some people. I was deliberately targeted and forced to crash at high speed. I just don't understand it. I keep asking myself, why? Why me? It just doesn't make any kind of sense.'

'Before you open up any more, I'd better warn you that I'm a senior detective in Dorset Police. I wouldn't want you to think I've somehow manipulated this meeting and tricked you into talking about your experiences.'

'Of course not. I've got nothing to hide anyway. Several detectives have already interviewed me. I've even got an alarm tag that I can activate if I feel under threat.' She looked again at Sophie. 'I don't remember your story cropping up in the local press.'

'No. It happened in Somerset, so I was taken to Taunton Hospital first. Then to Exeter for the specialist surgery. I've been here in Dorchester for about three weeks, since I got some mobility back. My next set of operations might be back in Exeter. My consultant is based there. It'll probably be a long haul.'

'I don't envy you. My injuries have been bad enough but I don't think they're as serious as yours.' Bryony paused, as if thinking hard. She drew a long puff from the fast-dwindling cigarette that rested between her fingers. 'So the detectives that interviewed me a few days ago. You know them? A detective inspector, Marsh, I think. And a woman sergeant.'

Sophie nodded. 'I'm their boss. Under normal circumstances, I mean. Not at the moment though. Official police procedures. I'm deliberately kept out of the loop and could end up on a disciplinary if I meddle in any way. Too many drugs, anyway. My head's all over the place. Even I wouldn't trust any decisions I make. Lovely, isn't it? That fuzzy marsh-mallow feeling.'

Sophie realised that Bryony was only half listening. The woman gave her a sideways look.

'How much of a problem is it if I haven't told them quite everything?'

'Might be serious. It depends on the relevance of what you've kept hidden.' She waited.

'It doesn't seem relevant, but it worries me. It's a bit sensitive and personal.'

'Better to tell them and let them decide. They're both very discreet, if that's what's worrying you.'

'You'll get to hear of it though, won't you? I thought the man looked familiar. He's been in visiting you, I bet. I must have passed him in the corridor at some time. Ginger hair?'

Sophie nodded warily. 'That's him. But he's a close friend. We've worked together for years. I sang during a cabaret slot at his wedding reception at Easter. Rather badly, to be honest. And, as I said, I'm not allowed to get involved.'

Bryony bit her lip. 'I'll phone them. It's been bothering me, to be honest.'

'The right decision. I'm Sophie, by the way.'

Her companion held out a hand to shake. 'Bryony.'

## CHAPTER 14: FLASHBACKS

The local police had swamped the small, sleepy resort town of Lyme Regis since the discovery of Robin Pryor's body near the coast path. Uniformed officers were knocking on doors, calling into shops, cafés and pubs, and asking holidaymakers if they'd seen anything suspicious on the morning of Pryor's disappearance. Sergeant Rose Simons and her sidekick, PC George Warrander, were on Monmouth Beach, talking to boat owners, along with chalet and beach hut residents. The area behind the shingle beach had provided the solitary sighting of Pryor on that fateful morning, as he climbed the steps onto the coast path. He'd been spotted by a chalet resident who'd identified him from his sky-blue walking jacket and red baseball cap. It was this strange colour combination that the police teams were asking about now, as they made an attempt to pin together Pryor's movements that morning. They struck lucky. A boat owner who'd not visited the beach since the previous weekend had been working on his boat on the day in question. He recalled seeing someone matching Pryor's description but also remembered something else. Another walker was some twenty yards behind their man and had climbed the steps after him. A woman, binoculars slung around her neck, and speaking into a mobile phone. George carefully noted the details.

'Is there any CCTV here?' Rose asked the man.

'In the boat park, I think,' he replied. 'I'm not sure whether it's council owned or private.'

'We'll find out. Thanks for your help. We'll be in touch if we need to check on anything.'

The two officers made their way to the boat park office and asked to see the manager, then explained their request. They were soon looking at a slightly fuzzy recording of the access gate to the boat park. It also showed a short section of the coast path as it headed west before turning through ninety degrees towards the flight of steps.

'Last Saturday morning, about ten,' Rose said, craning her neck to get a better view of the small laptop screen.

The manager selected the date, loaded the recording and fast forwarded through the sequence until just after ten, slowing it to a more reasonable speed.

There was Pryor, caught just for a couple of seconds, his back to the camera. And there was a woman, some fifteen seconds behind. She appeared to be wearing an olive-green walking jacket and jeans, her head hidden by a hat.

'Bingo. Can we get a copy?' Rose said, as George handed across a flash drive. The two detectives hurried back outside. Rose wasted no time in phoning Barry Marsh.

* * *

The detectives were huddled around a screen, examining the footage that Rose had brought across to the incident room.

'Can we tell who it is?' Tommy asked, as he tried to peer from behind Rae's shoulder.

'Doesn't look like it,' Barry replied. 'It can probably be cleaned up to give us a sharper image, but by the time she appears, we only get a view of her side and back. What you can do, Tommy, is to use it as a basis to get some measurements.

Print off a still image of her, then take Jackie with you and get her in the same position. Use that fencepost in the background as a comparison point. It'll give us a starter.' He paused. 'She's been careful with her appearance, don't you think? Covering her head and keeping her face hidden. But you can't really disguise things like height and body shape. We can use that.'

'Who's best to get it cleaned up?' Jackie asked.

'It needs to go to digital forensics. Can you do that, please? The problem is, they're overloaded with work at the moment, so it might take a couple of days. I'll phone Jimmy Melsom across in Bournemouth. He's a whizz with digital imaging. If he's not busy on some other job, he might be willing to do something for us today. If he's happy to help, I'll send him a copy. He owes me a favour or two.' He glanced at the time. 'I'll need to head off to the hospital. Bryony O'Neil has been in touch with a slightly odd request to see me. She said she wants to add something to her story. Rae, you can come with me. Rose, you and George follow up on that hypodermic that the search team found. Forensics should have analysed it by now. Then pay a visit to EcoFutures and the place next door, Hewton Distribution. If you think the same as me, that it was an attempt to get the lie of the land in that eco place, insist on seeing their security manager, Ian Duncan. Find out if he can justify not acting on it as a potential threat to them. Jackie, see if there's any trace of Pryor's mobile phone anywhere. I asked for a check on his recent calls, from his provider. Chase that up too, will you? We need a call log to see what was going on in the days prior to his murder. Let's move.'

* * *

Barry and Rae found Bryony in a small sitting room within her hospital ward.

'I'm being discharged,' she told them. 'I should be home tomorrow. The hospital admin people reminded me to inform you.'

Barry was perturbed. If this was all she had to say, why hadn't she just mentioned it on the phone rather than asking him to drive all the way across here to Dorchester?

'Rae can arrange transport home for you, if that's what your plans are. Remember I suggested that you might want to stay elsewhere, just as a precaution. Have you had any thoughts?'

She shook her head. 'Not really, though my brother can come to stay with me for a while if you think it would be safer than being on my own. Anyway, that isn't the main reason I wanted to talk to you. There are a couple of other things.' She looked down at the floor and fidgeted awkwardly. 'I wasn't entirely open with you originally. I failed to mention that I had a brief fling with Ian Duncan a few months ago, though it only lasted a short while. I was too embarrassed to mention it. It wasn't a good time for me, and I tried to purge it from my memory. I'm really sorry.'

Barry nodded. 'It does throw a different slant on things.'

'The thing is, I told him of that particular nightmare of mine. A man running out of the trees towards me, waving a big knife. It was a scene from a horror film I watched years ago. It obviously lodged in my brain. But I told him — I only remembered a few days ago.'

'Do you think he's capable of being involved?'

Bryony shook her head. 'No. I'm sure he isn't. He's a nice guy. My sense of judgement isn't that poor. But something else is bothering me. I've started getting flashbacks. The doctors warned me I might, as my memories return. The thing is, that woman who ran out and stopped my car. I've remembered something about her. I kind of assumed she was young when I first saw her. You know, a teenager. But I don't think she was, not now. She could have been in her twenties. Even thirties. It was when she was half in my car, holding the door open. I was shouting at her to close it, but she was ignoring me. And she looked tanned.'

'You said she had dark hair when you made your statement. And that she was pale, shocked looking.'

Bryony nodded. 'Yes, though her skin was kind of olive in colour. She had a kind of Mediterranean look. Her eyes were dark, too.'

The two detectives made a brief visit to see Sophie Allen before leaving the hospital and heading back to base. Barry gave her a quick summary of recent developments, including their chat with Bryony O'Neil.

'You know something,' Rae said while Sophie was pondering on what she'd been told. 'George was following up yesterday on what Justine told us about Robin Pryor and his recent take-up of playing darts in a pub back in Lyme.'

'Go on,' Barry said.

'Well, more than one person in the pub said that the woman he was with was Mediterranean-looking. Short black hair and olive-skinned. Big hooped earrings. It's in George's report. And he made a point of mentioning it to me. Quite a short, curvy woman. Probably in her thirties but could be taken for younger. One or two people said they didn't think he'd met her before that night. She made a beeline for him soon after he arrived.'

'Right. That's important. We need to trace her.'

'Someone also said that she was a bit touchy-feely with him. Very close. And something else that's just occurred to me. That woman caught by the CCTV was quite short from our check on the measurements. Well, to my eyes anyway. Could it be the same person?'

* * *

Rose and George were pacing around the area occupied by Hewton Distribution and EcoFutures, looking at it from all angles.

'It's pretty obvious, boss. It wasn't an attempt to watch Hewton at all. EcoFutures was the target.'

Rose stood back, surveying the scene. 'But why, George? What were they trying to do?' She turned to Glen Blackford, Hewton's security chief. 'What are your thoughts?'

He shook his head. 'It's what we said to the other two detectives. Odd. Maybe something scared them off. That would be my guess. Maybe they realised they'd been spotted. They haven't been back since. I've been keeping an eye out, just in case. Look, I need to be off. Find me if you need anything else.'

George waited until he'd left then offered an idea. 'Boss, we only have the eco place's opinion that whoever it was didn't come back. What if they did but weren't spotted? What if they've been keeping the place under scrutiny for some time? Before and after?'

'It's about the only thing that makes sense. Let's go and speak to their security person and see what he has to say. We've got to tread carefully, according to Barry. The guy might be under suspicion, and we mustn't give the game away. As if we would.'

Ian Duncan didn't say much when he met them at reception inside the EcoFutures complex. They walked with him to where the vehicle with the watchers had been parked.

'I really didn't think it was serious enough to warrant any action,' he explained. 'We haven't spotted anything ourselves. What's the problem?'

George spoke up. 'What if they did something other than just watching? Planted something? A hidden camera. A bug of some type. Isn't that serious enough?'

The security manager suddenly looked worried. 'Is that likely?'

'You tell me. It's your company, not ours. If you hold sensitive or confidential information, then there might be a risk, surely? Do you hold stuff like that?'

The man pursed his lips but didn't answer.

Rose took up the thread. 'If you want our advice, some kind of sweep might be in order. Identify the areas at risk and check them out. And keep us informed if you find anything. One of your staff has just been murdered and another scared witless in a potential assault. Do you see where we're going with this? It might all be part of a bigger picture. It might be more serious than you think, Mr Duncan.'

## CHAPTER 15: AN EVENING TO REMEMBER

Justine Longford still felt uneasy. She was sitting in one of Lyme Regis's pubs, chatting to Pete Bennett, her current boyfriend. Well, that's how she described him to her friends, even though she was a little unsure about the current status of their on-off romance. Was it really back on again? She'd told the police that it was. In reality, she was still unsure. The problem was that Pete was so laid-back about their relationship that she still wondered where they were heading and whether she'd ever really know when they got there. He was infuriatingly vague about everything. Maybe that's why he was a maintenance worker while she was a programmer and systems engineer. Different attitudes to life. Oddly enough, he was quite animated tonight.

'You told the cops about me? Why?' He seemed exasperated.

'Because they asked, of course.'

'Did you have to? I mean, what difference would it have made if you'd just stayed quiet?'

'What's the problem?' She was genuinely puzzled.

'I don't like being talked about, if you must know.'

'But they have to eliminate people, Pete. I told them you were in Spain when my flat was broken into, so there isn't a problem.'

He didn't seem reassured. 'See, that's the other thing. I reckon the whole thing was just down to your imagination. Seriously, who would break into a flat and not steal anything? There's no point, is there? Maybe it was just that time of the month for you. You know how emotional you get.'

Justine couldn't quite believe what she was hearing. She felt outraged.

'I wasn't on my period, Pete. How dare you imply that I'm just some weak-minded girly-type, ruled entirely by my emotions? I'm a fully qualified software engineer. I have a degree, a good one. And I earn twice as much money as you.'

'That's right. Rub it in, why don't you.' He sounded bitter.

'I've said it before. It doesn't bother me. I always thought that it didn't matter to you, either. Clearly, I was wrong to think that. I also mentioned to the police that we were getting on better second time around. I seem to be wrong in that as well. You're being really prickly tonight and I don't know why. Is it something to do with the police?'

He didn't answer, choosing to just stare at the tabletop instead.

'Are you on some kind of record somewhere? Is that what you're worried about?'

He finally looked up at her, rather moodily. Then he suddenly stood up and stalked away towards the bar area. Justine twisted around, trying to spot where he'd gone. Was he in the crowd at the bar or had he gone to the loo? Or had he left entirely? She peered at the figures lining the bar but failed to spot him. If he'd left then he really was a worthless, thoughtless worm. She'd explained to him what she'd been advised by the police, that she shouldn't be out alone as a precaution. She'd assured them that she was safe in the company of her friends. And now this. Would she need a taxi to get home? She swirled the contents of her glass, a white wine spritzer, watching as the ice cubes gently jostled each other. A shadow fell across the table and she looked up. Pete was back.

'I thought you'd gone,' she said.

'No.' He sat down. 'I wouldn't leave you on your own. I'll get you home.'

He still looked moody, angry even. But at least he hadn't left her in the lurch.

'I got into trouble with the cops when I was a lot younger,' he said. 'Shoplifting. Fighting. I'm changed now, though.'

'Do they know at work?'

He shrugged. 'I never told them. The cops will spot my record, as sure as night follows day. If they tell the bosses at work, I'll lose my job. I'm sure of it.'

'You can't be certain, Pete. If it was years ago, you deserve a chance. Is it relevant, anyway? You work in maintenance.'

He shook his head despairingly. 'It's not as simple as that, is it? It never is. Let's go.'

Justine didn't feel like arguing. The evening had been a disaster as far as she was concerned and had caused her to question whether Pete had any potential as a possible long-term partner. It was the first time he'd shown such irritability, and she was wondering how many other unpleasant character traits he had, hidden from view. Maybe it was time to call it a day. She continued the conversation once they were outside and had started the short stroll back to where she lived.

'I don't know where this is going, Pete. Us, I mean. I'm not sure we're suited to each other. Maybe we're looking for different things.'

He shrugged but didn't say anything. Justine realised something else about Pete. Despite knowing that she worked in the team led by Robin Pryor, Pete hadn't once talked about him or the nature of his death. He'd carefully steered the conversation away from any mention of anything that might connect to the tragedy. Was that out of consideration for her, not wanting to chance her getting upset? Or was there a different reason? And why hadn't he responded more strongly to what she'd just said about their relationship?

Oh God, she thought. Things are just too bloody complicated.

When they reached her block of flats, she merely expressed her thanks and turned towards the door to the building, leaving him to walk on to his own home. The main door had been left unlocked yet again, wedged slightly ajar by a thin wooden block, despite the prominent security notice in the foyer and her recent strongly worded request to the other tenants asking them to keep the building locked at all times. Why were so many people such utterly selfish and unthinking morons?

Justine slid in through the doorway and made her way silently along the short, carpeted corridor and up the stairs to the first floor. Why did she feel uneasy? She reached her door and stood outside, listening. Was that a slight movement she could hear? How could it be, at this time in the evening? The previous incident had been during the day, when she'd been at work. But this was different. She hadn't broadcast the fact that she'd be going out to meet Pete tonight, though she was back home earlier than expected. What should she do?

She retraced her steps to the main door, then went outside and phoned the detective who'd visited her, Rae Gregson. 'I'll be across right away, Justine. I'll call for a local squad to come out to you. They'll probably be there a good bit before me. I've got to drive from Wool, so it'll take me about an hour. Go somewhere safe. Maybe a neighbour?'

Justine didn't know any of her neighbours well enough to call on them with what she thought was a silly story about a creaking sound in her apartment, so she stood outside in an area of deep shadow, beside the bin enclosure, trying to stop her limbs from shaking.

Within ten minutes she caught the sound of a police siren in the distance. Thank goodness, though she guessed that they wouldn't be best pleased when they arrived and found her flat to be empty and still secured. She should have got the lock changed, as the visiting police officer had suggested.

As the siren got louder, she became aware of the nearby door opening and a dark-clad figure hurrying through it and running away through the car park to the roadway, almost colliding with the approaching police car. One officer leapt out and gave chase to the fleeing individual, while the other hurried across to Justine, who'd followed the fleeing figure despite shaking with fright.

'There's a good chance we'll have him,' the officer said. 'I'm Stephanie Biggs. My young colleague, Kieran, has a much better chance of catching that guy than me. You must be Justine? Are you okay?'

Justine could manage no more than a nod of her head. She found it difficult to speak clearly.

'Are you hurt in any way?' Stephanie asked.

Justine shook her head. 'I'm okay,' she managed to gasp.

By now, several of Justine's neighbours had come out of their apartments to see what the commotion was about.

'I need to check on my colleague, but I'll be back soon. Don't go into your flat. Wait with one of your neighbours.'

* * *

PC Kieran Mathieson kept himself extremely fit, with a mix of running and boxing to keep his muscles trim, strong and ready for action. He suspected that the man in front of him was less focussed on such activities, judging by the decreasing distance between them as they ran downhill, towards the River Lym.

'Stop. Police!' Kieran called again, as the man moved off the road onto a footpath that led north alongside the river.

He was definitely slowing. More caution was called for. Kieran knew that this was a time of danger for police officers in pursuit on foot, a time when the target might begin to panic and draw a knife. That's when things might move to an entirely different level.

The running man's pace had slowed to that of a trot. His arms were no longer pumping back and forward at his sides. They were no longer visible. What was he doing? Kieran slowed too and approached his quarry carefully. The man turned and a knife blade glinted in the moonlight.

'You really don't want to do that,' Kieran said. 'That makes everything so much worse.'

'Fuck off,' the man managed to gasp. 'Just go back and let me be.'

Kieran unclipped his small canister of incapacitating spray, holding it in direct view. He circled closer to the target.

'Drawing an offensive weapon on a police officer makes everything a lot more serious,' he said, loudly. 'Drop it now and take a step back or I'll use the spray.'

The man waved the knife in front of him. Kieran moved sideways, then sprayed into the man's face, momentarily blinding his quarry. He then stepped closer, avoiding the shiny weapon that was still being waved about, and grabbed his wrist, at the same time hooking his foot behind the man's ankle. The assailant tumbled over, unable to see clearly while coughing and sneezing. Within a few seconds, Kieran had him in handcuffs.

'I told you,' he said. 'That really wasn't a clever thing to do.'

He looked up as his squad-car partner, Stephanie, came into view.

'I'm too late again, I see,' she panted. 'Well done, Kieran. The girl's okay, by the way.'

'I can't fucking see,' the man was shouting. 'You've buggered my eyes!'

'I'll get some water on them if you just hold still,' Stephanie replied. 'Why didn't you just give up quietly? Why make it hard for yourself? No bloody sense.' She took a close look as she wiped the man's face. 'I know you. Joey Sturrock, local hard man. Not so hard now, are you?'

Another squad car soon arrived, with the officers taking charge of Sturrock. Kieran and Stephanie returned to the flats to check on Justine. She was in the apartment of her immediate neighbours, a retired couple, both slightly deaf. They had heard nothing, they told the two officers. Some twenty minutes later, Rae Gregson arrived.

'Is there somewhere you can stay tonight, Justine?' Rae asked. 'I've arranged for a forensic team to visit but they won't be here until the morning.'

The elderly couple looked at each other questioningly. 'You can use our spare room, Justine. We'd be really happy for you to stay. We don't know you well enough, even though we've been neighbours for several months now.'

Justine gave them a weak smile. 'Thanks. That would be great.'

Rae had a quick word with the two uniformed officers out of earshot, getting their account of events.

'Is there any chance you could get some of the paperwork done tonight? I'll probably be interviewing that man in the morning, once everything's been given the go-ahead from my boss. It'll be really useful to have all the facts to hand.'

'Of course,' Kieran said quietly. 'I don't mind doing it. I interviewed her a few days ago, after she reported another possible break-in. I thought she was reliable. A nice person, in fact, Sarge.'

'Okay. I'll take over from here. I'd still like a watch kept on the place, even though we have that guy in custody. There's something odd going on. Keep your eyes and ears open, won't you? Local gossip. You know the drill.'

The two uniformed officers left, and Rae returned to Justine.

'I think it's time I got a locksmith in,' she said.

'Best thing you could do, Justine. Go for a reputable company and don't compromise on the lock's quality. Tell them it's urgent and that the police are advising you. I'll try to see you again tomorrow evening.'

## CHAPTER 16: KEYS

It was the next morning and Rae was talking to Barry in his office. 'It's a puzzle, boss. But it's one that might open things up for us. I just can't help thinking that her boyfriend, this Pete Bennett, must know something. Her first evening out for some time and it just so happens that her flat gets visited. Again. It's too much of a coincidence.'

Barry pondered on what Rae was telling him.

'But what's the motive? Someone was there before. Nothing was taken, according to Justine. Why go back again?'

'I can see what you're saying, of course I can. We don't really know what's going on in any of this. But he arranged to take her out for the evening, and this happens. Their evening finishes early because of the row and she gets back to find this Joey Sturrock still in her flat.'

'That's what doesn't add up, Rae. If Bennett was involved, he'd have found an excuse to keep her out until later, some pre-arranged time. The fact that he took her home early tends to suggest otherwise.'

'But we'll still interview him? Get a statement?'

'Of course. We need to check the sequence of events and make a judgement about him, see if he's manipulating her in some way. I'm just a bit dubious. Things don't add up in my mind.' He paused. 'What's on record about this guy Sturrock?'

Rae glanced at the sheet of paper she held. 'Local bad boy. Petty theft, drugs, minor assaults, stealing cars. He's been in and out of trouble all his life.'

'Does this business fit his profile? A careful break-in, leaving next to no trace?'

'Not really. He usually leaves a trail a mile wide.'

Barry was deep in thought. 'Do you think he's been hired?'

Rae was silent as she contemplated this idea. 'It's the only thing that makes sense, boss. Someone wanted a local to do some kind of undercover checking but ended up with a careless halfwit.'

'Exactly. It's only a possibility, though. There are other, simpler reasons.'

'You want me to follow it up when I interview him? Try to pin him down?'

'Circle in to it, slowly. That's if he's at all responsive. My guess is that he'll zip his lip and give you the old *no comment* routine. Wouldn't you in his position?'

'I don't ever intend to be in his position, boss. But I take your point. If he is working for someone else, he'll have been given his instructions.'

'And told what'll happen to him if he does spill the beans. Get Tommy or Jackie to do some careful checking of his recent contacts. Someone might give us what we need.'

'Jackie's already found something interesting. This guy Sturrock? He lives right next door to a certain Billy Pitt. That was a name that cropped up early on, when we interviewed Justine after the first break-in. He worked for the building company that put the block of flats up, then became the maintenance officer and cleaner, part-time. Very part-time. She wondered if he still had access to keys. Worth following up, I think.'

'Absolutely. Give it to Jackie. She's a real boon, don't you think?'

Rae was just about to leave but paused at the door. 'Yes, she is. Boss, is there a problem with the DCI? I'd have thought she'd have been down to see us, even if she is tied up in that big operation up in Bristol. You know, just to get a handle on things.'

'I don't know, Rae. I just don't know. We've had phone conversations, but they've been a bit short. What was she like during that last case in Watchet?'

'Not at all relaxed. It was as if she was looking over her shoulder all the time. She kept asking me how Sophie Allen might view her decisions. It all felt a bit weird. Do you think she might be having second thoughts about WeSCU?'

Barry shrugged. 'I don't know what to think. And we've got enough on our plate, the way this case is developing. I haven't got time to worry about it.'

'You know who's just passed her inspector exams, don't you? And might be looking for a new posting very soon?'

Barry looked blank.

'Lydia. And everyone knows you're earmarked for a DCI role soon. It all fits, doesn't it? It could be great, boss.'

Barry shook his head. 'It won't work, Rae. The agreement about WeSCU was that the senior officers should come from across all the counties involved. What you're saying gives it far too much of a Dorset slant.'

Rae grinned impishly. 'Just saying.'

\* \* \*

Jackie Spring drew up outside the address she'd been given for Billy Pitt and took a good look at the rather run-down building in front of her. She'd wondered how low-paid workers could afford to live in a highly desirable picture-postcard town like Lyme Regis. Here was the answer, and it wasn't particularly pleasant. It looked as if the old Victorian-era house had been divided into a number of small bedsit rooms. Several old cars that looked as if they'd seen better days stood in an untidy parking area beside the house. Strangely, they stood alongside a gleaming Mercedes in a soft cream colour. How incongruous was that? She locked her car and made her way to the door. A list of twelve numbers was placed beside a vertical row of pushbuttons. Twelve? How was that possible in this ordinary-looking house? She pressed the button for number seven and waited. Nothing. She pressed it again. This time a small grubby grille crackled into life and emitted a low buzz.

'Yeah?' came a tinny, distant-sounding voice from the grille.

'Detective Jackie Spring, Wessex crime unit. Is that Billy Pitt? Can we speak please?'

Some muttered sounds came out of the speaker, although Jackie couldn't make any sense of them. She heard a click coming from the lock on the door. She pushed it open and went in, entering a rather dingy hallway, its floor covered by a threadbare carpet. A corkboard was fitted to the nearest wall, several sheets of faded paper pinned to it. The most prominent reminded residents to keep the building secure.

Jackie followed the directions to flats seven to twelve, given under an arrow pointing to the stairs. The stairway's carpet and walls were both faded but clean. The residents might be relatively poor but at least some were doing their best to keep their living conditions bearable. From her experience, that wasn't always the case.

She knocked on the door of flat seven. She heard movement inside and waited patiently while the door was opened, the face of a man who looked to be in his fifties peering at her suspiciously through the gap.

'What do you want?' he grunted.

'A few minutes of your time, please, Mr Pitt.'

'I've got a visitor. Can't it wait?'

'No. I'm a police officer. I only need a couple of minutes. It's important, Mr Pitt.'

Another mumbled grunt accompanied the door being closed further to allow a security chain to be disengaged. It then opened again, this time more fully.

'Sensible precautions, Mr Pitt,' she said, as she stepped inside a slightly gloomy room that smelled of stale cigarette smoke. The man who opened the door looked at her warily. He was of middling height, had mousey hair and was somewhat untidily dressed. Jackie refrained from wrinkling her nose.

'What's this about?' He was uneasy, peering at her suspiciously. Another man, taller, was lurking in the background. He had dark hair, smoothed back with oil, and was immaculately dressed in a pale-grey suit, white shirt and dark-blue tie. His black leather shoes gleamed.

'Maybe I'll be off, Billy. See you later.'

This second man, possibly in his late thirties, pushed his way past Jackie as he moved into the corridor. In a bit of a hurry, she thought to herself. I wonder why? There was something menacing about him. Or was it just her over-active imagination? Her gaze returned to the man she'd come to see.

'As I said, I'm Detective Constable Jackie Spring, Wessex crime unit. It's just a quick visit. I'm sure there's nothing to worry about, Mr Pitt. It'll only take a couple of minutes. Can we sit down somewhere?'

He led her into a rectangular multifunctional room, with a sofa against one wall, a small table with two chairs set opposite, and a worktop, small cooking hob and sink under the far window. A single door led off from one of the side walls. A toilet and shower, possibly. The sofa showed signs of also functioning as a bed.

The man gestured to the sofa, but Jackie had walked to the window, looking out in time to see a cream-coloured Mercedes pulling out of the car park. That other man had been quick, if it was him. Jackie ignored the suggestion to sit on the sofa and pulled out one of the upright chairs at the table. Pitt muttered something indecipherable as he sat down opposite her.

'I don't like being bothered,' he said, looking at her challengingly.

'Well, I can understand that. None of us do, do we? Not when we're busy. But things have to be investigated, Mr Pitt, and we need your help.'

Jackie had decided on an initially conciliatory approach on her way over. It did no harm to use a little smooth-talk to lull someone into a sense of false security. She was playing the innocent, as if she was unaware of rumours about his links to the local criminal community.

'So what's it about?'

'Keys, Mr Pitt. Missing keys. Specifically, missing keys to a block of flats on Belle Vue Avenue. I think you were employed by the builders who put them up. About five years ago, I'd guess. Is that right?'

He narrowed his eyes, staring at her as if he was trying to read her thoughts. Jackie gave him a gentle smile. Finally, he spoke.

'Yeah. But what would I know about keys?'

'You have one. You work as the maintenance officer and cleaner since the build was complete. The company closed down its operations in Dorset, I believe, and shifted to Hampshire. You didn't want to move, so stayed put. You worked for them while the flats were still on the market then offered your services to the new owners. You've been doing a weekly clean for about three years, haven't you?'

He nodded but said nothing.

'Where's your key right now?'

He stood up and retrieved a set of keys from the pocket of a coat that was hanging from a hook by the door. He laid it on the table in front of the detective.

'Which one is it?' Jackie asked.

He pointed. Jackie used a pen to push the keys apart slightly. The one he'd indicated shared a small ring with another two, both smaller. She used her phone to take several snapshots.

'What are the other keys?' she asked.

'Cupboards in the corridors,' he responded. 'One on each floor. For cleaning stuff.'

'Did you ever have access to the keys to the individual flats? The owners all say that they only got handed a single key each and had to get further copies made.'

'No. Anyways, why you askin' me this?'

'Break-ins, Mr Pitt. With no signs of forced entry. The culprits must have had copies of the keys.'

'Well, it weren't nuffin' to do wiv me.' He looked indignant but Jackie was sure it was false. 'You can't pin that kind of stuff on me.'

'I wasn't trying to, Mr Pitt. I just wonder if those missing keys could have found their way into other hands.'

'Not mine.'

He was glaring at her challengingly. Time to change tack.

'Joey Sturrock, Mr Pitt. He's a neighbour of yours, isn't he?'

The man eyed Jackie suspiciously. 'Yeah. So what?'

'Do you know him well?'

He shook his head. 'Not much. Just enough to say hello.'

'Doesn't he play in the same pub pool team as you?'

His eyes narrowed even more. 'What of it?'

'Surely that means you know him better than you've implied? You must chat to him regularly.'

He shrugged. 'Yeah, but it's nuthin' important. Look, what's this about?'

'We have him in custody, Mr Pitt. For breaking and entering. When he was arrested, he had a working set of keys in his possession, keys for the Belle Vue flats.'

'Yeah? Well, he didn't get them from me, if that's what you're thinking.'

'Give me a different explanation, then.'

'He's a bit of a Romeo, is Joey. Mebbe he's having it off with some bit of stuff who lives there. Know what I mean?' He was leering at her. No wonder he gave Justine the creeps.

'I knows a woman who gives her boyfriend a set of keys and tells him to surprise her. He creeps into her place some nights and slides into bed, silent like. Then gives her a good seeing to without warning. Mebbe not your thing, but some like it a bit rougher. Know what I mean?'

It took all of Jackie's self-control to maintain her neutral facial expression. Don't react, she told herself. That's what he wants.

'So if we find your fingerprints on those keys Joey Sturrock had, something must have gone wrong with our process. Or if your prints are found inside any of the other flats. Is that what you're saying?'

He sat forward with a jerk. 'What?'

Good. The reaction she'd been looking for. Get the creep worried and wipe that leering grin from his face. 'I didn't say we had, Mr Pitt. Not yet, anyway. Only time will tell.'

'Yeah, but I was one of the builders. My prints are bound to be on some surfaces, aren't they? I even put the finishing coats of paint on most of them.'

'But furniture would be different, wouldn't it? That would only go in after the apartments have been sold.'

No doubt about it. He was looking worried again. Job done. She'd better call in and warn all the flat owners to consider changing their locks, just as she'd suggested to Justine Longford. She called the incident room and reported events to Barry before setting out for the block of flats in question. She also told him of the luxury Mercedes.

'It stuck out like a sore thumb,' she said. 'Sorry, but I didn't get the registration.'

* * *

That evening, Rose and George were back at the EcoFutures premises, this time with a police digital surveillance expert, complete with kit. Barry had arranged clearance for them direct from Nicky Dangerfield. He'd told her that Ian Duncan may have known more than he'd been letting on, and that this visit needed to be kept under wraps. The security manager had left, along with most of the staff. Only Nicky accompanied them on their walkabout.

'What are you looking for?' she asked the technician.

'Won't know until I find it,' came the somewhat terse reply. 'Could be a hidden camera. Could be a listening device. It might be sensible to concentrate on the area used by that project team that's being targeted. Then, if we don't find anything, we move out from there.'

The small group moved inside the main building and towards the home of the Parantos Coastal Development team. Bella Ferarro, the police technician, switched on a couple of items of equipment she had attached to her belt as they approached.

'It's to pick up communication signals,' she explained. 'No one plants bugs that just store the data and have to be picked up to gain access to the information. If it's here, it'll be transmitting it. We're just trying to spot a rogue signal.'

'Don't you have to wave something about? A tracker of some kind?'

Bella shook her head. 'That would give the game away, wouldn't it? We assumed that you wouldn't want to alert whoever bugged you. Better to leave whatever we find in place, I would have thought. If I do find anything, it's important not to react in case we're being watched. This next step is quite important. I'll switch on my jamming device, but we won't have too long, otherwise anyone monitoring things will get suspicious. Ten minutes at best.'

During the next few minutes, four devices were discovered. Three listening devices in key locations, including the team manager's office, and a camera carefully placed high on a wall, giving a sweep of the main work room. Bella switched off the jammer and they returned to Nicky's office to discuss their findings. Nicky's shock showed.

'I can't believe it,' she said. 'How did they get in? And what are they after?'

'Secrets,' Bella responded. 'Whatever that team are working on, it's of major interest to someone. The monitoring stuff they planted isn't cheap. It's the latest stuff, really high quality. As to how they got in, I can help you there, even though I'm no detective. They've had inside help. Think about it. There's no other possibility.'

'So we've got a mole? Is that what you're saying?'

'Almost definitely. I don't see any other way. Someone being paid or blackmailed. Possibly both. That's the way these things usually work.' By now Bella was packing her kit away. 'It's your problem now. You and these fine upstanding officers of the law. My job's done, so it's home and beddy-byes for me.'

Rose was watching Nicky carefully. 'I think my boss needs to come back in for a detailed chat with you. This is beyond our remit and above our pay grade.'

They made their way back to the car park, leaving Nicky Dangerfield deep in thought. Rose caught up with Bella before she reached her car.

'Can you check two other places out? The homes of the two women who've been targeted?'

'That's already booked in for a few days' time. I'll keep you posted.'

# CHAPTER 17: SHOCK

It was such a relief to be back home. True, Bryony was by herself rather more than was ideal and the police seemed to be a bit grumpy about it, but it wasn't Bryony's fault that her brother wasn't able to join her until the next day. It was just lovely to be out in the fresh air and able to stretch her legs with a stroll to the local shops for the first time in weeks. Maybe stroll was a misnomer. She still needed an elbow crutch to lean on when her abdominal muscles became too sore.

Bryony rounded the corner from the main road into her own avenue and stopped dead. There was someone peering over the hedge into her front garden. Bryony shrank back against a wall, trying to stay out of direct sight. Who was this woman? It was difficult to be sure. She had her back to the road and was trying to look through the sprigs of privet that poked out in all directions. The stranger was wearing jeans and trainers, with much of her long black hair hidden under a dark-blue baseball cap. Bryony felt a shudder down her spine. It couldn't possibly be the young woman from the roadside entrapment, could it? With a feeling of increasing horror, Bryony realised that it might be her. She looked to be the right height and build, though Bryony could only see her back view. Bryony slid even further into the thick hedge, glancing around in a mounting sense of panic. She froze. There was a car parked about ten yards in front of her, with someone in the driving seat. A man, from what she could see. He'd have a clear view of the house and the woman peering over the hedge. Could he be with her? Might he be the same man, the one with the knife? Bryony closed her eyes and counted to ten, hoping that when she opened them everything would have returned to normal, with the woman, the car and the man inside it nowhere to be seen, all creations of her overstressed brain.

Not so. They were still there, with the woman turning to face in her direction. It was her, surely? It was just a little too far to be certain. Bryony's heart was hammering in her chest like a demented piledriver. She could feel perspiration beginning to trickle down her face. Her body felt hot with fear. This was all going very wrong. She slid carefully back the way she had come, trying to remain as close as she could to her neighbour's hedge, even thicker and higher than her own. She'd always hated this hedge before, annoyed at the way the house owner allowed it to grow outwards, blocking half of the pavement. Now it was a blessing. Once around the corner, she picked up speed and hurried back towards the local shops, gasping and shaking with fright.

Surely it was them? But why? Why would they be visiting her so openly, in broad daylight? She picked out her phone and tried to dial 999, her fingers shaking uncontrollably. After a hurried, half-whispered exchange, she made her way to the local library and settled herself into a seat in a corner, close to the librarian's desk.

Officers from a squad car were with her within fifteen minutes and took her to Lyme's police station. Meanwhile, a second car was despatched to her home but failed to find any sign of the unwanted caller.

Rae was waiting for Bryony in an interview room when she arrived.

'I should have taken your warnings more seriously,' Bryony said, her voice weak and unsteady. 'I just never dreamt that they'd still be interested in me.'

'If it was them,' Rae said. 'There could be an innocent explanation, Bryony. We're checking for any evidence as to their identity, but we may not find any.'

Bryony dropped her eyes. 'I feel a bit stupid. It was a good job I was out. Would I just have answered the door if I'd been in and they rang the bell? You know, without checking first? I'm worried that I might have.'

Rae shook her head. 'I think you'd have been more cautious than that. You'd have followed our guidance and used the security chain, I'm sure of it. You did everything right once you became worried, didn't you?'

Bryony looked glum. 'I didn't even think fast enough to get a photo of the car or note its registration plate. I'm useless at this. And I'm too trusting.'

'Look for the positives, Bryony. If it was them, they've put their heads above the parapet. We're combing the area around your house for witnesses who may have spotted them. And for any CCTV. Meanwhile, my boss is insistent that you move out to somewhere safe where we can keep an eye on you. Even if your brother had been with you, he might have fallen for someone's charm and opened the door.'

'Not Wayne. He's a bit grumpy, to be honest. He's suspicious of everyone and everything.'

'Well, you need to phone him and tell him that your plans have changed. We can't force you, Bryony, but you need to take this seriously. Where does your brother live?'

'Swindon. I suppose I could ask him if I can stay with him and his family.'

'That's ideal. I can get the local Wiltshire cops to keep an eye out. One of their detectives is a member of WeSCU, so it won't be a problem.'

Bryony bit her lip. 'I was hoping to go back to work. Help get the unit moving again.'

'That's not on the cards, not yet, not now this has happened. Surely you can switch to remote working? Huge numbers of people work from home now, even if it's only some of the time. I'll get my boss to speak to Nicky Dangerfield.'

'What about Ian Duncan? What's happening with him?'

Rae frowned. 'Don't contact him and don't speak to him if he tries to get in touch with you. Not until we've given you the all clear. We're still probing his background, looking for possible motives. We want all the facts before we interview him again.'

Rae returned to the incident room to report to Barry. It couldn't be a coincidence, could it, that the two women had both been visited again in such a short space of time? Surely something was stirring. But who, and why?

* * *

Barry and Tommy were interviewing Joey Sturrock, but progress was proving to be very slow. Was he scared of something? There was little bravado on display. His demeanour seemed haunted, as if he didn't know which way to turn.

'There's no escape, Joey,' Barry said. 'You still had the keys on you when you were caught. What's the point in denying you were in the flat? You left the door unlocked and the CCTV in the foyer catches you haring through the lobby and crashing through the doorway to the outside. It's cut and dried. So why not tell us why you were in there? What were you looking for?'

Sturrock shook his head. 'No comment,' was all he said.

'Who told you the flat would be unoccupied yesterday evening? You wouldn't have been there if there'd been any doubt.'

'No comment.'

'Where did you get the keys from?'

A shrug. He didn't even bother moving his lips to utter the two words that had formed the entirety of his spoken communication so far.

'Is something worrying you? Is someone leaning on you? Heavily? Have you been threatened? Intimidated?'

Sturrock's expression changed. He still said nothing but dropped his head. Not before both Barry and Tommy saw the worried frown that crossed his face. Nothing else changed, though. There was still no response to their questions.

They watched as he was taken back to his cell.

'Someone's put the frighteners on him, boss,' Tommy said. 'He knows he'd be better off coming clean to us. It makes no sense him taking the line that it was just him, and it was just a simple break-in. But he's scared. You can see it in his eyes.'

'But what was he after?' Barry said. 'That's what puzzles me. What might Justine have in that flat that they want so much? And why are they still targeting Bryony O'Neil?' He shook his head in frustration.

'Maybe it's just intimidation, pure and simple,' Tommy answered. 'That was one of the suggestions from a few days ago. They're putting the frighteners on two of the women members of that project team.'

Barry looked pensive. 'It's a possibility, I'll give you that. But a second visit to Justine's apartment, almost identical to the first? I keep coming back to the idea that there's something there, something they want but can't find. Something that wouldn't normally be viewed as a target for theft. We need to go back there.'

'Rose and George are already there.'

'We'll join them. I just wish I knew what we're looking for.'

* * *

Barry and Tommy were met by the two temporary unit members when they arrived at the apartment block. They both looked glum.

'Nothing so far?' Barry asked.

'Not a bloody sausage,' Rose said. 'Mind you, my guess is that guy who Kieran nabbed, Sturrock, was searching the place. It looks a bit disordered in there, like he didn't find what he was looking for. So whatever it is, it's not obvious.'

Barry thought back over previous cases where someone's home had been searched or ransacked by a criminal but with nothing stolen. What kinds of things had they been looking for?

'Might be a photo,' he said. 'One that shows someone or something that might be incriminating.'

'Hard,' George said. 'People just don't print out photos any more. They're all kept on phones or on SD cards.'

Barry was pensive. 'Let me phone Justine,' he said.

He explained that the detectives were in her flat looking for something of interest, possibly a photo, letter or document. Did she have any ideas? He listened to what she had to say, then put his hand to his head, remaining in that position for several moments.

'I don't believe it,' he said. 'All three of them were at a reception in the Parantos Embassy a month ago. Her, Robin Pryor and Bryony O'Neil. A few Parantos business people attended. There were photos. For pity's sake, why didn't anyone tell us?' He paused, thinking hard. 'I need to see Nicky Dangerfield, and in a hurry. Apparently, some group photos were taken. Bryony might have had copies as the admin lead.'

He phoned Rae. He needed a second experienced detective with him on this visit, there to assess Nicky's credibility.

# CHAPTER 18: DISCUSSIONS AND CREDIBILITY

Barry and Rae were sitting in Nicky Dangerfield's office. Barry thought that its décor reflected her personality, from his memory of their schooldays together: bright and vibrant. Today, though, she seemed perturbed, fidgety.

'I didn't know. It was meant to be Val Potter, the deputy project leader, who went on the embassy visit with them. I've only just found out she was ill that day. Justine went as a last-minute replacement. Look, Barry, I'd have told you right away if I'd known.'

The problem for Barry and Rae was whether to believe what they were being told. They'd suspected for some time that there was an insider, someone working for EcoFutures in some capacity, someone who was feeding information to outsiders. But who was it? Ian Duncan, the security manager? Nicky Dangerfield, the operations manager, speaking to them now? Or someone else, a person as yet unknown, possibly someone inside the project team?

'I know how this must look,' Nicky added. 'We must seem a right load of plonkers to you, but we do give a lot of autonomy to each development team to manage their project in the way they see fit. Even so, I can't understand how we missed it. All I can do is apologise. Do you think all this is connected to that visit in some way?'

Barry could see how worried she was. 'It seems likely, though we need to keep open minds. What I want to do is carry out a thorough check on everything in their work area. A search of every desk and storage unit. More importantly, a detailed check on all their computer equipment, looking at photos and documents. I want it done by our own forensic team and you need to keep it under wraps, Nicky. No one else must know what we're up to.'

'Do you know what you're looking for?'

'Not really, though we have some ideas. Our IT expert, Ameera Khan, is forensically trained. Give her a network and she'll burrow her way through it finding all kinds of stuff. Your own IT manager will have to be involved to give her the right network permissions but no one else must know. She'll be here tomorrow. We'll start on the rooms this afternoon when my team arrive. We'll need that suite cleared of personnel.'

Nicky sighed. 'Yet more delays to the project.'

'What exactly was their remit?'

'It's a river estuary that's a complete mess. The team were working on a total redesign that would improve and modernise facilities for the local fishing community but also include designated wildlife zones at the river mouth and for some miles upstream. It includes measures for flood prevention and water management.'

'A lot of money?' Rae asked.

'Yes. Their government has risked its credibility backing the idea. Our job is to turn the concept into a working development plan. Once it's approved, there'll be bids from builders and developers for actually doing the work. It's one of the most ambitious projects we've taken on. The next stage would have been for the team to fly out for a visit. Only Robin and Val, his deputy, went out for the initial scoping trip, as far as I know.'

'Maybe I need to have another talk with her,' Rae said. 'Has she been earmarked to take over?'

'In the short-term, yes. We haven't got round to deciding on the long-term way forward.'

'Who's we?' Rae asked.

'Me. The CEO. The strategy manager. Three of us.'

'Fair enough.' Barry glanced at the clock on the wall. 'Time to get started. Nicky, you stay out of this, other than smoothing the way for us. I don't want anyone from inside the company trying to run a parallel internal investigation and messing things up.'

Nicky looked at him somewhat suspiciously. 'You mean Ian Duncan?'

'I mean anyone.'

Rae gave Barry a sharp look. Was he becoming more assertive, with both Sophie Allen and Polly Nelson off the scene? About time, she thought.

\* \* \*

The team got to work. The remaining members of EcoFutures' Parantos unit moved to a different base within the building for a few days and were told not to access any work that was network-based, not until given the go-ahead by Barry. There were grumbles, of course. Val Potter, as the temporary unit leader, was particularly tetchy.

'But all our work is computer-based,' she protested. 'There's not much we can do without access to our computer system. And we're behind schedule as it is.'

Nicky tried to calm her. 'We have no choice, Val. Have some discussions with the rest of the unit as to who you'd like to join you once things are back up and running. I can pinch people from other projects on a temporary basis once you're ready. They'll help to make up for any lost time. But it needs to be people you trust and will fit in. That's item one on your agenda. Get your shortlist to me as soon as you can. Then carry out a review of what's to be done in the short and medium terms. Personnel needed for each item. Possible difficulties. As soon as you get the go-ahead from the police to move back in, I want you working at top speed right away. This is a high-priority project with lots of eyes on us. I want it delivered on schedule and to our usual high standard. I'll get you whatever and whoever you need. Just ensure the team are focussed. Are you okay with that?'

Val nodded her head. 'We'll do our best, Nicky. We can make use of charts and photos to tick off progress so far. Thinking about it, this is no bad thing. It's a big project. A detailed review at this stage could be really useful.'

Nicky smiled. 'That's what I want to hear. Think of the positives, not the negatives.'

'Okay, will do.'

'The other thing is, the police want to interview you again, particularly now you're in charge and have had time to reflect on things. It'll probably be the sergeant, Rae Gregson. She's the brunette with the bobbed hairstyle. Be absolutely open with her. Tell her everything she wants to know. But don't talk to your colleagues about it too much. I want them focussed on their work, not the police investigation. Clear?'

'Of course. I think it's called being circumspect.' Val smiled wryly.

'I know you can do all this, Val. It's about time you were given the responsibility that matches your ability. You go, girl.'

\* \* \*

Rae found the new manager of the Parantos unit, Val Potter, tricky to talk to. She spoke in a measured and controlled way. Maybe she was a died-in-the-wool scientist, cautious in her approach to everything. She was approaching middle age, wore her blonde hair cut short, had bright blue eyes and was dressed in informal but fashionable clothes. Her personnel file stated that she had a first degree in geography and a doctorate in ecology. Rae had Jackie Spring as a second when she interviewed her.

'I want to probe into the visit you made to Parantos with Robin,' Rae explained. 'Just in case something happened there that has led to what's occurred in the last couple of weeks. Two things, really. Whether anything odd happened, anything remotely suspicious. And the people you met while you were there.'

'I'll try,' Val replied. 'But we were only there for two days. And several rival companies were there too. Two, in fact. We'd put in an expression of interest and some rough ideas, along with a fair number of others, I expect. We'd done that without a visit, just based on the quite thin specification that their government had issued. They'd whittled the original expressions of interest down to three. That was when they wanted a detailed tender. It was us, a Belgian consortium and an American firm. That visit was an opportunity for us all to visit the site and gather more data. Then we all put detailed plans together. Ours won the contract. I wasn't surprised, to be honest. The Belgian team are good, but they don't really have our level of coastal expertise. The Americans had just landed a similar contract for Bolivia and didn't have the resources to do both at the same time. They withdrew.'

'So you don't think that rivalry from the failed bids plays a part?'

Val shook her head. 'No, not at all. The Americans didn't want it in the end, and the Belgians were relieved, if anything. One of their team told me they'd struggle because of a lack of specific experience.'

'Okay, think back to the few days you were there. Anything unusual? Something that may not have seemed particularly significant at the time but might now, given what's happened?'

Val shook her head. 'I've lain awake for hours at night, thinking back to that visit. But there's nothing. We were busy all the time. The people we mixed with were the Belgians and the Americans, plus a group of about three civil servants from Parantos who talked us through the project. We met the minister for an afternoon, all of us. I think it was obvious even then that we were more on-the-ball than the other two bidders. We asked more questions and were more focussed than them. That's it, really.'

Rae finished noting a few words on paper, then sat back. 'Okay. So you're pretty sure these events are not linked to that visit?'

'Yes. And it doesn't fit, anyway. It was just Robin and me. Yet this nasty business seems to only involve Robin, Bryony and Justine. They were the three who went to the embassy reception in London.'

'Did any of them comment on anything unusual once they got back from that visit? Anything you remember?'

Val shrugged. 'Not really.'

'Thanks, Val. You've been very helpful.'

Rae turned to Jackie once Val was out of the room. 'What did you make of her?'

'Seems honest enough on the surface. She didn't raise any of my hackles in an obvious way.'

Rae nodded. 'Same here. She seemed on top of things and that's no mean feat in the circumstances, though she was guarded. Maybe she always comes across that way. When we see Justine and Bryony we'll need to double check their memories of that reception in London. I wonder if we need a list of everyone who was there. Let's take one each. I'll do Bryony, you take Justine. Okay?'

'Thanks, Sarge. I mean, for showing faith in me and letting me do it on my own. I won't let you down.'

Rae smiled. 'I know you won't. If you do, you're out.' She winked at the most recent addition to WeSCU's ranks. It felt a bit weird being senior to a new recruit who was almost old enough to be her mother.

## CHAPTER 19: AWKWARD CUSS

Sophie Allen, sitting on a chair with a book on her lap, looked up as the door to her room opened. The familiar face of Dorset's assistant chief constable peered through the gap.

'Are you decent?' he asked.

'Well, it's a bit late if I wasn't,' she answered. 'Shouldn't you have sent a scout on ahead to check out the lie of the land?'

'You've been watching too many cowboy films,' he answered with a grin.

'Not much else to do in here. Books, TV, making mischief. That's my average day.'

'I can well believe it.'

'Come in and make yourself comfortable. The other two occupants have gone on a raiding party, looking for snacks. My job is to hold the fort and repel possible enemy ambushes.'

Jim Metcalfe pulled a chair across the room and sat down. 'You're looking better,' he said. 'You've got some colour back in your cheeks and your sense of humour seems back to normal. Any news of when you'll be out?'

Sophie shrugged. 'Maybe next week? They don't really like keeping me in, but I have to go through so much treatment each day that home care doesn't make sense at the moment. One of those things, I suppose. I could get really depressed about it, Jim, but I'm training myself in taking a more meditative and philosophical approach to life. Helped by the contraband that Martin sneaks in during his evening visits. I've regained a liking for Curly Wurlys. Do you want one? I keep them hidden in there.' She pointed towards the lower door on her bedside locker.

'I think I can survive without one, but thanks.'

'So, what's the bad news?' Sophie asked.

'What?'

'You're here, only a few days after your last visit. And this one is in work time rather than an evening or weekend. That spells trouble, in my view. Am I being given the sack at last? It's probably long overdue.'

Jim laughed, though it sounded a little forced to Sophie's ears. 'No, no. Of course not.' He cleared his throat, always a sign that bad news was coming, in Sophie's experience. They'd known each other a long time.

'It's about Polly. Polly Nelson. It's not what we thought.'

Sophie frowned. 'What do you mean?'

'We were told she was heavily involved in the take-down of an organised-crime group. That's only partly true. She's had to take some time off, Sophie. She's suffering from stress-related anxiety.'

Sophie was horrified. 'Oh, no. How is she?'

'Not sure. She's on a month's medical leave.'

'Is she at home?'

Jim shook his head. 'Her partner's taken her away somewhere for a complete rest. Wales is what we've heard. Snowdonia.' He was watching her carefully. 'Did you have any inkling that something like this might happen?'

'What? Are you mad? Of course not.'

Sophie was thinking hard. She'd known Polly for many years, having worked with her on several cases that had crossed the county boundary into Somerset.

'I first came into contact with her in that Dorchester case, the one with the children's bodies buried under a bush in someone's back garden. Then again in that nasty one involving the old commune in the Quantocks. She's got a good sense of judgement and has real determination. I'm a bit surprised.'

Some doubt was beginning to creep into Sophie's mind. Had Polly been just a little too brittle, a little too jumpy? Sophie had always put it down to her junior officer being eager to get a case solved. But was it, in fact, down to an inherent anxiety that Sophie had failed to spot in her desire to give another talented woman officer a helping hand in the promotion stakes? She needed more information. But there was no time for that at present with the current case seemingly getting more complex as each day passed. The Polly problem would have to be shelved for now, but not forgotten.

'This mucks things up big time. We were desperately hoping she'd be back soon to take overall charge. Barry must be feeling the pressure.' She was rubbing her brow with her fingers, and none too gently.

'That's why I'm here, to talk options with you, unofficially of course. The problem is that we've got plenty of foot-soldiers we can bring in, but that's not what Barry needs. We could temporarily free up Lydia from her role in Bournemouth. But the problem isn't at that level. We need someone of Barry's seniority, or above.'

Sophie watched him carefully, thinking hard. 'With respect, Jim, I think you're wrong. Barry is the right person, in the right place, at the right time. He's absolutely ripe for a DCI role, as you well know. And the worse thing we could do is to parachute some senior person in to take over. Someone who'd feel the need to muscle Barry aside. We could well lose him if we did that. Think about it. Gwen, his wife, works in Hampshire. I've been thinking for some time of finding a way of getting her closer. If you stick some plonker in, above or alongside Barry, the exact opposite could happen. Jack Dunning has just got his superintendent promotion. He'd love for Barry to join his Hampshire team as a DCI. And what you suggested would ensure that's what would happen. No, that's not the way. I'm going to have a chat with my consultant.'

'What? Why?'

'Because I've had enough of this.' She waved her arm around vaguely, indicating the room and the ward's nursing station in the corridor outside. 'If the local hospital at Lyme Regis can find someone who can do my daily physio treatment, then the problem's solved. I can go down there.'

'I can't sanction that, Sophie. That isn't why I came here today. It sounds too risky.'

'I know what I'm doing. If you must know, I've already been talking to my consultant about the possibility of something like it. And it'll only be for two or three days each week.'

'How do you plan to get around?'

'Wheelchair, of course. Thousands of people do each day up and down the country. Why do you think I've been practising so hard? WeSCU is my unit, Jim. I don't want someone else causing it to implode. Don't stand in my way.'

'You're an awkward cuss.'

'I know. You've been telling me that for years.'

\* \* \*

What Sophie had told the ACC was true. She'd already realised that there was probably more to Polly Nelson's absence than was immediately obvious. She'd formulated a plan in her head and gained her husband's agreement, if not full approval. Martin was the deputy principal of a large secondary school in Dorchester and came in for a visit each evening, before heading home. The plan was that they'd stay over in Lyme for two or three days each week, at a suitably adapted guest house, already identified, close to the police station. Martin's drive to work in Dorchester would be little different in distance compared to his usual drive from Wareham, although it would be in the opposite direction. Sophie had been preparing the groundwork in her conversations with her consultant, who seemed broadly happy with the plan, once she'd checked the facilities in Lyme's small hospital.

Sophie moved out of Dorset County Hospital the following day and waited until she was settled into the small guest house before phoning Barry with her news. He was dumbfounded.

## CHAPTER 20: GOOD AND BAD NEWS

'There's good news and bad news.'

The detective team were in the incident room at the start of their early morning briefing, mugs of tea and coffee at the ready. With those few words, Barry had their attention.

'Bad news first, please,' Rae said. 'Get it out of the way, then finish on an upbeat.'

Barry steeled himself. 'The DCI won't be joining us for the foreseeable future. She's been signed off on a month's sick leave. I don't quite know everything that's happened but there's been a personal crisis of some kind.'

'Oh, my goodness,' Jackie exclaimed. 'You don't know the details?'

Barry shook his head. 'And I don't want to pry. I'm sure she'll be in touch as and when she's ready, but she needs time to get better.'

'We're very stretched, boss,' Tommy said.

'I know. And that's where the good news comes in.' He paused, as if for dramatic effect. 'The chief super is coming in on a part-time basis, starting in a couple of days' time.'

Rae leaned forward in her seat. 'What? You're joking.'

'No. It's all fixed. She'll be staying in a bed and breakfast place just a few doors away from here, one with good wheelchair access. She'll be getting her daily treatment and therapy at the local hospital, here in Lyme, as an out-patient. Apparently, it's all been fixed.'

'But she can't even walk, not yet, not even with elbow crutches.' Rae was incredulous.

'Apparently she's been given the go-ahead to try getting about in a wheelchair and on crutches, as long as she's careful.'

Rae snorted. 'How likely is that? How did she manage to convince the doctors that this is a good idea? You and I know what she's like, boss. How likely is it that she'll toe whatever line they've drawn? I mean, seriously?'

'That's where you and I come in, Rae. We keep a weather eye on her. At the first sign of trouble, we tell Martin.'

What does he think of this plan?'

'Surprisingly, he's okay with it. He phoned me last night. My guess is that he's worried about her mental health, being stuck in a hospital room for weeks on end. He did say that she's been doing extra gym-based exercises and is probably fitter than she's been for some years. Maybe that has something to do with it. Look, Rae, if Martin's okay with it, then so am I. To be honest, I feel relieved. I'm not putting up any objections. It's two or three days a week, and her sense of judgement will be invaluable. We need her, Rae. With Polly out of the picture the alternative is for someone to be parachuted in to take over. Do we really want that? I don't.'

Rae frowned. 'Nor do I. I don't want to sound negative, boss. It's just that I worry about her. She can be a bit careless about herself at times. It will be great having her around. I know how she always buoys us up.'

'The other bit of good news is that Ameera thinks she's found something on the EcoFutures network. There are some photos Robin Pryor took at that reception at the embassy in London. They're separate to the official ones, by the way. She's only just called me with the news. We should finish the physical search this morning if we get a move on. And the detailed results from Robin Pryor's post-mortem are in, though I've still got to go through them.'

'Has Benny put a summary in?'

'Well, we already know most of it. But there's a tiny puncture mark on his upper right arm, consistent with a hypodermic. Traces of a strong sedative in his bloodstream.'

'Fairly conclusive, then?'

'I'd say so. Beaten up and drugged. The forensic people think he got away somehow but possibly collapsed a few yards further on. Maybe that's when he got the final blow that finished him. Covered up with some branches pulled off nearby undergrowth. Left to die in that hollow. Cold-blooded killers.'

'But why? It doesn't make any sense,' Rae said.

Barry shrugged. 'That's for us to find out.'

\* \* \*

The photos that Ameera had discovered in a folder on the EcoFutures computer network arrived in an email a little later. Barry opened them up on his laptop. There were six in total, all showing groups of people talking to each other during a buffet reception. They quickly identified Bryony and Justine in some of the photos, standing next to each other, chatting to others.

'Maybe this is why we've never found his mobile,' Barry said. 'Their file names tend to imply they were snapped on a phone. Is there something in these photos that created a real problem for somebody? But that doesn't explain why the other two, Bryony and Justine, have been targeted as well.'

'They might have taken photos too,' Jackie suggested.

'But they didn't,' Rae said. 'We've asked them.'

'Yes, I know. But maybe whoever's behind this doesn't know that, not for sure. Justine's place is searched, and Bryony is intimidated. Maybe the aim all along was to find out more, find their weak points.'

'We could get these photos projected on a big screen,' Tommy said. 'We could dim the lights and really look at all the details. There's a screen in the CID room down the corridor. Shall I try to get it organised?'

'Sounds good,' Barry replied. 'See what you can do.'

Within a few minutes Tommy had the system set up and the team found themselves looking at the images on a large high-resolution screen, allowing them to stand back and inspect the details that were showing up.

'We need to know who these people are,' Barry said. 'I need to speak to someone in the embassy. But we'll organise visits to Bryony and Justine first.'

Jackie and Rae were concentrating on a couple of figures on the periphery of two of the photos.

'Could she be the woman picked up by the CCTV on Monmouth Beach?' Jackie asked. 'A little on the short side. Dark hair. Olive complexion.'

'If that's the case, there's also the possibility she might be the woman who stepped out in front of Bryony O'Neil's car that night,' Rae added, screwing up her eyes in a vain attempt to make the picture clearer.

Barry turned to face her. 'Can you go through the case notes again, Rae? I'll do the same. Let's try looking at everything afresh, if we can. We've all been working on this since the start, when it appeared to be a simple set of probably disconnected occurrences. We've got to where we are now via a pretty tangled route. I'm worried we've missed something.'

'Sure thing. I was planning on spending the rest of the afternoon on catch up, so it would fit.'

'Then visit Bryony. She's staying with her brother in Swindon. Jackie, you see Justine. Show them the photos. See what they say. And remember, everyone, the chief super is planning on coming in tomorrow morning. Be prepared.'

Barry's phone pinged, indicating an incoming message. He looked at the screen and frowned.

'Ameera,' he said. 'Something important. The network folder that contained these photo files. It's been accessed by someone else, not just Robin.'

'Who?' Rae asked.

'That's just it. She can't tell yet. Whoever it was, they were using a guest log-on ID.'

## CHAPTER 21: CONFIRMATION

Jackie and Tommy visited Justine that evening. She'd moved out of her flat soon after the second break-in, opting to stay with an old friend who lived in Bridport, on the Dorset coast, some ten miles east of Lyme. Bernice Navarro had a small house in the old part of town, near the Tiger Inn. The two women had known each other since university days, where they'd found themselves close neighbours in a hall of residence. Bernice had offered Justine a room in her home as long as it was needed, an ideal solution to her friend's problem. The drive to EcoFutures only took twenty minutes or so, although she was remote working at present, following advice from the police to maintain a low profile. Bernice took herself off to the kitchen to allow the two detectives to talk to Justine undisturbed.

Jackie thought that Justine looked tense. Dark shadows under her eyes suggested that she hadn't been sleeping well since the events a couple of days earlier. No wonder, Jackie thought. You lead a normal life for many years, untouched by menacing events, and then, without warning, you find yourself in the middle of a whirlwind of intimidation and violence. The solid ground of your everyday life has somehow become quicksand without you noticing it, and you begin to wonder if anything is quite what it seems.

They sat in a cosy living room, yet Justine clutched at a cardigan that was draped around her shoulders. When she picked up her cup of tea, her fingers shook.

'You're safe here, Justine,' Jackie said. 'No one knows where you're staying. To be honest, we don't think you were ever under a threat of violence. That man, Sturrock, only made attempts to get into your flat when you weren't around. It's unlikely that you were ever in serious danger.'

Justine raised her tired eyes to the detective. 'But will someone else take over from him now? Someone far worse? And anyway, what about Pete? I know he's never been the most reliable of boyfriends, but I can't get my head round what he might have been doing, telling that man Sturrock when I'd be out. I trusted him. I mean, you do, don't you? You assume your boyfriend is looking out for you, not the opposite.' Tears began to gather in the corners of her eyes. She dabbed at them with a paper tissue, screwed up in her hand. 'The sense of betrayal is the worst thing. I can't really cope with it.'

'Talking it through will probably help, Justine. With us, I mean. We don't want you back at work until we give you the say-so. We've spoken briefly to Pete. We think he only passed on your details twice. And he was very ashamed of what he'd done. It's possible there might be someone else feeding information to this group.'

'Oh, no. I can't believe it. And how is the unit functioning? With me and Bryony not there, and Robin . . .' Her voice tailed off.

'Val Potter and the others are keeping things ticking over. Nicky Dangerfield is arranging for people to come in from other development teams, just to keep things going. No need to worry. They still aim to deliver the plans on time.'

Justine frowned slightly, something picked up by Jackie. But before she could speak, Tommy took over. 'Justine, we have a few photos of that reception in the Parantos Embassy. Robin took them on his phone. They're informal ones but he did copy them into one of his own folders on the network, a sort of store of background stuff for his own use. Could you have a look at them and tell us what you can?'

Justine nodded her agreement, dabbing once again at her eyes. She watched as Tommy spread the six images out on a tabletop, then she stood up and walked across to examine them.

'Yes,' she murmured, 'I remember Robin taking them now. You can see Bryony and me posing a bit, particularly in the last two.' Her voice was a little stronger now, and examining the images seemed to have caused her to regain some sense of purpose. 'We'd both planned our outfits for the reception before we left Lyme. It's a High Commission, by the way, not an embassy. That's because it's a Commonwealth country.' She moved the photos around, as if trying to reconnect with the event they recorded. 'They were lovely people. So welcoming. I remember Bryony saying to me how great the food was. There were some people from the Parantos government there. That's why the reception had been arranged, to coincide with them being in London. This group.' She pointed to the group surrounding the two British women in two of the photos.

'I think they're in the official photos,' Tommy said. 'There's a folder of them on your company computer system. These photos of Robin's aren't such good quality.'

'No. He wasn't the world's best photographer, to be honest. He had a habit of snapping things without lining them up properly in the viewfinder. He used to take photos of his rambles but didn't take enough time over them. You'd see what was obviously a stunning view, but it would be off to one side or not level. I wondered about telling him but never did. He was my boss, after all.' She pointed to one of the final photos. 'This one's like that. We asked him to take it to show off our clothes to best effect, but just look at it!'

The photo was quite badly tilted to one side, but Jackie did think that the two women looked glamorous.

'Who are these two people in the background?' she asked. 'They're not in the earlier shots.'

A man and a woman were caught in the photos as they crossed the floor.

'No idea. I don't remember them. It looks as if they were just walking through the room.' Justine closed her eyes for a few seconds, as if trying to imagine the layout of the reception. 'There was a small door on the other side. They must have been heading for it.'

Jackie glanced at Tommy and could tell that he had the same thought. In the final photo, the woman in the background was looking directly at the camera. She'd obviously spotted Robin taking the photo. Could this be the trigger that had set all the subsequent events in motion?

'Is there anything else worrying you, Justine?' Jackie asked.

'No, not really,' came the answer.

\*\*\*

Rae arrived at the house where Bryony was staying in Swindon with her older brother. Rae had forgotten quite how large the county was, with most of the population living in towns spread in a vast arc around the southern, western and northern edges. The centre was dominated by the huge expanse of Salisbury Plain, with its army training ranges. To be honest, Rae preferred living in neighbouring Dorset. Wiltshire held too many damaging memories for her, of events from which she'd successfully escaped some five years earlier.

Bryony's brother, Wayne, lived with his family in the Freshbrook area of Swindon, in the south-west part of the town, close to the M4 motorway. It wasn't hard to find his house, and there was convenient parking close by. The presence of young children was obvious: a tricycle in the front garden, a basketball net fixed to the house's side wall, a sand pit discernible in the rear garden, close to the house. They made their way to the front door and were welcomed by Wayne, with Bryony hovering in the background. Wayne and his partner, Billie, made the dining room available to the trio, keeping their small children in the lounge, watching television.

Rae looked carefully at Bryony as they sat down.

'You're looking better than I thought you would, Bryony. Less tense.'

Bryony gave a mild grimace. 'It's the kiddies, I expect. They keep my mind off things. They keep pestering me for stories.'

'I bet you love it, really,' Rae continued.

'You're probably right. It's a major change for me.' She paused. 'What is it you want to know? You said it was important.'

'The trip you made to London with Robin and Justine. We'd like to know a bit more about it. That's if you feel up to it.'

'Yes, of course. We'd got the contract for the coastal development in Parantos. A delegation of officials from Parantos were in London for trade and development talks, including a couple of their top civil servants who were also linked to the project. They suggested meeting for a question-and-answer session to clarify a few things. It was held in their High Commission. After it was over, they put on a reception with a buffet and a few drinks. I suppose it provided for more informal conversation. It can be useful.'

Rae spread some photos out. 'These are the official photos. Is there anyone here who wasn't involved?'

Bryony looked at the photos in turn. 'Not really. These are the people in charge of the project.' She pointed to a group of four. 'They're senior civil servants. Then this second group are the Deputy High Commissioner and his team.'

Rae set the photos aside and added the six that Robin had taken. 'These are Robin's photos, taken on his phone. Is that right?'

Bryony frowned in concentration. 'I'd forgotten. Yes, come to think of it, he did take some snaps. They're a bit fuzzy, aren't they? Typical Robin.' She frowned even more and began to look upset. 'Sorry,' she added. 'I forgot for a moment.'

'Take your time, Bryony,' Rae said. 'It'll still all be raw. Is there anyone in any of the photos who was not part of the group? Anyone unexpected?'

Bryony looked through them all again, then held on to the final two images.

'These two in the background,' she said. 'I think they were just walking through. No idea who they are.'

Rae passed her a magnifying glass. 'Could they be the couple who tried to attack you? They fit your description.'

Bryony examined the photos more closely, frowning in concentration. 'I don't know. I suppose it could be them,' she said.

'You can't be more sure?' Rae asked.

Bryony shook her head. She was looking pale. 'It's not clear enough for that. It could be them, but it might not be.'

'Justine told me last week that Robin talked about a woman he met at a pub in Lyme, someone he said he played darts with. Did he ever mention her to you?'

'No, but I don't think he told Justine that he played darts with the woman. He just said that he was there playing darts, and she was there watching. They got talking. Justine told me all about it over lunch later. We don't normally gossip like that, but Robin was always such a reserved sort of guy. It was a kind of *you'll never guess what* . . . kind of chat. And that's all she said. I didn't think anything of it.' Her eyes widened. 'Is it her? Do you think it might be this woman?'

'We don't know. But thanks for confirming Justine's story.'

'Why would it be them doing all this? What's going on?' She looked even more worried than before.

'That's what we're trying to find out. And you've been very helpful, Bryony.'

\* \* \*

Jackie was in the local Thai restaurant for a late evening meal with her current partner, Tony Fisher. He'd travelled down from Watchet to spend the evening with her. She speared another piece of curried duck and bit into it. Delicious.

'This is a great place, Jackie. How's the job going? I mean, really? You haven't said much about it over the phone.'

'Honestly? I love it, Tony. I know we're working long hours, but they fly by most of the time. I was really worried when I finally accepted the offer to join the unit, and then found that my boss would be Barry Marsh, the acting DCI, and not Polly. I hadn't really met him on that case back home. He was away on his honeymoon. But he's great. So calm and thorough. And I get on really well with Rae and Tommy. Rae's my immediate boss. But it's the work, really. It's right up my street. I did the right thing in taking the job, Tony. I know it's early days yet, but even so.'

'I was a bit concerned. You did sound tired on the phone.'

She smiled. 'You noticed then? I feel tired every evening. Work's pretty relentless. Everything has to be checked and double-checked, then cross checked.' She paused and leaned forward. 'I'm not too tired tonight, though. I've been trying to pace myself today. Are you staying over?'

'If you'll have me.' He put a hand on hers. 'I've missed you. Even more than I thought I would.'

'Same for me. But I was in a rut, Tony, back in Watchet. It was all too cosy. A part-time librarian using my hours as a volunteer special constable to give my life a lift. Maybe I just didn't realise it at the time. But I feel so involved here, in this team. I'm important rather than just filling in as an extra. I don't know how it will work out in the long-term but even if it all ends up going pear-shaped, at least I've tried. Thank God for that last case and the body in the harbour. I wouldn't have met them if it hadn't been for that. That was you, Tony. You were the one who came rushing across to find me that morning. It makes me love you even more.'

Jackie had never used the word *love* before in any conversation with Tony. Not even when the couple were at their most intimate. He squeezed her hand.

'I love you too.'

## CHAPTER 22: HIGH COMMISSION

Barry and Rae took an early morning train into London. They'd been fortunate in gaining a mid-morning appointment with a senior official at Parantos's High Commission, near Marble Arch. Carlos Martinez, a tall, dark-eyed man, told them that he'd been in the UK for just over a year and was hoping for promotion from his current role of Under-Commissioner to Deputy High Commissioner at some point in the future.

'I was here at university,' he told them as they walked from reception to his office. 'I love Britain but want to stay in my country's diplomatic service. My job here is ideal.'

He seemed an amiable yet focussed man. Once seated, with a coffee in front of each of them, he asked for more details about the information they required.

'I understand that it's a murder investigation. I'll give you all the help I can. But I don't see how it can possibly be linked to anything we're here for. Our main function is to serve the interests of our country, help potential tourists with information and offer aid to our own people who are in the UK, if they need it.'

Barry cleared his throat. 'We're interested in a reception that was hosted here about a month ago. EcoFutures landed a contract to design the new waterfront development and eco-park for your country's main estuary area. I think I've got the details right?'

'Yes, I'm aware of the plan. I wasn't closely involved in that reception, but I was there for some of the time.' He was frowning slightly.

Barry continued his explanation. 'The project leader at EcoFutures has been murdered. His two junior colleagues who were at the reception with him have both been targeted. Well, intimidated really. By someone unknown.'

'So, you suspect a link?'

'Exactly. I'd like your co-operation in getting copies of all documents relating to the event. In particular, guest lists. It's a process of elimination really.'

'I can see why I was chosen to deal with you. Police and crime matters come under my remit.' He stroked his chin. 'Of course, being a High Commission, you have no jurisdiction in here. It's just like an embassy.'

Barry smiled politely. 'I'm fully aware of that. Nevertheless, it's in our mutual interest to pursue the facts behind these events. Maybe they're due to different causes entirely and aren't linked, but we can't ignore this angle.'

Rae broke in. 'Really, what we want is to put names to faces and faces to names. Then identify their roles. Can you lay your hands on the relevant paperwork?'

'I'll see what I can do. Give me a few minutes.' Carlos left the room.

'Why didn't he just phone?' Rae said, indicating the slightly old-fashioned handset on the desk.

'Wouldn't you have done the same, in his position? With two cops watching you like hawks and listening to every word?'

Rae laughed. 'Guilty secrets.'

Barry shook his head. 'Maybe he's just being careful. He doesn't want to land someone else in the soup, needlessly. He won't even know if any paperwork was retained. I'm willing to trust him. Well, as far as it goes. Is it likely that any senior official here was involved?'

'You think it might be just those two in the photos?'

'Nothing else makes sense, does it? But what's at the root of it? We'll have to open up to one of the senior staff here if there is a link. But I'll need to get the go-ahead from someone on high if that's the case.'

Rae smiled mischievously. 'Good job the chief super's coming back in tomorrow, then. It's right up her street. Diplomats. Possible high-level shenanigans. She'll be in heaven. All these people she knows in the Met. And she's got that ace up her sleeve, hasn't she? That's if her pal Yauvani is still home secretary after the reshuffle. Isn't one on the cards?'

'You know more than me, Rae. I lost faith in politicians after the last round of budget cuts.'

They both looked up as the door opened and Carlos returned, with a smartly dressed young woman beside him, a folder under her arm.

'Angelika here did the planning for the reception. You're in luck. She still has the paperwork.'

Angelika looked nervously at the two detectives as she moved to the table and opened the folder.

'I don't know whether this will help but it's all I have.' She had a soft voice with a melodic lilt.

Barry leaned forward to scan through the papers that were revealed. Rae opened her bag and extracted a set of photos that had been taken at the reception.

'We'd like you to identify these people, if you can. These are official photos, snapped by your own staff. Sit down, please.'

Angelika leant forward to pore over the images. She picked a list from the papers and ran down it with her fingers. It contained both names and roles. 'I can do that,' she said. 'Everybody is here on the list somewhere.'

Rae took out a sheet of small adhesive circles from her bag. She stuck one on each person in the photo, above their head or on their torso. Pen at the ready, she turned to Angelika.

'Let's work down the list. As you identify each person, I'll number them on the sheet and on the photo.'

The system worked well. As Angelika trailed her finger down the list, then pointed to a figure in the photo, Rae added a number to each. The task took less than ten minutes to complete, with the two men watching on with interest.

'A mixture of High Commission staff, government officials and EcoFutures people,' Angelika said.

'That's everyone in the photo identified.' Barry was looking pleased. 'Our first major task. But there are two people on the list not in the photo. Can you explain?'

'They're High Commission employees. Junior staff,' Angelika said with little hesitation. 'They were assigned to the government team for the duration of their visit. They normally do office work but acted as guides to take the group around London.'

Barry turned to Carlos. 'Is it possible to see staff photos of them, please? Just for elimination purposes.'

Carlos was obviously a little unhappy with this request but finally agreed. He used his desktop computer to pull up their records from a staff database, then rotated the screen briefly to give the two detectives a view of each staff member. Neither were the people they were looking for. Rae reached into her bag once again and pulled out a large print of the final photo Robin Pryor had taken on his phone. She pushed it towards Carlos.

'Who are these two people in the background?'

Carlos frowned and shook his head. 'I don't recognise them. They don't work here. Angelika? Do you remember them?'

Angelika looked confused and worried. 'No, sir. They weren't in any of the designated groups and they're not on the list as far as I can tell.' She turned back to Carlos. 'Are you sure they're not staff? Could they have been temporary workers?'

Carlos was looking equally puzzled. 'I've never seen them before. I wonder who they are and how they got in. One thing's for sure, they couldn't have gained entry without being signed in at reception. I think I need to do some checking. Is it possible they were with the caterers?'

'The buffet food was all done in-house, sir. The catering manager was keen to show off the best of Parantos cooking.'

'I just don't understand this.' He stared at the photo for several moments. 'There must be a record of them somewhere. They wouldn't have got past reception without some kind of authorisation and signature.' He looked at Angelika again. 'You speak directly to the catering manager. Julia, isn't it? Press her hard if necessary. I'll do the same with reception and security.'

'Can we come with you?' Barry asked. 'I'll come with you, Carlos, and Rae here can go with Angelika.'

Once again, Carlos frowned. Barry sensed the diplomat's reluctance. He wouldn't really want some kind of mix-up to be brought to light in front of two UK police officers, but Barry was unwilling to sit idly by in Carlos's office and leave the questioning to someone inexperienced. He really wanted either himself or Rae to be present when staff were being probed.

'It really would help us. And we'll be very discreet, if that's what's worrying you. We're both experienced interviewers and can often tell when someone's lying. I realise we have no jurisdiction inside the High Commission, but this case involves the cold-blooded murder of a British citizen and intimidation or assaults on two others. We really need answers as to what's going on, and fast. And I'm becoming increasingly worried that someone inside the Commission might know something about it. The key question is, how did these two people get inside that reception room if they had no right to be there? Someone must know. They might even know that we're visiting today.'

Carlos nodded. 'Okay. I see your point. I'll do as you ask.'

He locked his office door behind him as they left.

\* \* \*

The reception area seemed calm and peaceful. The receptionist on duty, a young woman whose name badge identified her as Maria Castillo and who had signed Barry and Rae in earlier, was obviously intrigued by Carlos's series of requests – that he wanted to find out who'd been staffing the desk on the day of the reception, and if that day's entry log was still easily accessible. Barry stood back and observed.

Maria nodded enthusiastically to Carlos's request. 'Of course,' she replied. 'It's all on the computer.'

She rotated her screen so that Carlos had a clear view and worked on it for a minute or two, then sat back as a list was generated, showing all visitors on the day in question. Carlos made sure Barry could see the screen too. There were more than a hundred names.

'Could we start just with those associated with the reception?' Barry asked. 'Is it easy to pull them out?'

Maria nodded and set to work. A subset of the previous list appeared, which Maria directed to her printer. Once he had the paper copy in his hand, Barry compared it to the list Angelica had provided. They were the same. The three staff from EcoFutures were listed together, along with the times they'd signed both in and out. The delegation who'd flown in from Parantos were also grouped.

'Can you go back to the original list of all visitors and print me a hard copy?' Barry asked.

Maria looked to Carlos for permission, and he nodded.

With this much longer list spread out on the desktop, Barry and Carlos spent several minutes poring over it. A proportion were High Commission staff, others were Parantos nationals visiting the Commission for legitimate reasons, and yet more were UK nationals calling in to find out about tourist locations in the country. Finally, ten names had appointments with High Commission personnel. Nothing seemed out of order.

Barry folded the lists and slid them into an inside pocket in his jacket. Just as he did so he heard footsteps approaching from behind and turned to find himself facing a tall man who was standing too close for comfort.

'Who is this and what are you doing?' the stranger asked.

'Oscar, this is Detective Inspector Barry Marsh,' Carlos explained. He turned to Barry. 'And this is my good friend

Oscar Garcia, our head of security. Oscar, DI Marsh is investigating the murder of someone involved with the coastal development project. The victim was at the reception last month. There might be a link.'

The man didn't look impressed. 'Really?' he said. 'Is that likely? And he has no powers here inside the Commission. Surely you realised that?'

'Of course. But after DI Marsh explained the way his investigation is proceeding, I decided to offer him our help. It is possible that two unauthorised people attended that reception, if only for a minute or two.'

Garcia snorted. 'I don't see how.'

'Even so, it looks like it happened. It needs checking out and that's the decision I made.'

Barry could see that there was some degree of friction between the two men. Was it just linked to this particular incident or was it more long-term? He guessed the latter. He also judged that Carlos was the more senior of the two in terms of Commission hierarchies. Oscar Garcia came across as a rather more confrontational individual yet seemed to be holding himself back. But he didn't raise any immediate concerns in Barry's mind that he might have been involved in whatever incident had been initiated at that fateful reception. Rather that it was just a display of squabbling about status. He gave off none of the common signals that might indicate involvement in some kind of conspiracy. Would this prove to be a dead end?

* * *

Angelika didn't say very much as she and Rae made their way to the catering manager's office at the back of the building. Although she seemed a pleasant young woman, she appeared on edge and responded minimally to any question Rae asked of her. Julia, the catering boss, also seemed grumpy and somewhat hostile at being disturbed from her work. She told them that she was a staff member down today and really didn't have time to waste. Angelika coaxed her into giving them five minutes of her time, something for which Rae was grateful. She made the most of the opportunity, though not before she'd made an attempt to placate the woman with an ice-breaking comment.

'I love Central and South American food,' she said. 'Rice and beans with chicken. So tasty.'

Julia looked at her with a little more interest. 'It can vary so much,' she replied. 'I have my own family recipe. I made it for the reception you're interested in. They ate it all, those greedy people.' She seemed pleased though.

'Did anything unusual happen that day, Julia?' Rae asked. 'It's just that two people were spotted in the reception room that weren't on the list to be there. No one seems to know how they got in.'

Julia closed her eyes for a while, causing Rae to wonder if she was about to have a snooze.

Her eyes suddenly opened. 'Yes. Odd. I found the delivery door ajar, even though we didn't expect a delivery that day.'

'Who opened it? Did you ever find out?'

Julia snorted loudly. 'Of course not! No one ever owns up to something like that! It wasn't obvious, either. A little wedge was holding it open a crack. I wouldn't have noticed if it hadn't been a cold day. I felt the draught in my old bones.'

Rae refrained from smiling. The woman couldn't be much older than fifty. She took out the photo and showed it to Julia, pointing out the two figures in the background, noting the way the catering manager screwed up her eyes.

'I don't know her, but he looks like Pedro Hernandez.' She curled her lip. 'He was a cleaner here a long time ago. I never forget. He was stealing some food supplies from my stores and selling it to a market stall.'

Rae listened with interest as Julia became more animated.

'He got the sack. He deserved it, stealing from my stock.'

'What happened to him?'

'The last I heard he was trying to get another job in London. I didn't give him a reference though. Not after stealing from me.'

Julia seemed to have taken the incident personally. A woman of principle, Rae thought.

'Is there anyone who'd know more?'

Julia shook her head. 'I don't know. He wasn't a nice person, that man. His eyes always weighing you up as if you were for sale. Eugh!'

## CHAPTER 23: CHOCOLATE ECLAIRS

Jackie was interested to see how the following morning's briefing would pan out. It would be the first with Sophie Allen, the chief superintendent, present. Would she muscle in and take over, re-establishing her authority? After all, morning meetings up until now had been held first thing, at eight o'clock on the dot, but this one was to be delayed until well after nine to give her time to get in. Jackie felt more than a little nervous. She didn't know why. She'd met the woman before, back in Watchet, midway through that awful case with the man's body found washed up on the mud in the harbour. But that was when she was still working as a part-time special constable, not as a full-time member of Sophie Allen's own elite squad. And that case had been largely run by the DCI, Polly Nelson.

A bump followed by the squeak of an ageing door hinge woke her from her reverie. She looked up in time to see a wheelchair backing through the doorway. Soft blonde hair was showing above the chair's seatback. Jackie wondered if she ought to stand up and help in some way, but she was beaten to it by Rae, quick off the mark as always. The chair turned and a smiling Sophie Allen faced them, her arms clutching a box of shortcake biscuits and what appeared to be a bag of chocolate eclairs, judging by the coloured shape that was poking out of the top. A ripple of applause broke out among the other members of the team, so Jackie joined in. She watched as Barry strode across from his desk and gave the woman a hug, followed by Rae. Their genuine pleasure at seeing their boss was obvious.

'Well, here I am, everyone,' Sophie said. 'But don't mind me. I still can't get around very much, so I expect I'll be little more than a glorified tea lady. But, God, I've been looking forward to this moment. You have no idea.'

Jackie glanced around at the other unit members, Tommy Carter, Rose Simons and George Warrander, the latter two temporarily seconded into WeSCU to help out. Greg Buller, head of Dorset's so-called snatch squad, was also present for the briefing. They all seemed really happy to see Sophie. Moreover, they looked relaxed. Jackie realised that the chief super was still speaking.

'And can I say a big welcome to our newest member? I know we've met briefly before, Jackie, but I'm so pleased that you took the plunge and joined us full-time. I owe you a lot. It was your quick thinking that got Rae down to the riverbank when she pulled me out of the water. I owe you both my life. Anyway, let's not dwell on the past. Down to business, I guess. Over to you, Barry. You're still running the show.'

Barry gave a brief rundown of the previous day's visit to the Parantos High Commission in London.

'Pedro Hernandez, that's the name of the man we're looking for. He was a cleaner there some years ago but was sacked for petty theft. Added to which, he was unpopular with other staff. He tended to intimidate some colleagues, particularly women. Several of the staff identified him as the man in the background of Robin Pryor's photo. He and the woman had no legitimate reason to be there. They hadn't signed in at reception. It looks as though a rear door had been left ajar for them. There's got to be an insider. They're looking for who it could be.' He paused.

'This all came about because of our usual team effort. Ameera found those photos taken by Robin. Tommy and Jackie followed it up with Justine and she spotted the two strangers. They got a message to Rae, so when she visited Bryony, they could focus on it. That in turn meant that we could use it on our visit to London yesterday. What this all shows is the importance of teamwork and keeping each other informed.'

'Do we know anything at all about the woman?' Sophie asked.

'Jackie and Tommy had time to do some checking at the pub yesterday evening, the one Robin played darts in. It looks likely it was the same woman. She was using the name Bella. That doesn't match anyone at the High Commission or anyone they're aware of.'

'And we can't be directly involved in any internal investigations, can we?' Sophie said.

'That's why we didn't go in all guns blazing,' Barry replied. 'They could have just chucked us out. As it was, we got their co-operation.'

Sophie frowned. 'You played it right, Barry. But it still leaves me uneasy. An important part of the investigation is out of our control. We don't even have eyes in the place. Someone could be leading them up the garden path and we wouldn't know. It's a problem. I bet you if it was a Scotland Yard case, they'd be leaning on High Commission staff heavily, trying to muscle in, using their influence.'

Barry seemed unconvinced. 'They'd maybe try. I'm not sure it would work though. They can be a bit prickly in that place. Rightly so, I guess. Who wants the big boots of the Met trampling all over everything? It would be the quickest way to alienate the staff. But I do take your point about the fact we're in the dark. What can we do about it though?'

'I'll give it some thought. It's exactly why I've come back. For these sorts of knotty problems,' Sophie replied.

Barry continued with his summary. 'A few more things. Rose and George have managed to speak to Bryony O'Neil's previous travelling companion, Mel Jones.' He looked across the table at Rose, who took a sip of her coffee before she spoke.

'There's nothing suspicious about her not going with Bryony that night. She's recently moved to Weymouth. Right, George?'

George was looking fidgety.

'Anything to add, George?' Barry asked.

'Just that it was convenient for those two that Bryony was alone in the car. Could they have known about it in advance? If so, how? It makes you wonder, doesn't it?'

'Good point,' Sophie said. 'Someone knew she'd be by herself that night and seems to have fed the information to those two, this Pedro Hernandez character and his woman friend. We need to chase it up.'

'They all knew, everyone in the department. Bryony talked about her Zumba evenings a lot during office chit-chat and mentioned Mel's absence. We can tick that one off the list,' Barry replied. 'Can we have thoughts, please, about Ameera's discovery that someone else accessed those photo files on the EcoFutures network, using a guest log-on identity?'

'Why would someone do that?' Rose asked.

'Ameera thinks they might have tried to delete them. Remove the evidence. They couldn't, though. The ID they used only allowed them to view the files, not wipe them. She's noted the date and time of access. Ameera is back there today to see if she can trace the hardware that was used. I want Tommy to work with her and see if the mole can be identified. Jackie, you go too. See if you can find other evidence as to who it might be, sending out information on Bryony. She was clearly targeted by Hernandez and this Bella woman. Who was leaking stuff to them? We need to know.' He paused. 'Anything else, anyone?' He looked around in turn at the team members, but no one had anything to add. He looked at Sophie.

'I'm still not clear why Justine Longford was targeted,' she said. 'Where does she fit into the big picture and why was her place broken into twice? What's the motive?'

'Rae and I have talked about that,' Barry replied. 'Our guess is that it's all to do with photos taken at the High Commission. Someone's looking for any more, just in case Robin Pryor's weren't the only ones. Someone is paranoid about those two strangers he snapped.'

'So that's why the other woman, Bryony, caught sight of someone outside her house a couple of days ago? Any signs of an attempted break-in there?'

'None.' This was Greg Buller speaking up. 'One of Dave Nash's forensic officers has had a close look but nothing's out of place. Rose and I have had a chat about it. It's a bit puzzling why someone was there when she got home. It doesn't really make sense.'

'There's a lot about this case that doesn't make sense, Greg. But isn't that true of most of our investigations? Things only come together at the end. As far as I'm concerned, it's all looking good,' she said. 'With all these latest finds coming in, I sense that we're getting somewhere. Maybe I'm not needed after all. Except for the cakes, of course. Good work everyone, particularly you, Barry.'

Jackie was watching attentively. She was impressed by what she'd seen in recent days. What the chief super said was true. All that digging away was finally paying off. And there was a different feel to the investigation than the first one she'd been involved with, back home in Watchet. She'd got on really well with the DCI, Polly Nelson, but Polly had been more tense, more brittle in her relationships with the WeSCU members. Whereas Sophie Allen had them all in the palm of her hand. Added to which, Barry seemed calmer, more controlled, than Polly. Of course, he'd probably been trained that way by the chief, or used her as a role model. Jackie felt happy despite her tiredness. She realised that she'd made the right decision when she'd accepted the offer to join WeSCU. It was perfect for her. She was about to gather up the notes she had in front of her when she realised that Sophie Allen was speaking again.

'Of course, we don't know the whereabouts of this couple, Pedro Hernandez and Bella whatever. We don't know whether they've gone back to London or are still around here somewhere. Or whether they've left the country. Barry, we need to check with border security that they're still looking for people that match their descriptions. And we can give them their names now. Well, Hernandez, anyway. But if they're still around here, I wonder if there's a way of winkling them out? Thoughts, anyone?'

Rae spoke up. 'Maybe Jackie and I can have a night out in the local pubs tonight. Particularly the one where the woman snared Robin Pryor. Are you up for that, Jackie?'

'Of course. Pubs are my natural second home.'

'It's a date then.'

Barry closed the meeting. 'I want you all to be careful,' he said. 'Think about your own safety when you're out. I said earlier that we don't fully understand what we're up against. I've discussed it with the chief super here and we agree. It's beginning to smell like large-scale organised crime. Might be drugs related but not local level. Parantos has been used in the past as a route to ship out drugs from Colombia. We're starting to think they may have wanted to spike this development that EcoFutures was hired to plan.'

'And get the whole project cancelled?' Tommy asked.

Barry shook his head. 'I was talking to Carlos Martinez about it yesterday. Apparently, there's an alternative location. It would be less effective in terms of ecology and wouldn't attract so much international development money. But some shadowy figures back in Parantos are still pushing for it, even though it came a very poor second in the initial internal reviews. That's all he would say.'

142

## CHAPTER 24: DARTS

Lyme Regis's Appletree Inn was on the north side of Broad Street, an old and narrow thoroughfare that climbed uphill from the town museum. The street was lined with small shops of various types, from outdoor clothing to bakeries, bookshops and trinket shops with window displays set out to entice passing tourists. The pub, situated halfway up the hill, had low ceilings and old beams inside. It was popular with tourists and locals alike.

Rae and Jackie had dressed up a little for their evening out, although both were in trousers and low-heeled boots. They were aware that an evening out watching and listening might well turn into a very different type of occasion, where they could end up chasing someone down a dark footpath. And in Lyme Regis a high proportion of these had steep inclines. High heels and tight skirts were far from ideal clothing for such situations.

'Do I look okay?' Jackie asked when she met up with Rae outside the pub.

'Oh, yes,' came the reply. 'We'll knock 'em dead.'

Jackie crinkled her nose. 'Who do you mean, exactly?' she asked.

'No idea. But we'll use our natural charm and beauty to winkle out the information we need. That is, with a bit of luck and a following wind. To be serious, I have no real plan. I guess we start near the dartboard. We might even manage a game if it's not being used.'

They entered the pub and made their way to the bar.

'This is where I differ from the chief super,' Rae said, glancing at the beers and ciders on tap. 'She's a real ale fanatic. I prefer the fizz in a good lager, though I'm coming round a bit. I tasted that Dorset Gold that she's always going on about, and quite liked it.'

They ordered their drinks and took them across to the dartboard, currently not in use.

'Okay,' Jackie said. 'I'll give you a game. I'm pretty useless, though. I might go to pubs a lot back in Watchet, but I haven't played this since I was young. I suppose I throw the pointy end towards that board and hope for the best?'

'You've got it in one,' Rae laughed. 'That sums it up.'

The pub gradually got busier, and they attracted a small audience, mainly men. Some offered advice, others just watched. Rae and Jackie didn't bother to keep a score at first but one or two of the audience stood by the old chalkboard and kept tally, giving target advice when it became necessary. Jackie played a better game than she'd hinted at, although Rae was steadily moving ahead. She even received several ripples of applause, though whether it was for her darts playing or her figure-hugging jeans was unclear.

One man seemed particularly fascinated by Rae and Jackie, and their game of darts. He didn't offer any advice, but he was clearly interested, judging by his close observation of the two women. This didn't escape Rae's attention. When it was Jackie's next turn to throw, Rae moved close to where he was sitting.

'Do you play darts yourself?' Rae asked as she sat down next to him.

'A bit. Why do you ask?' He had a gruff voice and narrowed his eyes as he spoke.

'I just caught sight of you watching us.'

'My girlfriend runs the women's darts team here. She's always short of players. I was kind of scouting for her.'

'And your conclusion?'

He screwed up his face slightly. 'Maybe you've got potential, but you're not at match level. Your friend's just a beginner, isn't she?'

'To be honest, we're just having a bit of fun. We don't want to keep serious players off the board, so once we're finished we'll move away.'

'It's not a problem,' he responded. 'It's open to anyone when it's not a match night.'

'So, you're a regular in here? And your girlfriend?'

He nodded and took a sip from his glass. 'It's not exactly a town full of vibrant nightlife. Darts. Pool. Getting pissed. That sums it up, really.'

'Do you think strangers are made to feel welcome here? Or are they made to feel like outsiders?'

He shrugged. 'Do you mean this pub in particular or the town?'

'Both.'

'Tricky one. I s'pose the locals are split into three types. The posh buggers, retired moaners, and working folk like me who get treated like dirt by the other two. Not always a happy mix, if you ask me.'

'That's quite cynical, isn't it?' Rae was watching him carefully.

'Couldn't care less. It's what I think. What a lot of us think. It's not all rosy living in these coastal towns. Summer's ruined by all the bloody tourists and trippers. Winter's cold and wet but at least all the sodding second-homers have gone, with their posh cars and posher voices.'

Rae was wondering where this conversation was going. Was the man just another grumbler with a chip on his shoulder, sounding off about his own prejudices? Maybe she should open up about her reasons for being here.

'We're both police officers,' she said. 'I'm in here to see if anyone remembers an evening a few weeks ago when a man who works locally was playing darts and being watched by a woman he met.' Rae felt herself being scrutinised even more closely. 'He was the man found dead a few miles west of here, on the coast path. He was murdered.'

The man narrowed his eyes even more. 'I heard about that. Poor bastard.'

'Were you in here the night he was playing?'

'Why do you want to know?'

'We're trying to trace the woman.'

'Was she a honey trap, then?'

Rae shrugged. 'We don't know, to be honest. That's why we're trying to trace her.'

At this point they were joined by Jackie who had finished her last throw. 'You win. I guess I've got a lot to learn.' She glanced at the man sitting next to Rae.

'I'm Detective Sergeant Rae Gregson,' Rae said. 'My friend here is Detective Constable Jackie Spring. And you are?'

'Micky Robins. And I do remember who you're talking about. Middle-aged bloke with a moustache?'

'That's him.'

'Yeah, he was in here. The woman was a sultry-looking type. Obviously up to something, I thought. She was coming on to him quite strong. I even thought they were an item.'

Rae hooked her phone out of her pocket and opened the photo of the two strangers at the reception in the High Commission, zooming in on the woman's face. 'Is this her?'

'Possibly. Can't be sure though. She was olive-skinned like her in the photo, and even had short hair and enormous hooped earrings like her.'

'What gave you the impression they were already together?'

'She was sticking to him like a leech. Look, I've already told the cops about it.'

'So that was you who spoke to our colleague? What, a few days ago?'

'Yeah. So why are you here asking the same stuff?'

Rae pointed to her phone. 'We didn't have the photo then.'

One of the other men had been listening to the conversation. 'He went back to her hotel. I saw them leave.'

The detectives switched their attention to this second man. 'Are you sure? No one else has mentioned that,' Rae said.

'I haven't been here for a while. Bloody hay fever. Left me feeling too wiped out to come out in the evenings. It's my first night out for a week. But, yeah. They went in the old hotel down the hill. She had her arm around him and was leaning in close. They stopped twice on their way down and had a snog. I can remember thinking, lucky bugger. He's won the jackpot there. So he's the one who ended up dead? Not so lucky, after all. What's that insect where the female eats her mate after doing the business?'

'A praying mantis?' Jackie suggested.

'That's the one. Reminds me of them. Makes me shudder.' He added a dramatic shake of the shoulders to illustrate what he meant. Jackie thought it looked entirely staged and rather ridiculous.

Can you describe this woman, this femme fatale?' she asked.

'Quite short. Dark hair. Shapely. She was wearing a low-cut lacy top, tight black trousers, shiny ones. You know, the ones that look like leather. Maybe they were leather. High heels. A red zipper jacket. Her name was Bella, I think.'

Micky Robins seemed highly amused. 'You obviously took a lot of interest, Geoff. I couldn't have told you stuff like that. Take a fancy to her yourself, did you?'

Geoff obviously didn't find this comment funny. 'I just notice things, if you must know. It don't mean anything.'

'Can I have your name?' Jackie asked. 'And how we can contact you?'

The two detectives remained in the pub for a further hour but made no new discoveries. Their darts playing improved as they took the advice of the pub locals, and they were rewarded with several invitations to join the group again on future evenings.

'We'll give it some thought,' was all Rae would commit to. 'It's a long way from Wool, where I live. And Jackie lives near Minehead in Somerset, even further. We're only here on the murder case. Once it's solved, we'll be off. Nice place though.'

Rae turned back to Jackie and spoke quietly to her. 'I'll send Tommy to check out that hotel. See what the staff remember.'

When they finally left the Appletree, Jackie had an uneasy feeling that they were being watched, and not just by members of the darts-playing group. Was she just being paranoid? The thought that their real opponents were some Colombian-based drugs cartel was frightening.

## CHAPTER 25: SECRET DINNER

Sophie's phone rang. She glanced at the caller display, then closed the office door before answering it, keeping her back firmly in place against the door in case Barry tried to open it.

'Hi, Yauvani.'

'I heard you're back at work. Is that wise?'

'I got the go-ahead from my consultant. As long as I'm careful, there shouldn't be a problem.'

'Okay, I'll take your word for it. Can we meet? Normally, I'd suggest you come to London, but I expect that's out of the question.'

'Everything has to be fitted around my daily physio sessions. Sorry.'

'I can make this evening, for dinner, over where you are. I've had a meeting cancelled. Can you book somewhere good for us? Some discreet place where we won't be overheard. My car can pick you up. I'll message you beforehand.'

'Sounds good. I'll pick the brains of some of the locals to find somewhere. I'm in a wheelchair, YoYo, so it'll need to have disabled access.'

'As long as it's not fish and chips on the beach. I do have to draw the line somewhere.' There was a pause. 'I need you to bring me up to speed, Sophie. There have been rumblings.'

'I wondered. But we're getting a handle on it all.'

'I'm sure you are. I just want to see if there's anything I can do to help. It'll be good to see you anyway. Last time you were swathed in bandages and drugged up to the eyeballs.'

Sophie was trying hard to remember her friend's visit to the hospital, but nothing came to mind. She vaguely remembered Martin mentioning Yauvani's low-key visit, but she had no direct recollections.

'I can't remember a thing about that first week,' she said.

'Not surprised. Anyway, got to go. See you tonight. Low key, remember.'

With that, Yauvani rang off and Sophie was left staring at the screen in mild frustration. Martin had been set to join her this evening. How would he feel about being shouldered aside by the home secretary, particularly since he refused to ever vote for her party?

*  *  *

Sophie had been recommended the restaurant of a hotel that was situated at the top of the hill overlooking the town's flower gardens. It proved to be a good choice. Yauvani's driver and personal detective sat at a nearby table while the two women were shown to a window corner, with stunning views across the bay. Yauvani was wearing a sapphire-blue wrap dress, with matching jewellery and evening sandals. Sophie, unable to get into any of her favourite outfits, was feeling envious.

'I like it here,' Yauvani said. 'It could be a good place to bring my new partner. He says he likes the coast. What do you think?'

Sophie, as always when she met her friend, didn't quite know what to say. She knew that Yauvani was a ferociously single-minded woman, utterly dedicated to her career in politics. She'd never really opened up about her love life to Sophie before. Had something changed?

'I don't know, YoYo. I don't know your partner. Martin would love it here, but he's a bit of a wildlife freak. Is it your kind of thing, coastal walking? Tramping through mud?'

'I haven't a bloody clue. Never tried it. Maybe it's about time. I'm getting fed up with the life I'm in, though.' She looked Sophie in the eye. 'I'm thinking of standing down at the next election.'

Sophie was genuinely puzzled. 'Why?'

Yauvani sighed. 'It's what's looming on the horizon. All this culture wars nonsense. I can see it coming. Picking on harmless minorities and deliberately demonising them in a misguided attempt to gain votes. I bloody loathe it, yet I have to be seen to support it. It makes me sick.'

'I can understand that. You've got scruples, Yauvani. I saw that when we first met.'

'Well, that's a big weakness in a politician.' She took a sip of wine. 'Enough of this, anyway. That's our starter just arriving. Let's talk business.'

Sophie talked as they ate their way through the first two courses, giving a summary of the case so far, how it had expanded from what had initially seemed some low-level intimidation and abduction into murder and a likely international organised-crime group. Yauvani asked a few perceptive questions, then sat thinking, poking at her dessert.

'Have you considered the drug-smuggling angle?'

'It's at the back of our minds, yes. One of my team thought of it right away. It's one of the routes out of Colombia. Not a major one but it's there.'

'Well, your people seem to be on top of it, Sophie,' she finally said. 'I'll keep the Met off your back.'

'Was there a danger of that, then?'

'Oh, yes. Once your DI escalated it to involve the High Commission. It was the right thing to do, but it caused some comments in the stratosphere. I'll smooth the way. I have contacts with the High Commissioner. Apparently, he's straight-talking and a decent person. He wants to be kept informed but at an unofficial level. One of my people can do that if you keep me in the loop. Leave it with me.'

'Thanks. I wondered if it might come to something like this. I'm grateful, YoYo.'

'I don't have many real friends, Sophie. Normal people, I mean. Too many backstabbers in politics. I sometimes feel it's like an assassins' convention. What I'm trying to say is that I value our friendship. I know we have different political views, but I've come to realise that we have a somewhat similar moral outlook on life.'

Sophie was touched. 'I feel the same. What will you do if you leave politics?'

Yauvani shrugged. 'Business? Academic work? I haven't really thought about it.' She looked out of the window again, scanning the view that stretched beyond Golden Cap, on towards the Isle of Portland. 'Coastal walking? Even if it is a bit muddy.'

'As a hobby, yes. But I know that brain of yours. Mine's similar. It needs activity. It needs people. You've got to plan this, YoYo. Your background's in science, isn't it? Anything you can use there?'

'Too long ago, Sophie. I haven't kept up with it.'

'Michael Portillo does those TV travel programmes about train journeys.'

Yauvani's lips curled to such a degree that Sophie wondered if her dessert had gone sour.

'Maybe I shouldn't have mentioned him. What about writing?'

'No patience. That's always been my problem.'

'TV work, maybe?'

'Hmm. Now there's a thought. As long as it's nothing like who you've just mentioned. Something political, possibly.'

'Where politics meets science?'

'Hah! Science is based on evidence. Politics is as far away from that as it's possible to get! How would that work?'

Sophie felt nonplussed. 'I wish you hadn't told me that. It confirms my worst fears about the running of the country.'

'Eat up. We can toddle through to the lounge and have a couple of liqueurs. I've enjoyed this evening, even though we spent much of it talking business. It's always good to spend time with someone normal who's not in the Whitehall bubble.'

'Is it really that bad, YoYo?'

'You have no idea. Anyway, this evening's been great. I was worried about you, you know. Seeing you in that hospital bed, hidden behind all those bandages and not entirely with it because of the painkillers. What's the long-term prognosis?'

Sophie shrugged. 'It's still wait and see at the moment. I've got to behave, though, and not push myself too hard. Otherwise, they might insist on me going back in.'

'Is this the first time in your life you've done exactly as you've been told?'

Sophie nodded. 'Afraid so.'

Yauvani laughed. 'I can imagine. Come on, finish that wine. I can feel a cognac calling. I'll snooze in the car on the way back to London.'

# CHAPTER 26: IRONSIDE

Just where were Pedro Hernandez and his partner-in-crime, Bella? Barry was staring at their somewhat grainy photos on the incident board, vainly hoping that inspiration might strike, and an idea would occur to him that would help to solve the crime during the next twenty-four hours. Get real, Barry, he told himself. Life is never like that. Maybe it was time to take another look at the one person they'd been treating with kid gloves up to now.

Ian Duncan, EcoFutures' security manager, had not really been scrutinised closely since the start of the investigation. Could he be implicated in whatever was going on? Bryony O'Neil had insisted that she'd told no one else of that particularly bad dream of hers, the one of being lured into opening her car door to a manic-looking fiend wielding a knife. This didn't automatically make him guilty, but it painted a dark picture. Barry had decided to keep the man under unobtrusive observation rather than confronting him, in the hope that he might make a slip-up and reveal something more incriminating. But Ian Duncan had behaved faultlessly so far, showing no signs of behaving suspiciously. As Sophie Allen had said when he'd run through this strategy change with her, it was time to bring this tippy-tappy-toe approach to an end and go in all guns blazing. He went in search of Rae.

'It's time to go and put the screws on Ian Duncan. As far as we know, he hasn't put a foot wrong since we've been watching him. If he is involved, he must be feeling pleased with himself. Let's stir things up a bit.'

'I'm with you there, boss.'

The two detectives arrived at the EcoFutures premises half an hour later, unannounced.

'We're here to speak to Ian Duncan,' he told the receptionist. 'Right now, please.'

The man was out to see them quickly. 'Come into my office,' he said.

'I'd prefer somewhere neutral,' Barry replied. 'Maybe a meeting room?'

Ian Duncan frowned somewhat theatrically. 'Why?'

'So we're on a more equal footing,' came the reply. 'Alternatively, we could all go to the local police station. We're easy either way.'

'Meeting room one,' Duncan said to the receptionist. 'Keys, please.' He turned to Barry. 'I'll just pop back to my office to collect some files.'

'No, don't bother. We'll go directly to the meeting room. After you.'

The two detectives followed Ian Duncan to a nearby office and went in.

'What's all this about?' he asked.

'Let's sit down and we'll explain,' Barry replied.

He waited until the three of them were settled around a central table and Rae had her notebook at the ready, then spoke.

'There are a few things we need to check with you, Mr Duncan. We always look for discrepancies and things that just don't seem to fit comfortably with what we know. Let's start with that report that your premises might have been under observation. Two of our colleagues have already spoken to you about it, I understand. You didn't share their concerns.'

'No. I guess I was proved wrong in that instance. It happens to the best of us. I should have taken more interest. But it's all a question of priorities. I judged it not to be serious when I first heard about it.'

Rae frowned as she noted this particular comment.

Barry continued. 'You're a keen darts player, Mr Duncan.'

The man nodded, warily.

'Apparently you talked Robin Pryor into visiting the Appletree Inn last month for a few drinks and to get him to try out darts. But then you didn't appear. He had to fend for himself.'

Ian Duncan sat back in his chair, frowning heavily as if trying to dredge some memories up from the depths of his brain. 'A sudden family emergency, at the last minute. I'm sure I messaged him, but he obviously didn't get it in time. I apologised the next day.'

'Several witnesses said that there was a woman there who seemed to be expecting him. They hit it off and left together at the end of the evening. Her name could have been Bella or Belle. Ring any bells?'

He leaned forward slightly, shaking his head. 'No. Why would it?'

'Robin was dead a week later. Murdered along the coast path. It's possible a woman fitting her description was involved. Would you like to comment now?'

'I don't see what you're getting at. These are all just random events, not connected. Are you suggesting that I've been behind it all somehow? That's rubbish.'

As before, Barry refused to be drawn. Instead, he moved on. 'Let's switch our attention to your colleague, Bryony O'Neil. You had a fling with her last year. Why didn't you tell us when you had the opportunity?'

Duncan sighed. 'Usual reason. We're both married. We can't afford for it to get out. We agreed to keep the wraps on it. It wasn't really serious, anyway. It only lasted a month or two. Have you spoken to her about it?'

'Bryony said she'd told you about a particularly unpleasant nightmare of hers, one in which she was chased by a knife-wielding maniac late at night after being lured into stopping her car.'

Duncan looked bemused. 'I don't remember that. She's making it up.'

'Why would she, Mr Duncan?'

'How do I know? This is all so much total rubbish.'

'I'm giving you this opportunity to explain all this, Mr Duncan. Three seemingly disconnected events, but all of them are very relevant to our investigation and seem to involve you.'

The security manager gave him an angry look. 'But that's it. They are all disconnected. As far as I'm concerned, anyway. I'm just as puzzled as you are.'

Barry looked at Rae but she shook her head slightly. No more questions had sprung into her mind, then.

'Well, thanks for your time. We may be back in touch.'

* * *

'How did you get on, Barry?' This was Sophie, just arrived in the incident room in her wheelchair.

'I'm not sure. Either he really doesn't know what's going on or he's clammed up while he thinks things through. There's a good chance that he'll come round though, if that's the case. What other hope is there for him, if he's involved? Jackie, Rose and George have been following up on the people in the pub, getting statements. He's a regular there, he plays darts, and he encouraged Pryor along. That was how he met that woman, Bella. Though maybe Duncan is telling the truth and he's not involved. But that would mean someone else is lying to us. There is the possibility that he's been manipulated in some way.'

'Well, I'm here if you need me. He might open up to a woman, though I suppose you've got Rae for that. I just wonder how being interviewed by a detective in a wheelchair might change the dynamics. You know, the Ironside effect.'

'What?' Barry sounded genuinely puzzled.

'Ironside. Famous wheelchair-bound TV detective from the sixties, played by Raymond Burr. Or was it the seventies? My great aunt and uncle who I grew up with were addicted to it. I think there was a more recent remake, but it was rubbish.'

'Never heard of it.'

'Sheltered upbringing, Barry. Not enough exposure to the Hollywood take on life. It explains why you're so sensible. Sadly, I was corrupted from an early age. Let's not dwell on it, though. So you think we just leave him to stew for a while, our possibly mixed-up friend? It often works. I suppose it depends on whether they really have got to him in some way. These drug gangs, if that's who they are, can be really nasty.'

'If it is that, we can offer him safety in exchange for him turning, can't we?'

Sophie was non-committal. 'Only as a last resort. It's such a drain on the budget, Barry. That's the problem. New rules, I'm afraid. Try everything else first. In the meantime, we just wait and see, as you suggested. Any other new openings?'

Barry scratched his chin. 'Nothing much has come from that hotel liaison between Pryor and the woman after they'd finished their game of darts. We sent Tommy to check it out. False name and address but the description matches. She was gone before breakfast.' He paused. 'We've been mulling over what we've found out so far. Rae and I thought yet another visit to the EcoFutures place is called for this afternoon but with a change of focus. This time we want to see the remaining members of the Parantos unit together for a short while. See how they interact with each other while we question them.'

'What? All of them?'

He shook his head. 'Bryony and Justine are still working remotely. I don't want to put them at risk by bringing them in. No, just the remaining four. Val Potter was Pryor's deputy. She's taken over. There are three technicians, Simon, Nina and Nabila. We've already spoken to Val, but the others have just had quick visits. We need to suss them out a bit more. I want to see how they relate to each other, what the team spirit is like, if there are any obvious internal tensions.'

He collected Rae and the two detectives drove out to the company site in Axminster. They spoke to the development team members in their admin room, over coffee. The three technicians seemed very uneasy, but Rae thought that was to be expected considering the events of the past couple of weeks. The team leader murdered, and two other senior members intimidated or burgled. That would be enough to put the frighteners on anybody. Val Potter, only a day or two after taking over as the new leader, was much more at ease. But then she'd already been through a detailed police interview. This chat was different, though. As he'd explained, Barry wanted to see how the group members interacted with each other, although they couldn't form a totally accurate picture, not with Bryony and Justine still being absent.

The opinion that Rae had formed of Val, made previously when she and Jackie had interviewed the woman, was reinforced. She spoke carefully, and seemed thorough and well organised in her thoughts. She clearly had ideas of where she wanted the project to go, although she admitted that these hadn't been fully fleshed out yet.

'I have some changes to make to poor Robin's plans,' she admitted. 'But nothing significant. Not yet, anyway.'

Rae, watching keenly, saw a slight glance pass between the three technicians. They didn't speak, though. Val sat back after a short summary, presumably in order to let the rest of the team make some comments. They were reluctant to do so. The three technicians were all much younger, two in their late twenties with the man, Simon, probably a few years younger. He merely seemed bemused by the questions the detectives asked about relationships within the unit. Nina seemed jittery and Nabila looked wide-eyed and frightened, as if she was caught up in a bad dream. Only Val took the discussion in her stride. Was that surprising? She was middle-aged, after all, presumably with plenty of life experience. And she did have a point to prove, having only just been promoted to unit leader. She jollied the three younger people along, prompting them when required to do so, but they became steadily quieter as the conversation progressed.

Rae observed with disquiet. Something was wrong here. Could Val be trying to pull the unit in a different direction than before? Whatever forces were at work here, the unit seemed dysfunctional. Or was it just her imagination?

Barry threw in some questions about Robin's original ideas. Rae was intrigued by the way the three technicians, although still reticent, showed rather more positivity during this part of the discussion. Clearly, Robin Pryor had been a popular leader. Was it Val Potter's over-efficient methods that were to blame for their current lack of verve? Or was the unease down to something else entirely?

'Something not quite right there, boss,' was Rae's comment to Barry as they returned to the car.

'Glad you spotted it too,' was his reply. 'I'm not sure why, but I don't think they trust her. Interesting.'

## CHAPTER 27: MURDER ON THE CAP

Dorset's Golden Cap, halfway along the Jurassic Coast, is the highest point on the south coast of England, although it tends to be less well known than other high spots such as Beachy Head, places that have sheer, rocky cliff faces. Golden Cap doesn't have such a vertiginous frontage. The sloping face that fronts onto the sea is made of sandstone that glows gold in sunlight, hence its name. In good weather it's a favourite haunt of ramblers and other outdoor types, picking their slow way along the coast path, enjoying the peace and quiet that is often found within a protected area, several miles from the nearest busy road. In more malevolent weather conditions, it can seem desolate and lonely, eerie even, with dark clouds clinging to the summit.

Pitchfork Farm is the closest permanent habitation to the cap, lying inland to the northwest. Slightly closer is an old cottage, Shepherd's Rest, rented out as a holiday let, usually to walkers or cyclists. The small building occupies a picturesque, sheltered spot near a stream. Often empty in the winter months, it becomes more popular for weekend bookings as milder weather reaches the area at about the time of the spring equinox. As the late May half term holiday approaches, it tends to become fully booked and this busy period lasts through until the end of September.

Pitchfork Farm has a small number of arable fields but much of its work is centred on the hardy cattle and sheep that graze the high ground's upland pastures, including the area that surrounds the holiday cottage. It's a beautiful location — most of the time. But on wet and windy evenings like this, Bruno Lambert, the current tenant at Pitchfork, didn't feel so positive. He'd only just arrived back inside the farmhouse after a particularly busy day and was looking forward to a soak in the bath, a hot meal and a glass of cider. He'd hung up his waterproofs and had his arms around his partner, Sally, as she stood at the sink preparing vegetables. He nuzzled his lips into the back of her neck.

'Hard day?' she asked.

'Mm,' he murmured. 'Someone left the gate open near the lower field, close to Shepherd's Rest. Half the sheep got out and were all over the place. Two lambs were stuck in the fence down at the coppice. Terrified. Bloody careless walkers. They're okay now, though.'

'Well, you've got about half an hour. Better have your bath now.'

A distant bang sounded, coming in through the open window.

'What was that?' Sally said, puzzled.

Bruno glanced through the window, though its view of the surrounding land was limited by the proximity of the farm's outbuildings.

'It sounded like a gunshot,' he replied. 'Though I suppose it could have been a car backfiring. Odd.'

Sally stopped what she was doing and turned to her husband. 'There shouldn't be anyone shooting out there. Could it be down at the cottage? Shepherd's Rest has been occupied for some weeks now. Do you think we should check?'

They climbed the stairs to the spare back bedroom. It had a large window that gave a clear view of Golden Cap and its surrounding land. The wind speed had begun to drop during the past hour and the rain was diminishing in intensity. Even so, their view was somewhat obscured.

'Can't see anything,' Bruno said.

Just then another bang sounded.

'That's a gun,' he said. 'Sure of it.'

Sally peered through the glass of the window but couldn't see much. 'Over towards the Cap?' she suggested. 'I might be wrong though.'

'I'd better take a look,' Bruno replied.

'Well, I'm coming too. We'll take the Landie. I'll drive.'

Sally called to their two teenage children, both in their bedrooms supposedly doing their homework, although the sound of a TV show could be heard coming from their daughter's room. The two adults hurried back downstairs and climbed quickly into their waterproofs. Bruno extracted a shotgun from a locked cabinet in a small room off the hall.

'Lock the door behind us,' Sally said as she headed for the old Land Rover parked in the yard.

The lane Sally followed became rough as it approached the old building. Suddenly, a shiny dark-coloured SUV shot out of a sidetrack near the holiday cottage. She was forced to swerve onto the verge to avoid a collision. The vehicle accelerated hard and was soon lost to view.

'I didn't catch the registration,' Sally said. 'Did you?'

Bruno shook his head. 'The dashcam should be on though. Maybe it picked up something.'

Sally was looking worried. 'I don't like this, Bruno. Especially after that business with the dead body being found near the coast path out west, past Lyme last week. We need to be careful.'

Sally took the vehicle a few yards further to the pull-in by the cottage. They clambered out and somewhat hesitantly moved towards Shepherd's Rest. The lights were on and the front door stood open. Their calls went unanswered. There seemed to be no one around. They moved back to the front gate, and it was there that Bruno spotted a dark liquid stain on the white-painted surface. It was blood. Sally put her hand to her mouth in shock. Bruno reached for his phone.

* * *

A police squad car was on the scene within half an hour.

'Have you touched anything?' the first officer asked, looking at the couple suspiciously.

'Of course not,' Sally answered. 'What do you take us for? Idiots?'

'The report said something about two possible gunshots,' the second cop said. He was younger and sounded more amenable.

Bruno answered. 'That's right. The second was a few minutes after the first one. Maybe a bit more distant. We heard them both from inside our house, Pitchfork Farm, half a mile back up the lane.'

'So, is this your land?'

Bruno shook his head. 'That fence just back there marks our boundary. This cottage is a holiday let. We don't know who owns it, but it's managed by a local agency. Then, beyond the stream there, it's all National Trust land, right the way to Golden Cap.'

'Okay. You might want to head back to your house once we've got your details.'

Sally was unhappy at this suggestion. 'There was a second shot. We told you that. And it sounded a bit quieter, as if it was further on or more muffled, closer to the Cap. There could be a victim around somewhere. Maybe they're injured, not dead. I'm a nurse at Lyme Hospital. And Bruno knows the land around here better than anyone. Surely we should check, just in case?'

The older cop still didn't look convinced but the younger one nodded in agreement. 'Sounds sensible,' he said.

They all looked back along the lane as they caught sight of more blue flashing lights approaching.

'This might be someone arriving to take charge,' he continued. 'We'll just wait for them, then get going.'

Several more police vehicles drew to a stop and a burly police sergeant hurried over. She stood talking to the two cops for a few moments, then approached Sally and Bruno.

'Sergeant Rose Simons,' she said. 'Those two have told me of your suggestion. Sounds good to me, in the circumstances. My colleague is just getting some kit together, then we'll be off.' She looked around her. 'How long have we got 'til total darkness?'

Bruno shrugged. 'Maybe half an hour at best?'

'Okay, let's move.'

'I've got a shotgun in the Landie,' Bruno said. 'Should I bring it?'

'No,' came the abrupt reply. 'Not needed. PC Warrander here is firearms trained. Which way?'

Bruno spoke as they set off. 'The hard surface finishes here. It's just a farm track from now on. We'll go across the bridge then start uphill. There's a wooded area about a quarter of a mile up the slope.'

'Okay. We'll take it slowly, having a good look round.' Rose glanced at her younger colleague, who nodded his agreement.

The group of six moved off, following the deeply rutted path but also scanning areas of undergrowth nearby. The track started to climb, then entered the wood that Bruno had mentioned. He gave advice on which side paths were worth checking. The search was very much a compromise between the twin pressures of speed and thoroughness. If there was a victim and they were still alive, their chances of survival would be decreasing as time wore on and the temperature continued to drop. A couple of moss-covered posts marked a historic field boundary of some sort in the middle of the copse. The air smelled dank, reeking of rot and decay. Torch beams swept the area from side to side and Rose occasionally called out, then listened for a response.

They were almost giving up hope when a call came out from the searcher on the extreme edge of the search line.

'Someone here!'

A man's body lay on its side in a shallow ditch, a dark blood stain visible around his head. Sally checked for a pulse, but she knew she was wasting her time.

Rose Simons was already on the phone. 'I think it's him. Dead. Shot in the back of the head. George is just double-checking for me.' She paused, watching her younger colleague closely. He lifted his eyes to her and nodded. 'Yes. He's got a beard. Might be the one who stopped that O'Neil woman late at night a few weeks ago.'

## CHAPTER 28: GRIM MORNING

The following morning was a grim one. Not because of the weather, which was beautifully clear after a little pre-dawn light drizzle had cleared, but because of the body, still lying close to the muddy footpath. Dave Nash, Dorset's forensic chief, had made the decision to leave it *in situ* until first light, protected by a forensic tent, to allow more carefully planned photography and recording to take place at the largely undisturbed crime scene. Forensic teams had searched both Shepherd's Rest and its garden as well as they could during the night, and the area where the body was found was scanned by torchlight. A thorough search of the woodland and its pathways had also been left until after daybreak. The dangers of contaminating crime scenes and ruining evidence by fumbling about in the dark were well known.

The members of the police team were looking tired. Apart from Sophie, they'd all been at Pitchfork Farm and its surrounding area well into the early hours. A somewhat bleary-eyed teenage girl came out into the farmyard with Bruno well before seven, and found Rose Simons clambering out of her car.

'Olivia here might have something for you,' Bruno said.

'There's been two people staying in that cottage for a couple of weeks,' the pale-faced youngster told them. 'But they've been using separate bedrooms.'

Of course, the fact that she looked and sounded jumpy was no indicator of her usual demeanour. The events of the previous evening had been enough to give anyone the heebie-jeebies.

'Can you explain please, Olivia,' Rose said. 'How did you come to see them inside?'

'I'm doing a bird count this week. Local wildlife group. Alex is meant to be helping too but he's always got other stuff to do. Or so he says. I had binoculars to help. It meant I was looking out a lot more than usual.'

'You're quite sure?'

'Yeah. I thought it was a bit weird them staying inside so much. The weather's been pretty good. You'd think they'd be out walking or something.'

'Show me,' Rose said.

She followed Olivia upstairs to her room at the side of the house. The cottage could be seen through a gap in the trees.

'And a couple of times their car came past the farm on their way along the lane,' the girl added. 'It's what I said. They didn't go out much. Not this past week. Probably just for food and stuff.'

'So, they've definitely been here for longer than a week?'

'Yeah. A bit longer. Never stopped to chat, though. Kind of odd, that.'

'Okay. Thanks, Olivia. That's been really helpful.'

Rose reported the girl's account to Barry Marsh as soon as she could, then went inside the cottage to see how the forensic teams were getting on.

The interior of the cottage was surprisingly neat. Rose, now wrapped up in a sky-blue forensic suit, didn't know what she'd expected, but maybe not quite this level of tidiness. It looked unlived in. Had two people really been living here for several weeks? Wasn't the whole of the girl's story a bit fanciful?

But, of course, there was the near collision that Olivia's parents had experienced on driving out onto the nearby lane the previous evening after they'd heard the gunshots. Someone had been driving away in an almighty hurry.

A full-length mirror hung on the wall, close to the bottom of the open stairs. Rose was never happy to see her reflection while in uniform, even less so while wearing a forensic overall. It made her naturally stocky frame look even worse than usual, bulky and shapeless. But just look at George, she thought to herself. It didn't matter what he was wearing. He always managed to look slim and elegant, his hair in that slightly ruffled style that many younger men favoured. He and his girlfriend, Jade, always made such a great-looking couple when Rose saw them together, even if Jade was the taller of the two, by a whisker. Rose rubbed her cheeks. Concentrate, she told herself.

They climbed to one of the upper rooms, clearly converted from the loft-space. A dormer window looked south across the slight dip in the land, across the small valley and up the slopes of Golden Cap to the summit, about a kilometre away.

* * *

'The boss wanted to come up and pay a visit,' Barry said quietly to Rae as she joined the group at Pitchfork Farm.

'What did you say?'

'Told her to stay put. It's no place for a wheelchair, no matter how much she wants to join us. She'd just get in the way and cause mayhem.'

'I bet she wasn't happy.'

'Maybe not, but she's only been back with us a couple of days and she's already trying to push the boundaries. You and I, Rae, need to push back, firmly. It doesn't matter how she tries to wheedle us, the instructions from Martin are clear. She stays down in the town, in the incident room. The only real alternative is for her to go back into hospital. She'll probably try to get round you next. I thought I'd better warn you.'

'Okay, boss. Do you want to make me a sort of unofficial liaison officer, to keep her informed of what's going on up here? It'll keep her out of your hair, give you time to breathe. I promise to treat her with kid gloves.'

Barry looked taken aback and his face relaxed. 'Rae, that would be great. You won't mind?'

Rae smiled widely at him. 'No, of course not. I'd do any-thing for the both of you, you should know that. And I can be really delicate when I try. It'll only take a couple of short phone calls. I'll start now.'

Barry watched for a few moments as Rae walked across to a quiet corner of the farmyard, pulling her phone out. He felt a measure of relief. He wasn't confident enough to point out to his boss that today was meant to be one of her off-duty days, as agreed with her doctors. She shouldn't even be in the incident room. Rae had that little bit of extra openness in her relationship with Sophie Allen; she could say things that he daren't. Maybe it was a woman-to-woman thing.

He turned as Dave Nash approached him. 'The patholo-gist has just arrived. Do you want a word?'

Barry sighed, rather too loudly. Pathologists often had a slightly offbeat sense of humour, even decent ones like Benny Goodall. But was he in a position to complain? Murder detec-tives weren't really much better, if truth be told. Too much time spent in the vicinity of dead bodies and violent thugs.

## CHAPTER 29: EXPLORATION

The team reassembled in the incident room in Lyme Regis later that afternoon. Barry looked around at the tired but determined faces. What a great bunch of people. They'd spent half the night in the vicinity of that upland farm, carefully examining muddy paths by torchlight. And yet they'd all been back there soon after dawn, probing the grounds of the cottage, Shepherd's Rest, along with its surrounding area. He suspected that they all realised one important fact: the Lambert family at Pitchfork Farm were fortunate to have escaped physically unscathed. Things could have been very different for the farming family if the victim had managed to escape and had sought help at Pitchfork. Would the killer have pursued him to the Lamberts' home? Would he or she have left witnesses alive in such a situation? Well, this was somewhat pointless speculation. The killer, or killers, had succeeded in their aims, and such a drastic recourse had obviously not proved necessary.

'Let's make a start,' he said. 'Interim report from pathology. Over to you, Tommy.'

Tommy cleared his throat. 'Gunshot wound to the back of the head. Gunshot wound to the upper left arm. He was just under six foot tall. Middling build. Probably kept himself fit. Dark hair and beard. Maybe in his late thirties? Estimated time of death, between eight and nine. Death would have been instantaneous from that head wound.'

'That ties in with the second gunshot that was heard up at Pitchfork Farm,' Barry said. 'Go on.'

'Almost a professional hit, then?' Barry suggested.

Tommy shrugged. 'The pathologist won't comment on something like that.'

Sophie Allen had been watching and listening carefully. 'I'd go with that, Barry. Whoever it was, they knew exactly what they were doing. And to be as accurate as that in twilight, with the target trying to run away through woodland, is worth noting. But Tommy's right. Benny Goodall won't commit to anything outside his remit. He always says that to me, that it's not his job to speculate.'

'Okay. Let's move on. Initial forensic findings. Rae?'

'It was a handgun, nine mil. No surprise there. Pretty standard. But the second shot was in partial darkness and among trees and bushes. Quite impressive.'

'He might have tripped,' Tommy said.

'Even so. The killer must have been close behind, maybe closing in.' Rae paused. 'Two people had been in that cottage for several weeks, keeping a low profile recently. Maybe they guessed the heat was on and decided to stay in the cottage as much as possible in recent days. Maybe there was some kind of argument between them.'

'Anything about them from the search of the cottage?'

Rae shrugged. 'Not really. They were careful. But we did find his phone still in his pocket. It's with specialist forensics at the moment. It's registered to Pedro Hernandez. So the name matches what we know.'

'So it looks as though he's one of the two people we've been looking for, the couple in those embassy photos?'

'Probably. And we thought so last night when we first saw the body.'

'Anything else, anybody?'

Rose raised a hand. 'Nothing useful has shown up on the dashcam footage from the farmer's Land Rover. The reg plate of that other car was smeared with mud. It looked like a black SUV, maybe a Toyota. It's gone for analysis so we might get more information. But I'm not hopeful.'

'Well, you've done what you can, Rose.'

'Should we tell Bryony O'Neil and Justine Longford about what's happened?' Jackie Spring asked. 'With the man dead, aren't they safe to go back home?'

Barry looked across at Sophie. She took the hint.

'I think we should wait. There's still a killer out there, someone really ruthless. Maybe we've got some of our assumptions wrong. There's a tendency to assume that it's always the bloke who's the dangerous one in a duo like that pair. It's beginning to look the other way round this time. We don't have a clue as to who she is, other than that her name is probably Bella. And even that might be false. We don't know what her plans might be. We can't assume she'll stop now that Hernandez is dead. Too many unknowns, Jackie. Anyone else with any ideas?'

George coughed and raised his hand. 'Could it all be drug-gang related? Isn't this the kind of thing they do? Carry out an operation like this but then remove all the loose ends by killing them? Remember what Bryony O'Neil said she heard the woman say during that failed attempt at snatching her in her car. What was it? *What held you up?* If she was the driving force, maybe she didn't like that. And if she knows that we're onto the Parantos angle, she may be getting ready to do a runner but removing all the evidence first.'

'That's good thinking, George. It means we have to be extra cautious. Barry, can you warn the usual airport people? We need to be ready to catch her if she does decide to head abroad.'

\* \* \*

Rose Simons waited until the meeting was over and pulled George aside.

'You know that you're wasted working as a normal cop, George. I've told you that before. And I saw the way they all looked at you. They want you as a detective.'

'It's all too awkward, boss. What with me and Jade being together.'

'Yeah, but it needn't be. It's pretty definite that Kevin McGreedie is retiring, over in Bournemouth. Lydia Pillay is a dead cert to take over from him as DI. She'll be looking for new blood. It's ideal for you, George. Get in quick, that's my advice. Don't look a gift horse in the mouth. Now's the time.'

'Okay, I'll give it some thought. It does sound good when you put it like that. You're not just trying to get rid of me, are you, boss?'

'Bloody hell, George. You're a one! You're the best rookie I've ever worked with, and I'm not kidding you on that. No, you've got your future to think about. Don't let it drift, George. Act now. Have a word with Barry and get him to put a word in for you. He's always had a soft spot for Lydia. Better miss out her ladyship, though. You know, what with you and Jade. Keep it all above board. Better that way.' She paused. 'Listen, how about us going up to the area around the farm and cottage right now rather than leaving it until tomorrow? It looks like a nice evening. Just right for a walk in the countryside to get a feel for the whole area and the roads near there. And if we park in the right place, it'll be downhill, won't it?'

'Well, yes, boss. But we'll have to walk uphill at the end to get back to the car.'

Rose glowered. 'That's right, go ahead and spoil my happy mood with some bad news. You're a real spoilsport, George. Have I ever told you that?'

George sighed. 'Many times, boss.'

## CHAPTER 30: RUBBISH COLLECTION

Jackie Spring was attempting to check the booking records for the cottage, having contacted the letting agency, Lyme Coastal Cottages, with an urgent request. The young assistant who answered the phone seemed bemused by the information Jackie was seeking, so she decided to visit the agency in person. It was only a few miles away, in the coastal village of Charmouth. The company occupied a small office situated on the town's main street, squeezed between the pub and the fish and chip shop, two of Charmouth's biggest tourist attractions, she'd been told. No surprise there. Visitors to Jackie's hometown of Watchet also favoured pubs and fast-food outlets, and the same would probably be true for a hundred and one other small resorts dotted around the coast of Britain.

Jackie spotted a light on inside the agency's premises when she drew up outside, a good sign that it was open for business. An old-fashioned bell tinkled gently as she tried to enter, but she was forced to push the door against a sticking jamb. She almost fell in as it suddenly swung open to the force of her shoulder.

'Sorry,' a fair-haired young woman said as she looked up from her desk. She was smartly dressed and immaculately made up, with her sleek hair pulled back in a tight ponytail. 'I keep telling the manager that it needs looking at, but he hasn't got around to it yet.'

Jackie rubbed her upper arm, somewhat irritably. In her view, doors should open and shut as they were meant to.

'I'm DC Jackie Spring. I was on the phone to you a bit earlier, but I don't think you fully understood what I was asking for.'

'Oh, that wasn't me. That was the other assistant, Zoe. I'm Zara. She's just popped out. How can I help you?' the young woman said.

Jackie frowned. She wasn't entirely convinced by Zara's claim. Her voice sounded remarkably similar to the one on the phone, with the same soft Dorset accent.

Jackie held out her warrant card. 'I'd like to see recent booking records for the cottage close to Golden Cap, please. Shepherd's Rest.'

Zara's brown eyes widened, and her hand moved to her mouth. 'That's where those shootings happened, isn't it? Oh, my goodness.' She paused. 'Are you a murder detective?'

'That's what I was trying to explain on the phone, to your colleague. Zoe, did you say her name was? She didn't seem to understand.'

'She's a bit of an airhead,' Zara replied, giving Jackie a hopeful smile. 'No need to worry. I can help.'

She tapped a succession of keys on the computer that sat on her desk.

'There've been a number of bookings for Shepherd's Rest,' she said. 'Look.'

She swivelled the screen around so that Jackie had a better view of its display.

'Can you print it out for me?'

Zara clicked on a couple of icons and the printer on a nearby shelf whirred into life. A single sheet of paper appeared in the output tray. Jackie picked it up, examining its contents. The information was minimal, merely stating the names of the people staying, along with their date of arrival and the duration of their visit. The most recent booking had been for a month, but the name didn't correspond to that of the murder victim. Jackie frowned.

'Is this all there is?'

'It's what cottage owners usually want.'

'No home addresses? Payment details? Bank accounts? Card numbers? The name of the person who made the booking? Surely you have that kind of information stored somewhere?'

Zara looked wary. 'That's all sensitive stuff, isn't it? I can't go releasing that kind of information.'

'Well, Zara, this is a murder inquiry. That trumps any reluctance you may have about releasing *that kind of stuff*, as you put it. We have a killer to catch. You can help.'

'I'll need to phone the manager.'

'Please do so.'

Zara disappeared through a door at the rear of the office. Jackie soon heard the sound of her voice but couldn't make out what was being said. She soon appeared again, looking sheepish.

'I've got the go-ahead,' she said, somewhat embarrassed. 'Just got to find a way of getting you what you want.'

Her brow furrowed in concentration as she pressed keys and clicked on screen menus. Jackie stood to one side, watching carefully.

'That's it,' she said as a full set of details appeared on the screen. 'Print that, please.'

Again, the printer whirred. Zara swooped on the two sheets of paper that appeared. 'First time I've done that!' she said, triumphantly.

'Maybe you deserve a bonus,' was Jackie's somewhat sardonic reply. 'Though would Zoe need one too?'

Zara blushed and ignored the comment. 'Is that all?'

Jackie shook her head. 'Who owns the cottage?'

Frowning dramatically, Zara set to work once more. 'Ronnie Delphic,' she said.

Jackie noticed a slightly dreamy look in Zara's eyes.

'A nice guy, is he?'

Zara gave a start. 'What? Well, he's meant to be quite rich. He's probably a bit too old for me, though. No, it's his car. He's got this lovely cream-coloured Mercedes. It's just gorgeous.'

Jackie thought the young woman was almost drooling.

'Address?' Jackie prompted.

'He lives in Lyme. He owns a couple of other cottages. I'll get his address for you.'

A few seconds later, the printer pushed out another sheet of information.

'Anything else?' Zara asked, speaking in a breathy tone, as if this was the hardest set of tasks she'd been asked to perform all week.

'Yes. Who cleans the cottage between lets? We'll need to talk to them. I need a name, address and phone number.'

Zara scowled. 'Really? Are you sure?'

'Yes, I'm sure. I wouldn't ask otherwise.'

A now pink-faced Zara wrote some details on a pad, then tore off the sheet. Jackie looked at the name.

'Beryl Stebsworth,' she read aloud.

She looked again at the badge that Zara displayed on her lapel. Zara Stebsworth.

'Your mum?' Jackie asked.

The young woman nodded, looking miserable.

'Give my regards to Zoe,' Jackie said, as she turned towards the door, trying not to laugh. She'd just spotted three neatly labelled in-trays on a nearby shelf, one each for Brendon Stebsworth, Beryl Stebsworth and Zara Stebsworth. There wasn't one for a Zoe Stebsworth.

\* \* \*

Beryl Stebsworth was almost as far away from Zara in appearance as it was possible to be. Short and slightly tubby; wild

178

and curly greying hair; flushed cheeks; ill-fitting and badly co-ordinated clothes. Jackie wondered if the mother-daughter link was imaginary until she heard Beryl speak. Her voice was almost identical to Zara's and she had the same clear local inflexion to her words.

'Come in,' Beryl said. 'I wondered if I'd be getting a visit, seeing that I clean the cottage that's in the news. Such terrible events. I don't know what to think. No one does. And so soon after that other tragic death, along the coast path to Seaton.'

Jackie followed her through to a small lounge, neat and tidy.

'I've just been at your office, speaking to Zara,' Jackie said. 'Was it you she phoned for advice?'

'My husband, actually, though he was here at the time, so I heard what you wanted. He left for the office just afterwards. You probably passed him on the way.' She paused. 'Zara's sensible really, though she can be a bit uncertain when it comes to anything unusual. She's a bit of a daydreamer. She writes short stories as part of some sort of project for a local arts collective. Sort of fantasy fiction, I think.'

'Good for her. I hope it leads somewhere.'

Jackie wondered whether to ask if Zoe, the supposed other office girl, really existed, but thought better of it. Better to get on with the important stuff.

'When was the last time you were inside Shepherd's Rest?'

'Let me see now. It was on the Friday, just over a week ago. It was just to drop off some clean bedding and towels, and collect the rubbish. I'd usually do that every Saturday but the people there had asked me not to. But you can't go more than a week on dirty linen, can you? We only keep one spare set in each cottage, so after a fortnight I need to collect the used sets and drop off some fresh. They weren't very happy about it, though. I do remember that.'

'What do you mean?'

'I don't know, really. They just seemed a bit tense. Probably my imagination.'

'Who did you meet?'

'A man and a woman. I assumed they were a couple from the booking but I don't think they were, not after meeting them. Both bedrooms had been used. And she was definitely the boss.'

Jackie turned to a fresh page in her notebook. 'Descriptions, please?'

'He was tall and had a beard. He didn't say much. She was quite short. Her skin was very tanned. Either that or it was her natural colouring. She wore really big, hooped earrings. She had a foreign accent, sort of Spanish-like. She seemed angry with him for some reason. Almost as if they'd just had an argument. He didn't say much but he had an accent too. I asked him if there was anything they needed but he just shrugged and said, ask Bella. He pointed to the doorway to the kitchen. That's where she was.'

'Bella? Are you sure?'

'Yes. I thought her name went with her appearance and accent. Kind of Spanish-looking.'

'And you collected the rubbish?'

'That's right. It was in black bin bags. There was a lot of it. I don't think they went out much. To be honest, I wasn't very happy about their rubbish. We try to encourage visitors to sort through it and put it into the right containers, ready for recycling. They didn't bother. It was all dumped in the main bin.'

'Isn't there a garbage collection contract with the council or some other company?'

'There should be. There is with all our other properties. But the refuse company is always moaning that they can't get past parked vehicles in that narrow lane, so quite often they just back up and go away without emptying the bins. To my mind, it's just an excuse. It saves them a good twenty minutes on their run.'

'So, what happens to the rubbish you bring back?'

'I sort it here or at the office. Put it in our own bins.'

'And did that happen with the stuff you collected that day?'

'Some of it's gone. Some's still waiting. Out the back here, in fact.'

'Keep it. Don't let anyone touch it. I'll have a forensic officer come across as soon as I can, to collect it. Stay away until we give you the all clear. The cottage is owned by someone called Delphic, is that right?'

'Yes. I think his first name's Ronnie.'

'Zara said he has a luxury Mercedes.'

Beryl shrugged. 'I wouldn't know. But I'm sure it's true if Zara said so. She's a bit obsessed by upmarket cars. She wants one for herself. Don't know where she intends to get the cash though. We're not exactly flush with money.'

'I do need to check that we're talking about the same people up in the cottage. Could you check these sketches please?'

Jackie showed Beryl images of the couple from Pryor's photos at the London reception.

'Yes. That's them, the two I spoke to.'

'Thanks. Do you have any other office workers, Beryl?'

The woman looked puzzled. 'No, it's just the three of us. Me, Brendon and Zara. We're a family business. Why?'

Jackie felt like laughing because of Zara's obvious flight of fancy, but refrained from doing so. 'No reason. Thanks for your time, Mrs Stebsworth.'

As soon as she was out of the door, Jackie called Barry to report her morning's findings about the cleaning of the cottage, along with the name Zara had supplied and the information about the cream-coloured luxury Mercedes. Surely it must be the same one she'd spotted a week before, parked outside Billy Pitt's flat? So the well-dressed and intimidating man who'd been with Pitt at the time of her visit might well have been this Ronnie Delphic, owner of the cottage.

Jackie, of course, didn't know Barry at all well. He'd been away on his honeymoon during the Watchet investigation. Even so, she thought that he sounded both pleased and relieved over the phone.

## CHAPTER 31: FRESH EYES

With the rest of WeSCU out following up on various leads, Sophie and Barry had time to discuss the case in detail over cups of tea.

'My guess is that we're approaching the endgame, Barry,' Sophie said, sipping her hot drink, then leaning back in her wheelchair. They'd finished summarising the ramifications of the case. They were now speculating. 'Someone's panicking.'

'Linked to the visit Rae and I made to the High Commission? That's when things changed.' Barry was looking pensive.

'Exactly. You'd made much more progress than they'd anticipated, and more quickly. They got really worried that you'd soon be knocking on doors and making arrests. Better to get rid of all the traces before too late. Hernandez died as a result. Maybe he was seen as a weak link.'

'So you think we got close to the main people?'

'I have no doubt. You might well have met one of them at the High Commission. There's got to be an insider there, hasn't there?'

Barry's brow furrowed in concentration. 'We only spoke to half a dozen people. You're saying it was one of them?'

'Probably. Almost definitely. You got them scared. That's why things have escalated.'

'Whoever it is might have fled the country.'

'Unlikely. It would really draw attention to themselves, wouldn't it? My guess is that they'll wait and see. Be ready to run at short notice but not actually do it until we make a move. Time for us to be sneaky, Barry. Play our cards really close. Lots of undercover digging about everyone you met in London. But I agree with you about someone from the eco place being involved too. It's likely there's an insider. I think you should still leave someone checking on the history of that recent victim, while he was in Lyme. Hernandez. Surely someone has seen him somewhere around. Him or the woman. Bella, isn't it? Maybe Jackie.'

'That's what I was thinking. Jackie's coming on well. Still finding her feet in some respects. But she's a good listener and thinks about what she learns.'

'She seems quieter than in that last case, across in Watchet.'

'Maybe more responsibility. It's her full-time job now, not just a day or two a week as a special constable. I know I wasn't involved but my guess is that she could afford to indulge in a bit of whimsy up there. She knows it's serious now. She'll be fine.'

'And you, Barry?'

'I'm good. That long break worked wonders. Well, until I got back and suddenly found you were in hospital, lucky to be alive.' He looked at Sophie suspiciously. 'Why are you asking?'

'Just thinking of the future.' She paused. 'Possibly bad news expected from my consultant, I'm afraid. I think she's worried that my leg won't ever heal fully. Worst case scenario, I might be on crutches or in a wheelchair from now on.'

Barry looked shocked. 'That's awful. There must be some hope, surely?'

Sophie shrugged. 'Gradual improvements, probably. But I'm not getting any younger, Barry. I have to be a realist about it.'

'What are you saying?'

'If the worst comes to the worst, I'll have to think of chucking this in. Not immediately. A few more months yet, maybe even years if I'm lucky. I told you ages ago what my long-term plan was. A university tutoring job somewhere. I've been running away from it for some time but it's time to face facts. I swore I'd never do this if it became a desk job. And in reality, that's what it could be if I try to soldier on. I'm a bit superfluous to the investigations anyway. You don't really need me. This is what I've been training you for, Barry. You're in an ideal position to take over.'

'But you deal with all the political stuff. I couldn't do that.'

'Nor should you. I'm sure Polly will get over this stress-related problem. She can come back and take over in a more managerial role. My guess is that she's had enough of running investigations, and that's part of her anxiety issues. You're ready to take on a DCI role. She's about ready to step up to being a super. And I can stutter on to the next part of my big plan. Complete my doctorate and see where it takes me.'

'You used to say, back to Oxford.'

Sophie crinkled her nose. 'Well, that was then. It's off the list now, for a few years at least, with Jade being there. I don't want a job within ten miles of my daughter. My sanity's at stake here.'

He stayed silent for a while, frowning and running his fingers through his hair. 'I don't know what to say,' were the words he finally uttered.

'You don't have to say anything. Only Martin knows, so keep it to yourself. The last few days have been great, Barry. Being involved again, offering advice. But in my heart of hearts, I wondered if it was over. And I really, really don't want a desk job, moving up into the top hierarchy. *Administration*.' She pronounced the word slowly and carefully, as if it was toxic. 'Polly would be good there, though, which is why I think things will work out. But not me.' She watched him carefully. 'Whatever happens, I want you to know that I'll always treasure the time we had working together. You've moved from a young DS dealing with minor offences to an experienced and highly capable DCI, ready to take charge of a Major Crime unit. I'm so proud to have been the guiding hand in much of that.' She sighed. 'Maybe I'm just being too pessimistic.'

'It's funny in a way. You always appear to be an optimist but are a pessimist at heart. I'm the other way round.'

Sophie laughed. 'Maybe that's why we've always got on so well.' She flipped through the notes she'd made at the earlier briefing. 'Ronnie Delphic. Do you think he might be the key to it all?'

Barry shrugged. 'There's only one way to find out, isn't there? Who should we put onto it?'

'Leave it with Jackie, since it was down to her efforts that the name cropped up.'

Barry smoothed his hair back down. 'I'm worried that Jackie's arrival has upset Tommy's place in the team a bit.'

'Listen, Barry, it doesn't do Tommy any harm at all to get an occasional motivational nudge. It stops him from becoming too complacent and comfortable.'

Barry laughed. 'You're a bit of a schemer, aren't you?'

'Of course. But it might be a good idea to have Tommy involved in something tangible. Put him onto a bit more probing into that security bloke at the eco place. Surely he's involved somehow? Hasn't anything else shown up yet?'

Barry shook his head. 'Nothing. Either he knows he's under scrutiny or it's not him after all.'

Sophie became pensive. 'In which case it's someone else there. What's the operations manager, Nicky Dangerfield, like? Isn't she an old pal of yours?'

Barry grimaced. 'I wouldn't put it like that. She was a classmate back in primary school. Then her family upped sticks and left. They moved to London.'

'What was she like back then? Do you remember?'

'I've been thinking about that. All I remember is that she was really clever. Top of the class, I think.'

'Rae said she was a bit of a looker. So she's got it all. Beauty and brains. A high-powered job that ought to carry a good salary.

Would she put all that at risk? Unlikely, I would have thought, but since we don't really know what's driving these murders we can't afford to make assumptions. Is she married or single?'

'Not married but in a long-term relationship, as far as I recall. No family, not as yet.'

Sophie remained silent for a few moments. 'Give her to George. Tell him not to contact her but to do a bit of digging around. Take it a bit wider than before. Fresh eyes, Barry. Always a good thing. Anything else about Ian Duncan that Tommy ought to know?'

'He's still not changed his tune. He says that Bryony O'Neil never told him about that nightmare of hers, that she's making it up. Everything we have on him is circumstantial at best.'

He ran his fingers through his hair, a sure sign that something was worrying him. Sophie raised her eyebrows and waited for him to explain.

'What if Duncan's telling the truth? What if it wasn't him Bryony told about the nightmare, but someone else? Or she just made the whole thing up?'

'You mean she might be stringing us along?' Sophie leant forward, resting her chin on her hand. 'You've obviously been thinking about this. How does it pan out?'

'Let's imagine she's involved somehow. Don't ask me how deeply because I haven't got that far yet. The gang want to put the frighteners on her to keep her in line. Maybe they see her as a weak point, or she's been asking for more money or has been threatening to pull out. Whatever the reason, they need to pull her back into line. That's why that peculiar late-night event was staged. It was just meant to scare her. But it went wrong, and she crashed her car. In hospital she had time to think. She knows you're in there and starts dropping hints that she hopes will get to you. It gives her an escape route, you see. Neatly pointing the finger elsewhere.'

'Could she have been that involved?'

'She's got the knowledge. And she's a very capable person, by all accounts. She was at that High Commission reception.

And she was keen to go on the initial scouting trip to Parantos, along with Robin Pryor and Val Potter, but Nicky felt that she wasn't really needed at that stage. But something interesting. Apparently, she made a flying visit for a couple of days after the contract was awarded to make admin-level contacts. No one told us.'

'What?' Sophie was incredulous.

'Exactly. No one at EcoFutures gave us that bit of information. Ameera spotted a sub-folder on their system just yesterday. It only had a few documents in it, so she took a look. Only Robin Pryor, Val Potter and Bryony herself had access. That's where she found a single document written by Bryony subsequent to her trip there. Nothing incriminating in it, but even so.'

'Worth checking out with Nicky Dangerfield, do you think?'

Barry nodded. 'It seems a right mess, to be honest. But maybe not. Each unit at the place might have a lot of autonomy to work as they see fit. A quick follow-up visit by a team member might not be very unusual.'

Sophie was frowning. 'But why didn't she tell us? That's very suspicious, Barry.'

'Could there be other stuff we haven't been told? That's what I wonder. I think we need another detailed look at all of them, the whole team. Maybe Rae can take it on with a couple of the others. We might even need to bring Bryony in. Take her out of her comfort zone. What do you think?'

'I've got a therapy day tomorrow and can't get out of it. I'd like to be around, since we met at the hospital. Can you wait until the next day? Keep tabs on her until then?'

'Of course. It'll give us time to gather more background. Maybe better to keep this to ourselves for now?'

'Who went to see her last week?'

'Rae. Bryony's staying with family up in Swindon, well out of harm's way. She's working remotely.'

'Okay. Ask Rae to collect her and bring her in. Keep it relaxed and low key. Give her the gist of all this but tell her to keep it to herself for now. Is that good enough? You and I can do the interview. Well, you. I'll just observe.'

'And keep George on checking Nicky's background?'

'I don't see why not. What harm does it do? And there's still a chance the insider at EcoFutures might be her. That leaves Rae to do the deeper digging into Bryony.' She paused. 'It's a bit unsettling, Barry. The fact that she might have been stringing us all along. It's those big innocent eyes she has. But what's in it for her? That's what I don't understand.'

'Money? Influence? But maybe they've been leaning on her. Heavily. Maybe she's more terrified than we thought.'

## CHAPTER 32: BEAUTIFUL VIEW

Jackie Spring didn't quite know how to react. She felt confused. Should she be pleased that she'd been given the job of finding out about this new person whose name had cropped up, Ronnie Delphic? Or bothered by the fact that she'd been landed with the seemingly most difficult task? She felt oddly reminded of her schooldays when duties had been handed out by the school. Some fellow pupils had loved being given responsible roles. Others had moaned about the time they'd be expected to put in, often picking up sympathy from those who'd been left out completely. Jackie had tended to sit on the fence, undecided which path to take in case she lost friends. She was equally confused now.

Was this current task some kind of test, part of her probationary period? She wasn't particularly experienced at the kind of database and internet searches that other members of the team seemed to consider as second nature. In the end, she went to see Rae to have a quiet word. She felt insecure. Unlike the others, she'd not had an opportunity to get to know Barry previous to this case.

'I'm unsure where to make a start, boss,' she said. 'The DCI has asked me to dig into the background of this man

Ronnie Delphic, but I'm a bit of a novice. I don't want to mess it up.'

'I'm sure you won't, Jackie. Two ways in, as far as I can see. Social media is often really useful. But also some local probing in person. That's once you've found an address and maybe a place of work. I'd guess that's why he's given it to you. You're good at chatting to people and getting them to open up with what they know. Added to which, it was your lead, from that person at the letting agency.'

'Zara Stebsworth. She just gave me his address.'

'She may have more information that she could provide about him, so see her again if you need to. Have a wander around where he lives. Make up some cock and bull story, and speak to neighbours but keep it low key so he doesn't get to hear of it. You're trying to find out what kind of person he is, what his interests are, what he does for a living. That kind of thing. Check out your plans with me first. Tommy might be able to help with the social media part. He's a dab hand.'

'Okay. Thanks, boss.'

* * *

Delphic. An unusual name. One to conjure with. What could its roots be? Did it have Greek origins? Jackie could imagine it being the name of an academic, maybe a professor of ancient literature or biblical studies. Professor Ronnie Delphic. Maybe not. The image was ruined by the first name, Ronnie. She tended to associate that name with spivs, swindlers and pickpockets, but not for any logical reason. Realistically though, how can a name given at birth define and control a person? There are probably thousands of perfectly decent Ronnies up and down the country. Good honest citizens, all.

This particular Ronnie, in addition to owning the holiday cottage near Golden Cap, also owned several other rental properties, operated a taxi company and ran a café in Lyme. Fingers in lots of pies, then. He lived on the west side of town, not very far from Billy Pitt, the man she'd interviewed a few days earlier about his access to door keys. Delphic was the owner of the luxury Merc she'd seen parked outside Pitt's apartment. There could, of course, be all kinds of reasons why Delphic had used his car to visit Pitt, despite living so close by. Maybe he'd been elsewhere first, dropping in for a quick visit to Pitt before heading home. Maybe he'd been feeling unwell or was nursing a leg injury. But, in the end, her thoughts kept returning to the same explanation. That Delphic was an arsehole who liked to flaunt his wealth and wouldn't dream of walking a couple of hundred yards because of the damage it would cause to his rich, cool-guy reputation. And as she delved further into his social media posts, that explanation became increasingly likely. To Jackie's mind, his posts were narcissistic, arrogant and shallow. Certainly not the kind of considered comments that a professor of Anglo-Saxon literature would make.

With Rae's agreement, she headed out of the police station and walked uphill towards the area where Delphic lived. It was always good to be out in the fresh air, particularly when it carried the salty scent of the ocean. Jackie was approaching the area where her quarry lived when she realised that the cream-coloured Mercedes just turning out of a driveway in front of her was driven by Ronnie Delphic himself. He glanced along the road then swung eastwards, towards the town centre.

Jackie watched him go. Should she seize the opportunity? It took her only a moment to decide. She reached his driveway and veered into it, then almost stopped dead when she saw the view that opened up in front of her. This street must be close to the open land above the cliff edge. The vista was nothing short of beautiful. Another street of luxury villas, a thin band of trees, then the sparkling blue of the sea. The views from the rear windows and garden must be spectacular. She walked quickly to the front door and rang the bell. Would there be anyone in?

A shadow appeared on the other side of the frosted glass pane and the door opened slightly. A woman's face peered out, her hand pushing back a mass of peroxide blonde curls.

'Sorry to bother you.' Jackie was improvising wildly. 'Is this the house and gardens due for a makeover for a TV drama?'

'I don't know,' came the reply, spoken in a local accent. 'I'm Paula, the cleaner. You'd think I'd know, but he never tells me anything.'

'It's a murder mystery. I really thought it was here.' Jackie was trying to peer into the hallway.

'I'll ask. The owner's close friend is in. She might know.' The woman disappeared from view.

The cleaner had left the door wide open, and Jackie let her eyes wander over the room. A full-length mirror hung on one wall and, in its reflection, Jackie could see inside the front room. A woman was standing near the window. She had an attractive olive skin tone and short dark hair. Jackie could also make out a gleam of reflected light from large earrings hanging close to the woman's neck. She was talking quietly to someone, presumably the cleaner, who then returned to the door.

She was curt. 'No. Not here. You're mistaken.'

Jackie apologised and backed away quickly. She phoned the incident room as soon as she was clear of the property. This supposed partner of Ronnie Delphic looked to be very similar in skin tone and hair colour to the woman captured on the CCTV image on the footpath from Monmouth Beach that Saturday morning several weeks earlier, when Robin Pryor had been murdered.

* * *

'Well done, Jackie. That's great work.' Barry was full of praise for WeSCU's newest recruit.

'What does it mean for us, boss?' Rae asked.

'To be honest, it means that we're probably still in business. I was beginning to think that this strand had come to an end after Hernandez was shot. As George pointed out, it had all the hallmarks of a clean-up operation, getting rid of the people who had murdered Pryor and scared the daylights out of Bryony O'Neil. The super and I thought whoever did it had scarpered quick, probably back to London. But now this. She was quite young, you say?'

Jackie took a few seconds to reply, thinking through her recollections of the short time she'd spent watching the woman in the mirror. 'In her late twenties or early thirties, I'd guess. She was suspicious, though. She was standing watching through the window as far as I could see from her reflection. Very alert.'

Barry was pensive. 'This might change things. We were planning to interview Delphic very soon. Ask him who could have been using the cottage. But now we probably need to take a step back while we probe a bit deeper. He might be more involved than we thought.'

'I wonder if we need full surveillance on his house?' Rae suggested.

'I think so. This could be a bit of a breakthrough. Who could she be?'

# CHAPTER 33: BACKGROUND PROBES

Tommy had spent several hours on a computer, probing even deeper into the background of Ian Duncan. He was aware that some of the other WeSCU detectives thought that the man might be involved somehow in the violent attacks on staff members. He was ideally placed, as the security chief. He'd had a brief fling with Bryony O'Neil and learned of some of her fears. He'd verged on bluster during his most recent interview with Barry and Rae, and seemed to have had no real explanations to counter their concerns.

The problem was that Tommy didn't find anything in his background that might provide a pointer to his involvement in two murders. Tommy had probed his home and family life, his hobbies and his friendships. The man's social media postings were actually quite thoughtful, far from the shallow and misogynistic comments associated with some men working in the security industry. He'd even mentioned to other EcoFutures staff that he was involved with fundraising, raising cash for a leukaemia charity after one of his nephews had been diagnosed some years earlier.

Tommy double-checked the man's family background. He lived in Axminster, in a fairly new house on a recently built estate. Tommy drove around the area. A smallish family home, unobtrusive, with a few children's toys and games abandoned on the lawn. Ian Duncan's wife worked as a classroom assistant in the local primary school, the one attended by their two children. Tommy had a walk around the immediate area and spotted the trio approaching the house, school having finished for the day. They seemed to be a pair of amenable youngsters, who appeared to be talking to each other as they walked. No sibling animosity on public display here. Maybe they'd been well brought up. Mrs Duncan stopped to chat to an elderly neighbour.

Tommy returned to the incident room and reported to Barry, who listened carefully to what he had to say.

'It's all useful background, Tommy. In a way, it's what I half expected. He could be innocent of what we suspect. Or he might be embroiled in it up to his neck. I was hoping something might jump out at you but clearly not. The thing is, if everything is so tickety-boo at home, why did he have that fling with Bryony? Did he make the running or was it her?'

'I'm no good at relationship stuff, boss.'

'I didn't mean for you to find out. I was just speculating. Maybe we need to push him harder about it. But I'll wait until the others report back. There's got to be an insider at EcoFutures, but who is it? They're being very clever, whoever they are.'

Tommy shrugged. 'What about the unit's deputy? What's her name, Val something or other?'

'You mean Val Potter? Worth another look, Tommy, so get busy. There's got to be an insider in the place.'

* * *

George Warrander wondered if this was make-or-break time for his plans to become a detective and he felt a little apprehensive. Added to which, how do you go about investigating someone when you're not allowed to visit them or speak to them? He did understand the reasons why, though. He guessed the investigation had reached a hands-off phase, when the unit couldn't afford to spook anyone by dropping clues about who their main suspects were. Better get on with it.

Nicky didn't have a criminal record but that was to be expected. Would anyone get to be a senior manager in a specialist and high-powered organisation if they'd had some kind of tussle with the law, even early on in life? George didn't think so. Her family had moved from Swanage to west London when she was eleven, just at the right time for the start of secondary school. Nicky had gone to the local state school, but this was in Sutton, a very upmarket suburb. She'd done extremely well and had gained a place to study Environmental Science at Exeter University. Maybe she'd preferred living in the southwest and had taken the first opportunity to return to the area.

George looked at the short list of jobs she'd held before her appointment at EcoFutures. There had been a gradual change to the more managerial side of environmental work as she worked her way through a number of positions in a series of companies. Water, agriculture, ecology. Both public and private organisations.

George listed Nicky's jobs by date. There was a missing year between school and university. She'd probably done a gap year, maybe working abroad somewhere. Isn't that what so many youngsters did? George hadn't. He'd come from a poor background and just couldn't afford to go gallivanting around the world. He'd worked in a local hardware shop for a year, saving hard to minimise the need for large student loans during his forthcoming degree course. And Jade, his girlfriend, had gone direct from school to university, though she was studying medicine, a particularly long degree course. George was aware that many medics made the same choice. Not being able to earn any decent money for five or six years was surely enough. Why voluntarily delay it for another year? He dragged his brain back on track. Was there a way of finding out what

Nicky had done during that year-long gap? Would it be on her job application from when she'd first joined EcoFutures? If so, how could he see it without straying into illegal territory or alerting her to his inquiry?

He checked through some of the background documentation and discovered that Barry had been given a remote link to the staff records system at EcoFutures. George went to see him and got the access code and password.

He came out of Barry's office feeling reassured. He'd been told to follow up on the same ideas with the other senior people in the Parantos unit, starting with Bryony O'Neil, then join Rae with a similar check on Val Potter. George wondered if something had come to light. Barry had seemed animated and more determined, even if he had been tight-lipped.

Rae seemed pleased to get another helper on the task of building up a set of more detailed pictures of the backgrounds and lives of the key EcoFutures personnel. She listened closely to what George had discovered about Nicky Dangerfield, including the missing year before starting her degree course when she'd volunteered at an orphanage in Uganda.

'That's something I hadn't considered,' she admitted. 'Gap years. Maybe we need to do the same for any of them who went to uni. Tell you what, George. You look at Bryony O'Neil. I'll do Justine Longford.' She glanced at the time. 'Sorry. Got to go. Quick meeting with Jackie.'

\* \* \*

Rae and Jackie were back in the area around Ronnie Delphic's property, exploring the neighbourhood on foot, looking for possible vantage points from which the large house could be unobtrusively watched. It was a luxury property, built in an L shape with open lawns and shrubs to the rear and side.

Rae realised that they couldn't let this unknown woman in Delphic's house slip through their fingers, particularly if she was also the woman in the photos taken at the Parantos High

Commission, something Jackie was fairly adamant about. The two detectives discussed this very point as they quartered the area.

'It makes sense, in a way,' Rae said. 'I did wonder if there was more than a single woman involved in the violence, that the one who flagged down Bryony O'Neil and caused her to crash her car was someone different to the one involved in the actual murders. But it's beginning to look like this woman might be the active force behind everything.'

'I'm a bit bemused, boss. It's all so complicated.'

'Real life, Jackie. Most murders are pretty low-level. You know, man kills partner. Ex-lover kills someone out of jealousy. Drunk yob knifes someone in an argument about something petty. But just sometimes we get involved with serious organised crime and it's a completely different ball game. That's what this unit specialises in. The cases that aren't so simple. The ones where the killers might actually be working to a plan, involving extortion, fraud or large-scale money-laundering. Real evil.' She stopped and looked around. 'This is the ideal spot. See how a car parked here has a good view down the hill to the house? And we can see both front and rear? That's always the sign of a good location. And the hedges and trees close by mean a car sitting here doesn't stick out like a sore thumb.'

'So you think this might be a good lead? I haven't started some kind of wild goose chase?' Jackie adjusted her sunhat. She usually preferred to be bare headed, but had opted to wear headgear today to avoid being recognised if the cleaner or either of the house's occupants were to pass by. Her curls were tucked up not-so-neatly inside the pale green fabric. She also had large, bright red sunglasses perched on her nose.

'Definitely worth following up. I'll stay for a short while, Jackie. But I need to get back to check on progress. I'll send Rose up once she finishes her current task at the farm. Meanwhile, we want photos of anyone you spot at the house, front or back. So we'll shift the car here, then you stay inside. Alert. Clear?'

Jackie nodded solemnly.

'Good. You'll be fine.'

\* \* \*

George was back at his computer, probing the years before Bryony O'Neil started university, trying to find clues in her teenage years. She'd grown up in Gloucester, had attended local schools before starting her degree course at Bristol. George double-checked the dates. Sure enough, there was a missing year between school and university, just as he'd found with Nicky Dangerfield. But with Bryony there was no mention of what she'd done for the year. Her CV, supposedly still on file at EcoFutures from when she'd first applied for her post, wasn't in the batch of material they'd been given access to. Curious.

## CHAPTER 34: DREAMY LOOK

Jackie was relieved by Rose at the end of the morning. They'd only had minimal contact with each other before, so spent several minutes chatting after the burly sergeant slid into the passenger seat.

Rose wiped her flushed face with a tissue. 'Phew. Could do with an hour or two sitting down. Not getting any younger. What about you?'

'This is all new to me, Sarge. I'm the newbie in the team. It's all a learning experience.'

Rose screwed up her face. 'I've got mixed feelings about this detective lark. It makes a change from the usual rubbish that George and I spend our time on, but I don't have the right mindset for it. This is okay, sitting here watching that house. I can cope with that.' She paused for a few moments and scratched her nose. 'How've things been with you? Come in by the back door, haven't you?'

'I know. A few months ago, I was a special, up in Watchet. I still live there. Well, most of the time. I got offered this job at the same time as another bout of redundancies were about to happen in the library service. It was a no-brainer, really. I'm sort of training on the job. It's been a bit stressful, but I love it.'

'Yeah, well, they're a good lot to work for. George and me, we've been sort of involved with them in an on-off way for years. I reckon they've got their eyes set on George for some detective job or other once this one's over.'

'How will you feel about that?'

Rose shrugged. 'Bound to happen. And I mother him too much, I know I do. Anyway, time for you to get back. The boss wants you to find out more about Delphic's background. I'm to tell you to pay another visit to that letting agency place. Okay?'

She slid out of Jackie's car and returned to her own, taking the camera with her. Jackie took a sip of water and drove off east, towards Charmouth.

The bell tinkled as she opened the door from the street, just as before. Zara was on the phone, dealing with a booking enquiry by the sound of it. She looked up at Jackie and frowned. Jackie sat down in a chair close to Zara's desk and waited until the young woman replaced the handset. Jackie thought she looked uneasy.

'Yes? How can I help you?'

'Zara, do you know Ronnie Delphic personally?'

'Um, well, a bit, sort of.'

'Why didn't you tell me? You must have known he owned that cottage. Why go through all the rigmarole of printing out that stuff and acting as if you didn't know?'

Zara shrugged and looked miserable.

'I hope you haven't mentioned my visit and the fact you gave me his name.'

Zara looked even more worried. 'He phoned earlier, wanting to know if anyone from the police had been in contact.'

'What did you tell him?'

Zara dropped her eyes. 'That Zoe was dealing with it.'

Jackie was exasperated rather than annoyed. 'But there isn't a Zoe, is there?'

Zara shook her head. 'No. But I use her name in awkward situations. I don't like people pressuring me. It makes me feel really tense.'

'So you invented Zoe as a person to blame?'

'Yeah. Though Mr Delphic only knows Zoe. I started going to his nightclub last month and I sign in using her name.'

Jackie was intrigued. 'And does Zoe have a different personality to you?'

'Well, a bit. She's a bit more . . . out there. And she talks to people a lot. I'm shyer.'

'Has Mr Delphic tried to contact Zoe since you gave him that information?'

Zara frowned deeply. 'How could he? She doesn't really exist, does she?'

'So he hasn't learned anything from you about my visit?'

'No, nothing.' Zara shook her head energetically to emphasise the point. 'I wouldn't.'

'What else can you tell me about Ronnie Delphic? You must have been thinking about it since we spoke yesterday.'

Zara sighed. 'I heard that he owns more places than people realise. He's got another nightclub in Exeter, a big one. A lot of students use it. And he's got more cafés, in Seaton and Sidmouth. He's really rich. He's got a luxury villa in South America, that's what I've heard.'

Zara had a faraway and somewhat dreamy look in her eyes. Jackie could imagine how this young woman felt about coming into the orbit of a wealthy and influential older man, particularly one who owned the type of nightclubs that attracted large numbers of young people, especially if one was situated in a much more populous city like Exeter.

'Steer clear while we're investigating these murders, Zara. Something really nasty has been going on. I promise to give you the all clear if we find that Mr Delphic isn't implicated in any of it. Is that a deal?'

Zara nodded, somewhat reluctantly. 'I suppose so.'

'Did the person who mentioned his holiday home in South America say where it was?'

Zara screwed up her face in concentration. Somewhat melodramatically, Jackie thought.

'Can't remember. I think it had a British connection, though.'

\* \* \*

Barry had cleared the way for George to visit Nicky Dangerfield at EcoFutures. She seemed somewhat exasperated by yet another visit from a detective.

'What now?' she asked, a harried look on her face.

'We have a link to your network,' he explained. 'It should give us access to all the staff files. But I can't find Bryony O'Neil's CV from when she first applied for her job.'

Nicky seemed taken aback. 'What? It should be there.'

She used her own laptop for a few minutes, then frowned deeply.

'That's weird. You're right. Maybe she didn't supply one. She was already here when I started.'

'Would you still have paper copies on file somewhere?'

Nicky shrugged. 'Don't know. But I'll find out.'

She lifted the phone and made a call to the HR manager, explaining the nature of the request. She listened carefully before turning to George.

'We're going for a look-see. I'm intrigued.'

The personnel manager had a slim card folder ready for them. Nicky spread the sparse contents across a desktop for closer examination. She pulled out a neatly printed CV.

'Here it is.'

George had a quick look. It was exactly what he wanted. 'Can you get it copied for me please?'

He was worried. Had someone been deleting electronic copies of documents to prevent incriminating facts coming to light? Barry needed to know. The EcoFutures system needed to be made secure against any future access from within. They couldn't afford for more material like this to be wiped.

Once he was outside the building, he called the incident room and spoke to Barry. Their own computer whizz would need to put a lock on everything to prevent more stuff being deleted. What was her name again? Ameera?

He was intrigued by Barry's response.

'It's fine, George. Ameera mirrored everything they have on their staff when she first visited. It's all safely on a drive in her office at HQ. She also installed a bit of spyware on the EcoFutures system. It watches all activity and logs who's doing what. Useful, eh? If that file's been wiped recently, Ameera can tell who did it and when.'

\* \* \*

Barry, George and Rae were hunched over a table, looking at Bryony O'Neil's decade-old CV.

'She did a gap year after school,' George commented. 'In Belize, part of a Commonwealth link programme. It's fairly close to Parantos, isn't it? Is it relevant?'

'Could be. I called Ameera about it. She's doing some checking of the copies she's got to see if it's been wiped recently. If it has, then the answer must be, yes, it's relevant, though I'm not entirely sure how. If it hasn't, well, I'm not sure what it means. Maybe some junior office person never got round to scanning it in a decade ago.' Barry shrugged. 'We've just got to wait. But, George, it was a good idea to go searching for possible gap-year information. Make sure you do Val Potter as well. You never know what might turn up. One of us will call you when Ameera gets back to me.'

It was only five minutes later that George saw Rae approaching his desk. He looked at her expectantly.

She shook her head. 'No. It looks as though it was never scanned in. Sorry, George. It was a promising lead.'

He returned to the task in hand. Val Potter, the new leader of the Parantos Development Unit. The checks on her background had been understandably sketchy so far. After all, she hadn't been intimidated in any way, nor had she been at the High Commission reception. She hadn't ruffled any feathers and seemed to have fitted into her new role extremely smoothly. According to the information in front of him, Nicky Dangerfield held her in high regard.

George was relishing his new role as a stand-in detective. Rose was right. This was right up his street. Probing people and their motivations. He was beginning to lean even more strongly towards a decision that would follow his boss's advice, and apply for a role as a detective in Lydia Pillay's probable new unit. Maybe he should talk to his girlfriend, Jade, first. Didn't she know Lydia personally?

# CHAPTER 35: HYDROTHERAPY

Sophie Allen was at a series of therapy sessions. They were mainly in the therapy pool and their purpose was to maintain flexibility in her damaged leg without putting the limb under too much stress. She'd begun to look forward to them, but for all the wrong reasons. Her therapist was a slim and extremely fit-looking young man in his early thirties with a gentle touch and an engaging manner. Sophie, normally confident and outgoing with people, found herself somewhat tongue-tied in his presence.

'I don't think you should be as pessimistic as you are. About your injuries, I mean.' He gave her a soft smile as he gently manipulated her outstretched leg, the warm water lapping around them. 'As far as I can see, it's healing well. You've got more movement. When I first tried this weeks ago, you were grimacing in discomfort. Now you're not. And I can rotate it further. I'm really pleased.'

*So am I*, Sophie thought. *But for all the wrong reasons. This is heaven. If only I was twenty years younger.* She sighed deeply.

'Sorry. You gave a deep sigh just then. Was that last turn too painful?'

Sophie shook her head, her eyes now open. 'No. Not at all. I feel quite calm. Relaxed.'

'I think you have your level of overall fitness to thank. These are serious injuries. Normally, you'd be looking at long-term disability. But everything's gone right, as far as I can see.'

'I really appreciate your help in these sessions. I'm sure they're making a difference.'

'Sometimes hydrotherapy works, sometimes it doesn't. You're one of the lucky ones.'

'You can say that again.' She could still feel his firm but gentle grip manipulating her leg, massaging the muscles. She closed her eyes again, momentarily.

'Yes. I understand you were close to death.'

*That isn't what I meant,* Sophie reflected. *Maybe I need to force my brain onto a safer track.*

'Do you report my progress back to the consultant?' she asked.

'Yes, it all feeds in. It's all part of the process. Nice costume, by the way. Is it new?'

Sophie felt her face turning pink. 'Well, it's summer. I do like to look my best.'

Why had she said that? Would he now think that she'd bought the swimsuit especially for these sessions? She had, of course. It gave her a near perfect shape, especially around the bust. She hadn't even told Martin, her husband, about her sudden online purchase. Her mind was all over the place. How ridiculous. She could imagine a suitable tabloid headline. *Sad Fifty-two-year-old Goes Gaga Over Handsome Young Therapist!*

She realised he was speaking so dragged her mind back to the here and now.

'Well, I must say that you obviously look after yourself well. My mum is the same age as you and she's far too out-of-shape. She ignores all my advice.'

Sophie felt crushed. Here she was, fantasising about this delicious young man as a potential toy-boy, and he merely compared her to his mother. Really! What a letdown.

He was still speaking. 'I've had to start dropping gentle hints to my partner, too. He's put on a bit of weight lately. Too many carbs.'

Ah. This bit of information changed things. Had he really said the word *he*? Or had she misheard? Another fit, good-looking bloke who turns out to be gay. What a waste. Sophie felt deflated. 'Oh, well. At least you're doing your best to help them. You can take a horse to water . . .'

'Hmm. But then, beauty is in the eye of the beholder, isn't it? We need to look below the surface, don't we? As human beings, I mean. You can get beautiful people who are far too self-obsessed. Looks can be a trap, can't they?'

Sophie felt even more deflated. Was she too self-obsessed? She didn't think so. She just loved clothes and liked to look good.

'Mind you, that doesn't apply to you. You always look good, and you come across as a very caring person, the way you talk about your family and friends during our sessions.' He gave her a tentative grin.

Sophie smiled. They were back on safer ground.

He looked at the clock on the wall above the small pool. 'Session nearly over. Same time next week?'

'Yes, of course. Have you got a busy afternoon ahead of you?'

'No. I just do a half day on a Wednesday. A relaxing afternoon in the garden is overdue.'

Sophie took her time drying off and changing after the session was over, lingering over the hairdryer and examining herself closely in the mirror. Too many lines on her face. And was that yet another grey hair peeping through? She finally lowered herself into her wheelchair and made her way out to the reception area, just catching sight of her therapist leaving the building. He was arm-in-arm with a shapely brunette in a summer dress and sandals. Sophie wondered if he'd tuned in to her thoughts while in the therapy pool and had taken a precautionary way out of a potentially sticky situation. She sighed. Pre-menopausal fantasies had a lot to answer for. She guided her wheelchair towards the nearby police station. Time to get to work.

George was lurking close to Barry's office in the incident room, obviously waiting for him to finish a phone call. The young trainee looked on edge.

'Something important, George?' she asked. 'Can I help?'

'Val Potter,' he said. 'She did a six-month stint in Parantos during her pre-university gap year. It was at a coastal development base. I don't know any of the details though.'

Sophie turned her chair to face him, fully alert. 'Now that really is interesting. Why hasn't she mentioned it to us, I wonder? She's had plenty of opportunities.'

\* \* \*

Rose Simons, in plain clothes, was still watching the area around Ronnie Delphic's house from her vantage point on the slope uphill from his villa. It was quiet and peaceful with only an occasional passer-by, often walking a dog. One fit-looking pensioner walked by leading a spaniel on a lead. She passed the Delphic house, walked past two more properties, then turned off the pavement into a driveway. Or did she? Rose's first assumption, that the woman had entered the villa's garden, may have been mistaken. Through the binoculars it looked as if she was walking down some kind of narrow gap, between two sets of fences.

Rose looked at the detailed map she had. It didn't show any kind of footpath at this point. Could it be a new fixture? She climbed out of the car, walked on another dozen yards or so and then crossed over. Yes. A narrow gap existed between two houses. Maybe a footpath had been planned but never fully incorporated by the council. It had a rough, dirt-based surface that was weed infested, not tarmacked. Where did it lead? She remembered Jackie's description of the fine view from Delphic's driveway, looking beyond his house. This was the same, beyond the houses on the next road, where the rough path seemed to continue. She spotted the blue water of Lyme Bay. The path must lead to the clifftop. Rose glanced around quickly then hurried on.

She could see the dog walker ahead, allowing her pet to sniff around the base of some bushes. The narrow track she was on merged into a clifftop path that ran at a right angle. It looked as if it led downhill in the westward direction, presumably to join the coast path proper. If so, it would have been so easy for a couple of people to make their way onto that path on the fateful day that Robin Pryor had been murdered, particularly if the woman following him had been in contact by mobile phone.

Rose backtracked, walking quickly back to the car. She called the incident room and reported her findings to Barry.

'They're not official public footpaths,' she said. 'Not on the map. But my guess is that they're well used by locals. And Delphic's place is right there, only a minute or two away from a shortcut down to the coast path where Pryor was ambushed, further along. It's the ideal spot to move from when they got the signal. It all fits, Barry.'

She returned her attention to keeping watch on the suspect house. Maybe there was something in this detective lark after all. It had its moments.

\* \* \*

The problem for Sophie and Barry was when to bring Val Potter in for questioning. The evidence against her was circumstantial at best. Would more detailed scrutiny alert the other major players and cause them to quietly disappear before the police were fully ready? And who were they? There were strong suspicions against Ronnie Delphic and the woman sheltering in his house, whoever she was. Ian Duncan, the security manager, was still in the frame. Bryony O'Neil had switched from being viewed as an innocent victim to a potentially manipulative puller of strings. The two detectives were increasingly sure that Nicky Dangerfield wasn't involved, but she still needed to be treated with caution. And the two local thugs, Joey Sturrock and Billy Pitt, fitted in somewhere.

The guess was that they were only involved at a low-level, hired just for the break-ins. They probably didn't know the big players. After all, they were still alive, a sure indication that they were small fry.

Their thoughts were interrupted by the incident room door opening. The familiar figure of Ameera Khan, Dorset Police's IT expert, hurried in.

'I thought it was better to speak to you directly,' she said, somewhat breathlessly. 'I've found something on an old backup from EcoFutures I was checking. Something important to the project was wiped from the network, just a week before all the odd things started happening. Let me show you.' She pulled out a few sheets of paper. 'Several things. Firstly, the person who was logged onto the network when Robin Pryor's secret High Commission photos were first accessed, was Val Potter. When an attempt was made to delete them, two days later, the people logged on were Bryony O'Neil and Val Potter. Two attempts at deletion were made, both unsuccessful.'

'Very useful,' Barry said.

'More importantly, when I did an automated comparison of the files on two consecutive backup records there was a discrepancy. A folder had been deleted. I checked the date against your timeframe projection. It was two days before your victim, Robin Pryor, went missing. He was unusually active on the network the next day, the last day before his disappearance. It could be that he was looking for that missing folder, even though it wasn't his.'

'What do you mean, it wasn't his?' Sophie asked.

'It had been created by Val Potter. It was in a semi-hidden location that wouldn't have been obvious to anyone. I wonder if something aroused his suspicions and he went on a computer network hunt, looking for it. But it had already gone.'

'What could it have been?' Barry wondered. 'Causing this amount of violence and intimidation?'

'I've got it,' Ameera replied.

'You've what?' Sophie gasped. Both detectives were sitting bolt upright in their chairs in astonishment.

'We live in the era of cloud computing,' Ameera explained, opening her laptop. 'The EcoFutures servers work with mirrored drives and other clever stuff. Whoever the culprit was, they thought a physical deletion from the system would be enough. But the original network designer had built in an additional cloud backup. I found it. Here's the folder that went missing.'

She opened the folder that had been deleted, now safely stored on Ameera's laptop. They all strained to see the main file held within it.

*Parantos Coastal Development Proposed Location Change*

'What is it?' Barry asked.

Ameera pushed a printed copy of the document across the desktop towards him and Sophie, followed by a small flash drive.

'It looks very much as if Val Potter wanted to shift the entire project to a new location fifty miles along the coast. That's all I can say from my brief look. Here's a paper copy and an e-version. It's your baby now.'

# CHAPTER 36: A LAWYER, PLEASE

Sophie and Barry flicked through the brief report once they were joined by Rae, summoned from her current task. With her degree in marine engineering, she might have a better understanding of the principles of waterside developments. She'd brought an atlas with her.

At first glance, it looked as though the most useful sections of the paper were the outline on the first page and the summary section some four pages later. The middle part of the report was more technical in nature, with discussion of river flows, tidal reach and cost-benefit analysis. Barry turned back to the outline and read it aloud.

*Parantos Coastal Development: Proposals for a Location Change. By Valerie J Potter B Sc, Ph D.*

*This discussion paper proposes that the Parantos government should be approached with a view to moving the planned development to the estuary of the River Opanara from its current planned location on the River Mara. There would be significant savings that, in the opinion of the author, would outweigh the fact that the development would be further from the capital and the main centre of population. Ecological benefits would be high. The development would benefit a deprived area. Funding might be available from non-government sources.'*

Rae opened the atlas and traced the locations of the two rivers on the detailed map open on the tabletop in front of them. The original location was centred on the estuary of the country's largest river, close to the capital city. Barry frowned. He extracted a paper that WeSCU already held, passed over by Nicky Dangerfield on their first visit to EcoFutures several weeks earlier.

He read another extract out loud, tracing the words with his finger as he did so.

*'The Parantos government wants the development to provide both a major ecological boost to a run-down part of the estuary and give easy access to the population as an area of beauty and sustainability for use in research, education and leisure.'*

'That makes sense,' Rae said. She was looking at the atlas's data about Parantos. 'The planned site is directly downriver from the capital, and it has almost a third of the country's population within fairly easy reach, according to this atlas.' She googled the country on her phone. 'And according to this, the riverside area has become neglected. It used to export a lot of guano-based fertiliser, but the source became depleted more than a decade ago. If I was in the government, I'd want to find a way of boosting the area too. Sounds sensible.'

Sophie broke in. 'Which beggars the question, why does Val Potter want the location changed? Doesn't her proposal move the goalposts entirely?'

Barry frowned as he re-read the summary at the end of the report. 'I'm no expert, but this doesn't sound a strong case to me. It's certainly a cheaper option but it has nothing else going for it.'

Rae was chewing the end of her pen. 'It's closer to Colombia and the trails the drug gangs might use. That's my guess. Look.'

She traced the route with her pen.

Sophie leaned forward. 'Oh, you cynic, you. But you might just be right. So, this could all be down to pressure from some major smuggling gang or other? That's what you're saying? I have to say, it fits. Nasty people using nasty methods to influence a legitimate government initiative for their own benefit. Could she be on their payroll?'

'And this paper might be the first stage in a planned campaign,' Barry added. 'I wonder if Robin Pryor somehow got wind of its existence. Maybe at that reception in London. Once Potter realised that the idea had seeped out, she deleted this document from the network, covering her tracks. Then people started to get killed or intimidated. Maybe we need to see everyone again and focus on this. People may have heard whispers about this second plan and not fully realised what they were hearing.'

'And bring her in,' Sophie said. 'We need to push her a bit. Put her under pressure. We certainly don't want her out there, roaming around, doing who knows what. If she's not one of the architects of this mess, then she's in danger. If she is involved, then she's a danger to other people.'

\* \* \*

Val Potter's reaction to being brought into the police station veered between outrage and bemusement. What was real and what was a construction? It was impossible to tell. Rose Simons and George Warrander had brought her in but had refused to be drawn during the short journey. She was left in an interview room for a while with just a solitary and silent uniformed constable for company, standing by the door.

Meanwhile, Sophie, Barry and Rae had a discussion about the line of questioning and who should take the lead. In the end, they decided that both Barry and Rae should be involved.

'I'd like to be there as an observer,' Sophie added. 'I know that's unusual, but I want to see whether the presence of a woman in a wheelchair alters the dynamics in any way. I'll just sit in the corner, minding my own business.'

Barry was unsure about the effectiveness of Sophie's presence but didn't voice his doubts. Would his boss actually be able to remain silent in such a situation? Unlikely. But although Val Potter was now a significant suspect, she hadn't been formally arrested. He'd been insistent on a low-key approach, judging that a formal interview at this stage might be counterproductive. He guessed that she'd clam up totally in that situation.

He and Rae walked into the interview room and moved towards the table, taking seats opposite Val, who frowned as she watched Sophie's wheelchair enter the room and take up a position in the corner.

'This is Chief Superintendent Sophie Allen,' Barry said. 'She's just here to observe.'

'I don't understand. Why have you brought me here?' came the reply. 'I was told this was to be an informal interview. Do I need a lawyer?'

'That's an option open to you, Dr Potter. Really, we wanted to chat to clear up some loose ends, relating to new information that's come our way. We need to keep everything above board too. It's not to our benefit for a person of interest to feel they're being tricked in any way. In that situation, we'll always advise for a lawyer to be called in.'

Val seemed placated. 'I'll help you, of course I will, up to a point. But not if I think I'm being harassed or targeted in any way.'

Barry nodded reassuringly. 'Of course. The first issue is that we discovered you are not a stranger to Parantos. You spent your gap year there, as a teenager, between school and university. You worked as a volunteer on an environmental scheme. Is that right?'

Val was frowning and didn't answer immediately. 'Yes, I did. It's a Commonwealth country so it was less complicated getting a placement. I just used the system, put in my interests. That project came out. So did others. It was the one I landed.'

'Why didn't you mention it to us?'

'I didn't see the relevance. It was more than twenty years ago. To be honest, I'd forgotten about it.'

'It wasn't on your CV when you first applied for your job at EcoFutures.'

'No. They only wanted degree level and post-university stuff. Most of my references were related to my doctorate.'

'And that was about what?'

'Mangrove swamps in the Caribbean.'

'And that is relevant to what you're doing now?'

'Absolutely. A great fit with the current project, in fact.'

Rae broke in. 'How long have you been working for EcoFutures, Val?'

'Eighteen months.'

The detectives already knew this but wanted confirmation.

'Does that correspond with the preliminary plans for this project?'

'I think so. The company was keen to recruit people with the right experience in this type of work.'

'So you could say that the team was created specifically for this project?'

Val shrugged. 'Only partly. But then, I don't know the ins and outs of top-level management.'

'Had this particular development been talked about in Parantos for some time? I mean, within government circles there?'

Again a shrug. 'It's possible. I wouldn't know. Maybe Robin was more in tune with its history.'

'What are your thoughts on the plan? Are you onside with it, if that's the right expression to use?'

Val narrowed her eyes. 'I don't know what you mean.'

'Does this plan, as sketched out in the original government proposal, and as fleshed out in detail in the bid put together by your team at EcoFutures, the one that won the contract, does it have your wholehearted support?'

Val hesitated and fidgeted. She was beginning to look uncomfortable. 'I don't know why you're asking me that question. Of course it does.'

'Were alternative plans ever considered? Maybe in a different location, or at a lower cost to the Parantos government? We are in tight financial times, after all, right across the world.'

'I'm not aware of that, not in any detail. Look, is this really anything to do with your investigation? Aren't you meant to be looking for Robin's killers? How does that possibly involve what you're asking me?'

Barry cleared his throat. 'Motive, Dr Potter. Always of prime importance in a murder enquiry of this type. Why was Robin killed? Why were Bryony and Justine targeted? Why was one of Robin's possible killers themselves murdered a couple of days ago? How does it all link together? That's what we ask ourselves.'

Val hesitated a few seconds before she replied. 'I can't help you with that. How could I?'

'We've come across a discussion paper, Dr Potter, one written by you. We'd like your thoughts on it.' He pushed a copy of the recently discovered proposal, the one that suggested a complete shift of the entire focus of the development project elsewhere, across the tabletop. Val Potter glanced at the title page. Her face paled noticeably.

'I'd like to request for my lawyer to be present before I'm asked any further questions.'

'Of course,' Barry answered. 'As you wish.'

\* \* \*

'What do you think?' was Sophie's instant question when the trio returned to the incident room.

Barry spoke first. 'She's involved. I guess I underestimated her until recently.'

Rae nodded her agreement. 'Without a shadow of doubt. It fits with what we observed when we spoke to her and the rest of the team last week, before we were sidetracked by the latest shooting. The three junior technicians are edgy in her company. More importantly, I'm not sure they fully trust her.'

'I agree,' Sophie said. 'She's a clever woman, shifting her approach depending on the circumstances. Her body language reflected that. Rae, go and speak to those technicians again. Take Jackie with you. Keep pushing them until you break down their reluctance to talk. If they know more than they've let on, now's the time to find out. Then we'll move on Bryony O'Neil. We need to do the same with her as we've just done with her boss.'

## CHAPTER 37: SQUASHED TOAD

Jackie Spring heard footsteps as the three technicians approached
the conference room at the EcoFutures premises to meet with her
and Rae. Nicky Dangerfield had rounded them up and accompanied them to see the two detectives, who were already comfortably settled at the room's central table. Jackie could hear the
operations manager's voice as the group approached the door.

'Just answer their questions to the best of your ability,' she
was saying. 'Do it for Robin's sake. We need to get this sorted
once and for all and find out what's been going on. Find me if
you need me, okay?'

Nina led the trio as they sidled into the room, looking
worried. Simon was the last to enter and he left the door open.
Jackie rose to close it.

'Sorry,' Simon said, turning around to look at her. He
looked both scared and guilty, as if he'd already committed
a capital offence. He was probably guilty of little more than
stealing someone else's milk from the fridge.

Jackie gave him a reassuring smile. 'Don't worry,' she
said. 'We know this is very unpleasant for all of you.'

She sat down again, aligning her pen with the open page
of her notebook on the pristine table surface and waited for

Rae to begin. Her own role was to watch, listen and note what was said. Maybe add an occasional question. Act in a reassuring way to help put them at ease.

Nina was the senior of the trio, and it was to her that Rae spoke first.

'Nina, if you could give us a brief summary of your role in the unit and how long you've been involved, that would be really useful. Then we'll ask the same of Nabila and Simon. And please don't worry. You're not high on our list of suspects.'

'But we are on your list somewhere?' This was Simon, looking alarmed.

'Of course. That's bound to be the case, isn't it? Until we make an arrest and start charging people.'

Nina, a fair-haired and pale-skinned young woman, poured herself a tumbler of water from a jug on the table and nervously cleared her throat before starting to speak.

'I'm a biologist by training. I've been with the unit since it started. My role is to plan for biodiversity in the development, trying to identify factors that might seriously affect native populations, then plan to minimise those effects. This project has the backing of all the big environmental organisations. We have to keep them onside. That's one of my jobs. I've also got some test tanks of water set up in the lab, mimicking the real conditions. You know, salinity, pH, temperature. That kind of thing. I can see the effects on plant and insect life if anything varies. That's about it, really.'

'Thanks,' Rae said. 'What about you, Nabila?'

The young woman's eyes were still nervous, and she had trouble speaking, her voice little more than a hesitant whisper.

'I'm the team's microbiologist. I work mainly alongside Nina, using water samples from her tanks. I'm tracking populations of microbes. I also get monthly samples sent across from the site in Parantos. Different locations. I can track changing populations.' Nabila was starting to relax and warm to the task of talking about her work. 'People don't often realise how much everything in a water-based ecosystem depends on the microscopic life living in it. It's at the bottom of the food chain. Everything else depends on it. No microbes mean no tiny insects. Then, no bigger insects. No fish or birds. Basic science, really.'

'Thanks, Nabila.'

Rae turned to Simon, tall, gangly and still very edgy. She gave him an encouraging smile.

'I'm a hydraulics engineer. Water flows, currents, tides. Shapes of river beds. Piers and jetties. How all this might affect local animal and plant populations.' He stopped.

'Where do you do your research?' Jackie asked. She wanted to keep him talking.

'I mainly piggyback off some work done by Exeter University in the River Exe estuary.'

'Do they know why you're involved?' Rae asked.

Simon shook his head. 'Not really. We partly fund their project so I'm on the team. But I don't let any details slip out, just that our work is somewhere in the Caribbean. Nicky Dangerfield was adamant about it. And you don't cross that woman, trust me. She's seriously scary when she's angry.'

'When you were interviewed a week or two ago, we were focussed on Robin Pryor. Things have obviously moved on a lot since then. We want to know whether there was any friction inside the team over policy.'

The three technicians glanced at each other. Jackie, observing carefully, wondered if they'd already discussed this very point between themselves before the meeting.

'What do you mean?' Nina asked.

'Had a more senior unit member suggested a location change?' Rae replied.

A short silence followed. The trio exchanged glances again.

'We did pick up on some disagreements,' Nina finally said.

'Can you explain?'

'It wasn't definite. Nothing was said at official meetings so there's nothing in minutes as far as we know. But something was going on. At times we could sense the tension between the unit's senior people.'

222

'Who?' Rae asked.

Another glance. It was as if Nina was seeking the approval of the other two before committing herself to an explanation.

'Mainly Robin and Val. Sometimes Bryony.'

'Can you give me an example?'

Nina frowned. 'There was one time I walked into the admin office. I heard Robin saying, *No way. That's bonkers. It wouldn't work.* He and Val clammed up when I went in, but they'd clearly been arguing. Another time Robin stormed out of the office looking red faced and angry. I went in. Val and Bryony were in there, talking really quietly. They shut up as soon as I walked in the door. They pretended to be busy, but it was a bit faked, I could see it. It all worried me.'

Rae turned to the other two. 'And you? Similar?'

They nodded.

'Val was nagging him about something,' Simon said. 'I couldn't tell you what, though.'

'I liked Robin a lot,' Nabila volunteered. 'He was really good to work for. But something was troubling him in the last few weeks. And I thought it was Val, too. There must be a hidden side to her. Don't understand it. She was really good for my first year or so here. But in the past few weeks, well, I've changed my opinion. I can't help thinking she's up to something.'

'And Bryony, too?'

'Can't be sure. I get on well with Bryony. I think, what's got into them?' she paused. 'I wanted to say something when you were first here. But I felt it would be disloyal.'

The other two nodded in agreement.

'Did you ever hear talk of a possible location change? For the project, I mean. To a different river. The Opanara, I think.'

A silence followed, in which the three junior staff looked at each other once again with expressions that reflected mixtures of guilt and relief.

'There have been rumblings,' Nina said.

'It would be ridiculous,' Simon added. 'Everything I've done is based on the main river. A year's work down the drain if it changed to the Opanara. Coupled with the fact it wouldn't actually work. Not in the same way.'

'Who proposed the change?'

Nina glanced at her two colleagues again before replying. 'That's what we've been talking about. It was never raised in any formal way, not at a meeting. I first heard it during chit-chat over morning coffee. Maybe early last month.'

'Same with me,' Simon added.

Nabila looked torn. 'I may have heard something earlier than that, but I can't be sure. I was working late to finish off some specimens. I heard voices coming into the lab, women's voices, talking quietly. I'd have said something but for some reason I felt uneasy, as if I was eavesdropping. I was sure I heard the name River Opanara. I stayed quiet and they went.'

'Who was it?'

'It sounded like Val and Bryony. But none of it made any sense, not at the time.'

Nina took a sip of water. 'She hasn't been sleeping well.'

'Who?' Rae asked.

'Val. She got quite tetchy for a while, though she tried to keep it hidden. Then there was a spell when she and Robin were glaring daggers at each other. Then he vanished and she got even more tense. It was all a bit weird. I didn't really want to think about it. I thought, it's none of my business.'

'Has she vanished too?' Nabila asked.

'Who?' Rae said.

'Val. She's not in today but she didn't tell us in advance.'

'No, she's safe. No need to worry.'

'Are we being targeted? You know, one by one, like in an Agatha Christie?' Simon asked.

'No, we don't think so. We're happy for Justine to return to work now. She'll be in tomorrow, I expect.'

'What about Bryony?' Nina asked.

'Not sure,' Rae replied. 'It's a question of wait and see, I guess.'

*  *  *

Back in her room in the local bed and breakfast, Sophie's phone rang.

'Hello, Yauvani. Something important?'

'You could say that. I have a name for you. Isabella Perez. That's Isabella with an S, not a Z. She's the daughter of a local gangster chief in Parantos. Apparently, she's a dab hand with a gun. All types of guns. And knives. And, believe it or not, hypodermic needles filled with poison. She flew out of the capital to Mexico a couple of weeks ago. It looks as though she travelled from there to New York on a false passport. And there the trail goes cold. We have someone working with the FBI. They're confident that they'll trace her subsequent flight. Let's assume it was across here. I've got people trawling through the flight records at Heathrow and Gatwick, trying to spot someone with her appearance.'

'Which is?'

'Late twenties, shorter than average, dark hair cut short. She favours big, gold, hooped earrings. Must be a woman after my own heart. Oh, except for the fact that she shoots people she doesn't like. Sadly, I can't do that. Even as home secretary. Not yet, anyway.'

'She might be the woman we have under surveillance in a house on the outskirts of Lyme. The description matches. And whoever carried out the murders is pretty ruthless. Is the father involved in the drugs trade?'

'Everything. Drugs, booze, theft, embezzlement, fraud, intimidation, murder. You name it and he's in it. Apparently, nothing sticks to him though. He uses other people to do his dirty work. They get caught; he slithers away. His favourite trick is to somehow slip a squashed toad through the front door of potential trial witnesses. Everyone in Parantos knows what that means. Perez has his eye on you. They quickly withdraw their statements after that.'

'A toad?'

'Exactly. Apparently, he has bulging eyes. The daughter doesn't, though. She's a bit of a looker by all accounts. I'll get the security people to email you a photo of her once one arrives. And a short resumé about her. Oh, and don't contact the High Commission about her. Or anything else, come to that. Perez might have an insider there.'

'Thanks, YoYo. This is all brilliant stuff.'

'They're both lethal, Sophie. Take care, please. All this information comes from Paul Baker at the Met, by the way. He's happy for you to get in touch with him, just as an adviser you can use if you want to. He's taken on that kind of analysis and intelligence at the Yard. And he's a good guy, as you already know from that nasty business a couple of years ago. Okay with that?'

'Of course. And thanks. I'm grateful. All the pieces are starting to fit together now.'

## CHAPTER 38: TOO MANY DEATHS;
## TOO MUCH DECEPTION

It was now well into the second day of the surveillance on Delphic's house, the one that might be sheltering the elusive dark-haired woman. Was she Isabella Perez? And might she be, as Yauvani Anand had suggested, a notorious killer back in her South American homeland? The police were now watching the house twenty-four hours a day but there had been no signs of her coming in or out.

'What's she hanging around for?' Tommy Carter asked of George Warrander. 'If she's done the job she came across for, why didn't she scarper immediately? Don't assassins usually plan their escape and leave the country within hours of killing someone?'

'I think you might have answered your own question,' came George's reply. 'She might have more to do.'

Tommy turned and looked at him aghast. 'God. I hadn't thought of that. So she might have another target?'

George nodded. 'I overheard Barry and the chief super talking about it just before I left the station.'

'Who?'

'Well, who's locked up in a cell and impossible to get to?'

Tommy frowned. 'Val Potter, the new boss of the unit. But hasn't she been working on behalf of the crooks? Why would they want her dead?'

George shrugged. 'Maybe they didn't like her backtracking – that's if she did start to change her mind. Or she's still working for them, but they want to keep the pressure on her. Knowing there's a killer still around is probably a good motivator. Or maybe she isn't the problem at all. There are still doubts about Bryony O'Neil, aren't there? She's currently in hiding. Once she's back at work this woman might make a move on her. And what about these peripheral figures? Ronnie Delphic. Billy Pitt. Joey Sturrock. They might be viewed as loose ends, needing to be tidied up at some time.'

Tommy looked at George carefully. 'You know you've got the right type of brain to be a detective, don't you? I've heard the others saying that. I can see why.'

George laughed. 'Well, I think I've finally made the decision to apply.'

'The timings a bit wrong, isn't it? Jackie seems to have nabbed the empty slot in WeSCU. That would have been ideal, wouldn't it?'

George shook his head. 'Absolutely not. I'll stay in Dorset but try to get into the Bournemouth squad. Lydia Pillay is meant to be taking over. I couldn't work directly for the chief super.'

'Whyever not?' Tommy seemed puzzled.

George smiled. 'Because of Jade. It would just be too awkward.'

Tommy nodded sagely. 'Yeah, I'd forgotten.' He peered through the car windscreen towards the house. 'That's Delphic coming out. What does he do for a living?'

'Fingers in lots of pies. Bars, clubs and cafés mostly, across this area and into Exeter. He's a bit of a bad boy, apparently.'

\* \* \*

Back in the incident room Barry, Rae and Sophie were having a similar conversation about Isabella Perez. The longer she remained, the more likely it was that she had another target in mind. But surely she'd realise that the net would be closing in on her? Did she really think that British police were so slow at reacting to such serious crimes as murder and intimidation?

'She'll be tense, that's my guess,' Barry said, scrutinising the photo of the Perez woman that had been forwarded to Sophie by Paul Baker. 'She'll be weighing up the options. Stay and attempt to complete the tasks. Clear the decks, as it were. Or cut her losses and leave. Tommy's just phoned in with the same thoughts.'

Sophie raised her eyebrows.

Barry continued. 'Well, he was honest enough to admit that it was George who came up with the suggestions.'

'We've got to make a judgement too,' was Sophie's response. 'We can't leave her there, tying up our people, having to keep the place under scrutiny day after day. Do we even know she's still in there?'

Rae replied. 'We managed to get a couple of acoustic listening sensors planted onto some of the windows late last night. Someone's there, moving around, and it isn't Delphic. He left early this morning. Rose tailed him. He went to Exeter, to one of his clubs.'

'So if it is her, we have to ask ourselves, who might her target be? Is there anyone who stands out, other than Val Potter?' Sophie looked at her two colleagues.

Rae responded immediately. 'Maybe Bryony O'Neil. Nothing is clear, as far as that woman is concerned. She's led everyone a merry dance. She might be viewed as a weak link, if she's involved.'

'I agree,' Barry said. 'Interestingly, Tommy added that point too. George thinks she's the likeliest other target. We've got Stevie Harrison keeping an eye on her while she's in Swindon at her brother's. It might even be this Delphic man, although we think she's staying in his house. Though he's the one with the link to Parantos, with that villa he owns there. So maybe he's safe.'

Sophie made her mind up. 'Get Stevie to pull the O'Neil woman in, not least for her own safety. Send Jackie up there too. They can bring her down here and we'll give her a grilling, put the pressure on. I don't like people who try to lead us on. At the very least, she's guilty of wasting police time. Wasting my bloody time, in fact. I don't like being manipulated.' She paused. 'Barry, when you've got a moment, contact Lydia. Tell her what George has just come up with. He's a natural for her squad in Bournemouth.'

'Has she got the job then?' Barry asked.

'Just heard this morning. Matt Silver messaged me. I think a celebratory party might be in order. It's about time we had an excuse for another one. I've felt trapped for months with this bloody leg injury.'

'A party? You're not planning to sing again, are you?' This was Rae, now putting a hand to her mouth after the last words came out. She had a look of horror on her face. 'Sorry, sorry! That came out all wrong. I really didn't mean it the way it sounded.'

Sophie gave her an icy look. 'I am fully aware of my own weaknesses, Rae Gregson. I'll have you know I've been taking singing lessons during my convalescence. And by the way, do you still want a future in this unit?' Her voice seemed to break up, distorted by a mix of anger, intense frustration and dammed-up emotion. 'This meeting's over.'

She turned her wheelchair and quickly left the room.

Rae was left open-mouthed. Even Barry looked confused.

'She's obviously a lot more fragile than we thought,' he said, standing up and pushing his chair back. 'I think you hit a nerve. I'd better catch her before she leaves the building.'

He hurried out, leaving Rae by herself in the meeting room. She felt like crying.

\* \* \*

Jackie Spring had set out early for north Wiltshire in order to collect Bryony O'Neil and bring her in for questioning. She'd rendezvoused with Stevie Harrison, a Wiltshire detective sergeant and occasional WeSCU member. He usually operated out of Salisbury, in the south of the county, but had spent the past few days some forty-five miles north, in the industrial town of Swindon, keeping an eye on Bryony, still staying with her brother's family. Stevie shared the unease of Barry Marsh, who'd phoned him with the changed plan for Bryony. A determined assassin would be able to trace her too quickly to her current whereabouts. She had no other family, after all. Where else was she likely to go but to her brother's home? No, holding her for a few days for questioning would be in her own interest as well as that of the police.

Jackie slid out of her car and walked the few yards to where Stevie was parked. She knocked on his window.

'DS Harrison?' she asked. 'I'm Jackie Spring. I hope you're expecting me.'

'Right. So, we're bringing her in? Barry sounded under pressure on the phone. What's been happening?'

'We've found out more about the probable killer and it's not good. We think she's holed up in a house in Lyme, keeping a really low profile. But we can't be sure. If it's not her, then she's roaming around somewhere else, maybe planning to remove all the loose ends before heading back to Parantos or wherever. Anyway, Barry is sure Bryony knows more than she's letting on. Shall we get her?'

When the two detectives reached the door, Bryony opened it a crack and peered out. She looked pale and drawn, Jackie thought. She let them into the hall.

'Why?' Bryony asked. 'Why do you want me back in Lyme?'

'We have some questions for you, Bryony. Besides, we think you're too vulnerable here. It's partly for your own safety.'

'Haven't you got the killer yet? Surely you've had plenty of time?' She had a hand to her face, scratching at her cheek. Her eyes were wide and fearful, her voice quivered.

'The goalposts keep moving. Too many people have been leading us astray for too long, that's what it looks like. Might you be one of them, Bryony?'

The woman dropped her eyes. Then her whole body seemed to sag, and she started crying.

'I'd never have got involved if I'd known,' she said through her tears.

'Maybe save it until we're safely in Lyme,' Stevie replied. 'We haven't cautioned you yet. At the moment we're just planning to question you informally, but it needs to wait until you're at the station.'

Jackie spoke. 'You have a bag packed ready?'

Bryony pointed to a weekend case, tucked up against the wall. 'Another move to another supposed safe place. But none of them are, are they? Not totally. This is a nightmare, all of it.'

'Well, let's hope it's all over soon. Too many deaths. Too much deception.'

Stevie looked at Jackie with interest. That was a heartfelt comment coming from his new colleague. Impressive.

Bryony then astonished them both with her terse reply, spoken bitterly as she drew herself up to her full height. 'It's that fuck of a man Ronnie Delphic. He's a sewer rat.'

She spoke no more until they reached the police station at Lyme Regis.

## CHAPTER 39: UNBRUSHED TANGLE

Rae was desperate to find Sophie Allen and explain to her that the comment she'd made had just been a throwaway one, carrying no significance and no importance. But she couldn't find the boss anywhere and there just wasn't time to go on the hunt for her. All the strands they'd been investigating for weeks had suddenly sprung into life and might be about to coalesce into some kind of fuzzy climax. Rae worked with an acid knot of worry in her stomach. How could she have been so insensitive, so thoughtless? God, the woman had nearly died, had suffered terrible injuries to her thigh and hip, had spent several weeks in a hospital bed and more than a month in arduous and probably painful physiotherapy. This was the woman Rae looked up to above all others. Her boss, yes. But also her mentor, her saviour, the person she almost worshipped.

She shook her head, trying to free herself from her worries and get on with the job. That was the only way open to her to find a way back into the chief super's good books. By doing her job and doing it well.

Ronnie Delphic. Jackie had just phoned in to say that the man may have been involved deeper than they thought, judging by Bryony O'Neil's comment when she'd been picked up in Swindon. It would be almost another hour before she arrived in Lyme, though. She went to find Barry. He was looking troubled.

'I still can't find her,' he said. 'And she's not answering her phone. I called Martin, her husband, and he's on his way across. He was coming anyway but he's set out early. His guess is that she's had some bad news from someone in her medical team and that's why she was so touchy.'

'Do we need to send out a search party? Boss, I'm so sorry. I hate myself for what I said. It was so bloody insensitive of me after everything she's gone through.'

'It was you who saved her life, Rae. She'll remember that. And yes, I'll allocate some of the uniformed troops to keep an eye out for her.'

Rae passed on the update from Jackie, her concern that Bryony's comment about Delphic might mean he was more deeply embroiled in the affair than they suspected.

'I wonder if we should lift him, boss. Right now. Before he returns to his house. He's in Exeter, visiting one of his clubs. That will isolate the Perez woman, if she's in there. If we do it now, Rose can get him here at about the same time as Jackie and Stevie arrive with Bryony. Jackie thinks she's ready to spill the beans. We've still got contacts in Exeter who can give Rose a hand.'

'Then we'll have a go at Delphic with whatever we've learned? Sounds like a good plan, Rae. Get the preparation done so we don't waste any time.' He pushed a printed set of photos across to Rae. 'Just arrived from the immigration authorities. What do you think?'

She took a glance. Two figures, caught on camera, probably at airport security.

'It looks like those two on Pryor's photos from that London reception. And he looks like the man shot in the woods near that cottage.'

'Exactly. Pedro Hernandez and Isabella Perez. Now confirmed by the Parantos government security unit, according to our contact in the FBI. They arrived on a flight from Florida almost three weeks ago.'

Rae took a closer look at the images. 'Just a few days before this all kicked off. Did they supply any intel about them?'

'Just that he's a low to medium level crook. She's something else entirely. Hernandez has only appeared on the scene recently, according to the intel. That fits what we know. He was employed here, in the High Commission, until a couple of years ago. The catering manager there refused to give him a reference after he was sacked. He was caught stealing from her stock, then selling it on via a local market stall. Small-scale stuff, really.'

'So he went back to Parantos and got embroiled in the Perez gang? It makes sense to choose him to come back over here and start intimidating staff at EcoFutures. He knows Britain.'

Barry nodded in agreement. 'My guess is that Hernandez was ahead of Pryor on the coast path when he was killed. Isabella Perez was behind him and was probably the one who actually killed him.' He pointed to the photos. 'But maybe something else didn't go to plan and Perez decided to remove anything and anyone who might incriminate her. He had to go.' He glanced at his watch. 'I'm heading out to meet Martin. I'll be back soon.'

\* \* \*

Barry walked the short distance to the small hotel Sophie had been staying in and spotted her husband, Martin, in reception. He didn't look particularly anxious.

'Sorry, Martin. It's all a bit hectic. I need to explain.'

Martin shook his head. 'No, you don't. I was coming for a visit today, so you haven't dragged me away from anything important. Sophie messaged me about twenty minutes ago and assured me she was okay. Said that she just needed a few hours thinking time on her own.'

'She didn't seem overstressed or worked up?'

'I don't think so. Why?'

Barry decided to keep explanations to a minimum. What was the point of going into unnecessary detail if there wasn't much of a problem after all? 'Just a bit of internal friction in the unit. We were worried an offhand comment had upset her.'

Martin shook his head. 'I don't think that's the cause. She's been worrying about the prognosis for her leg injury. That and the painkillers she's on are still playing havoc with her moods. She'll be somewhere quiet having some time for reflection, that's my guess. She's worried about things in the long-term. I know she is, even though she works hard to hide it. The thing is, Barry, she's much more complex than people think.'

'I know that.'

Martin shook his head. 'No, you don't. Not the depth of it. I know there are things she hasn't ever told me, stretching back to before we met. What is it some psychologists say? That our childhood experiences can map out our future feelings? Sophie is a classic example of that, but she doesn't talk about it, not to me. I think she confides in Hannah a bit more. But I think, even then, that she only releases what she feels safe with.'

'She's not answering her phone.'

'I know. Look, Barry, she has these darker spells. She's adept at hiding them. I've just got to trust her. Do you really need her at the moment?'

'Not really. We'd covered everything just before this happened.'

'Well, she'll know that. Just give her a bit of time and a bit of space. She trusts you. Just get on with whatever was planned.'

He moved aside and thumbed a message on his phone. It wasn't long before a reply sounded.

'She's fine. She said, tell Barry the Perez woman will be thinking about running. That was it.'

Barry turned away just as his mobile phone rang. It was Rae, still in the incident room.

'Boss? Ameera's just been in contact. Someone accessed those photo files of Pryor's on the EcoFutures network earlier than she first thought. Bryony O'Neil. This was a couple of days before Val Potter tried to delete them. And something else very interesting has come in on an email for George, but he asked for me to be copied in. The gap-year ecology project Val Potter was on in Parantos about twenty years ago. It was on the estuary of the same river. The project collapsed a month or two after Val finished her placement. Friction with a local criminal gang. There might be a connection, boss.'

* * *

The first suspect to arrive at Lyme's police station for questioning was Bryony O'Neil.

Barry thought that she looked awful. Her hair hung lifelessly around her neck in an unbrushed tangle. Her eyes were sunken into their sockets, which were dark rimmed. She looked tired and listless.

Stevie had a few words with Barry as Jackie led Bryony into an interview room.

'She's ready to talk. No doubt about it. She's been blaming someone called Ronnie Delphic, then moaning about some of her work colleagues. Not accepting any responsibility herself, though. We advised her not to say anything that might be incriminatory until she got here. She needs legal guidance. Her brain is all over the place, if you ask me.'

'Thanks, Stevie. I think we need to strike while the iron's hot. One of the local lawyers will be here any time now. Thanks for helping to bring her down here. Did anything strike you?'

'Not a problem. And yes, something was obvious. She's scared stiff of something or someone. Whether it's this man Delphic or not is hard to say. Anyway, I'll leave it to you.'

By the time Barry joined Jackie in the interview room a short time later, a lawyer was present, sitting beside Bryony. She had a half-empty mug of tea in front of her and the few mouthfuls she'd already swallowed had clearly had a rejuvenating effect. She'd also found time to brush her hair and, probably, rinse her face. Consequently, she now looked slightly further away from death's door than half an hour earlier. She looked at Barry resolutely.

'I haven't been entirely open or honest with you. I'm sorry for that. But I was under threat. I was frightened that I'd be next. That's what I was told.'

'By who?'

'Ronnie Delphic, for one. I've had an on-off relationship with him for nearly a year. It's the usual story. Really nice to start with, then he turned nasty. Threatening. By then I'd gone too far at work. Found him some information he wanted. Once I was stupid enough to do that, he had me where he wanted me. Owning up would have lost me my job so I had to keep quiet. Keep him quiet too by going along with what he wanted.'

'Which was?'

'It wasn't always clear. For a long time, it was just updating him on the project. Then he wanted me to think of ways of sabotaging it. That started just a couple of months ago. Could I find ways of altering plans and ruining trials? That kind of thing. I said no, I wouldn't. But he kept on. Told me that someone else more senior was also involved, but he wouldn't tell me who.'

'Was there any truth in what you told us about Ian Duncan? That you'd told him about that dream of being attacked at the roadside? Did you actually have a relationship with him?'

Bryony sighed. 'Yes. I'm not proud of my flings. They happen. Maybe they wouldn't if I'd ever found the right guy for me.'

Barry couldn't hide his disbelief. 'But you're married. Isn't your husband in the navy?'

'Out of sight, out of . . . You know. It was a mistake anyway. He wants a little dutiful wife back here at home, spending her days dusting and cleaning, and socialising with other navy-officer wives. That's not me. Never has been. I've got my career. Well, I did have. Then Ronnie Delphic came into my life.'

Barry frowned. 'I'd like you to finish what you were saying about your relationship with Ian Duncan, if you don't mind. That dream?'

She looked blank for a second or two. 'Oh, yes. I did tell him, but it was when we were chatting about favourite and least favourite films. Lots of stuff came up. He could well have forgotten about it.'

'So when you claimed that Ian Duncan must have been involved, that was an exaggeration? Nothing more than conjecture?'

Bryony dropped her eyes. 'Yeah. I guess so. He's a nice guy really. Seriously overworked. Tense. Stressed.' She sighed. 'He didn't deserve it. What I implied about him. I'm really sorry if it's got him into trouble.' She dropped her eyes and studied her fingers. 'I'm not a nice person when I get too stressed. I wish I'd never met Ronnie Delphic. He's a devious bastard. He manipulated me and I walked right into his trap.'

'Are you saying he's the architect of all this? Everything that's happened?'

She shrugged. 'He's working for someone, that's my guess. I don't know who. Someone even worse than he is. They must be. I can't believe that it's him killing these people. He's not that bad.'

'But you don't know who?'

She shook her head. 'No.'

Barry was very aware of an absolute truth that often applied to the partners or lovers of murderers. They just couldn't bring themselves to believe the worst about their chosen companions. The thought that the person who shared their home and bed might be a killer was, in their minds, an impossibility. They helped with the grocery shopping, swept the garden path, put the kids to bed. How could they possibly be a murderer? He switched his thoughts back onto a more direct track and fired a different question at Bryony.

'Robin took some snapshots at the London reception, the one you attended with him and Justine. He stored them in a folder on the EcoFutures network. Were you aware of them?'

'I know he took some photos, yes.'

'Why did you try to access them?'

Bryony stiffened. She'd been co-operative up to now. Was that about to change?

'Justine told me about the photos. I was curious to see them.'

'Did you try to delete them?'

A frown crossed her face. 'Why would I do that?'

'Just answer me, please.'

'No.'

'Are you aware of anyone else from the unit trying to delete them?'

'No. Why would anyone want to wipe them?'

'That's what we're trying to find out. It was two days before your roadside incident. Could there be a link?'

'I don't see how.'

'You were logged onto the network when the attempt was made. The times match.'

Bryony sat in silence for a few moments, staring at the tabletop. She was rubbing the fingers of her right hand together but stopped when she realised that both Barry and Jackie were watching her.

'Val Potter was logged on at the same time as me.'

'How do you know?' Barry quickly retorted.

'We were both in the same room. I found the photos and viewed them. I told Val. She came across for a look.'

'And then what?' Barry asked.

'What do you mean?' Clearly Bryony was still playing the injured innocent.

'Did you try to delete them?'

'No.'

'Did Val?'

A pause. 'Yes. She's senior to me in the hierarchy. Maybe she had the right permissions to delete stuff from that folder.'

'Did she manage to do so?'

'How would I know? Maybe. Maybe not.'

'But neither of you were logged on as yourselves. You were deliberately using guest log-ons. Why was that, Bryony?'

Barry found himself on the receiving end of a deep scowl. 'You can't possibly know that. You're guessing.'

'Afraid not. We employ a forensic computer expert. She can turn the simplest computer log-on process into a gold-mine of information. And she's been through that network with a fine-tooth comb. So we know when you're lying to us. You had a problem, didn't you? You both wanted those photos deleted but you couldn't use your own IDs because the network logs would flag it up. So you tried a variety of guest log-ons between the two of you. None of them worked, though, did they? We found the photos when we examined the network folders, something neither of you wanted. That led us to the two people who were caught on camera at the embassy reception, when they didn't want to be identified. They were the two involved in the set-piece against you, weren't they?'

Bryony nodded a reluctant agreement, as if she was still wondering how much Barry already knew.

'So it wasn't just Ronnie Delphic, was it, manipulating you? Feeding you instructions? Was Val Potter also making suggestions?'

Bryony nodded again.

'Can you answer, please, Bryony? For the purpose of the recording.'

'Yes. Val was telling me what to do.'

'Why? What was the aim? What was this shadowy group trying to achieve?'

Bryony shifted uncomfortably in her seat. 'They wanted the project in Parantos shifted to an entirely different location. I don't know why. I never really bothered to find out.'

'Didn't Val tell you? Or should I say, didn't you ask her? I can't believe you'd have put your career at risk without asking why.'

'Some influential people in Parantos wanted the change.'

'Drug-running gangsters. Is that who you mean? And is that where the money that's found its way into your savings account during the past three months has come from? That secret account that you didn't tell us about?'

Bryony turned pale.

'And why did you make a short visit to Parantos, just after the contract was signed? You didn't tell us about that either.'

Bryony held her head in her hands.

'Was that the occasion you were issued with orders by the people you were secretly working for? Is that when the planning was done? Isn't it the case, Bryony, that you're in this far deeper than you've let on? Here you are trying to blame everyone else, and claiming that you're just an innocent victim, when in fact you're in it right up to your neck? The real problem for you was the fact that even the people organising all this didn't fully trust you. That's why they organised the little charade at the roadside that night. A non-too gentle reminder that you needed to remember your place. Both you and Val were bribed by the Perez gang once you signed up for the plan. Val had twenty-five thousand deposited in a savings account. You had fifty thousand. What kind of picture do you think that helps to paint?'

## CHAPTER 40: ACCESSORY TO MURDER

Rae and Stevie were in the other interview room with Val Potter, having called her up from the cell she'd been locked in for several hours, partly for her own safety. This time a lawyer was present. The eco-unit deputy leader really didn't look well. Her hair seemed greyer, her face more sunken, her eyes tired and lacking any sparkle.

Rae led the questioning while Stevie took notes. 'Look, Dr Potter, we've uncovered plenty of new information in our inquiry and you're implicated in much of it. Why not cut your losses and come clean with us? I have to be honest with you, things don't look good for you, not from where I'm sitting. We have conclusive proof that you withheld evidence. That you orchestrated a campaign to get the estuary development project moved to a different location. That you attempted to delete files from the computer network. That you have a savings account squirrelled away with more than twenty thousand pounds in it, all deposited in recent months. And that's just for starters. It's time you were honest with us. If there's something we need to know, something that explains all this, now's the time to tell us.'

Val suddenly erupted into sobs, as if a dam had burst, one that had helped to keep her emotions in check for a long time. She held her head in her hands. Rae pushed a box of tissues across the tabletop and Val finally took several, wiping her eyes and blowing her nose, long and loudly.

'They told me they knew where my daughter lived. They held that over me.'

'Where is she?'

'In a student flat in Southampton. I had to keep her safe. She's all I have.'

'Why didn't you tell us?'

'Because they told me not to. Isn't it obvious?'

'No, it isn't obvious. You didn't tell us you had a daughter when we first spoke to you. Yet I remember asking you about family. Who was this? Who was issuing threats against your daughter? Give me a name.'

'Ronnie Delphic, though he said he was just the messenger. I remember what he said. *Don't cross them. They're nasty people. Do what they say.* So I did. What mother would do any different?'

'How did you meet this man, Delphic?'

'In Parantos. It was when I was there with Robin on the short fact-finding trip, early on. Ronnie Delphic hosted a sort of party for us at his villa. One of their government officials took us. We didn't think anything of it at the time. Not even when he told us he lived here in Lyme Regis for much of the time.'

'So what do you think now?'

Val rubbed her eyes. 'His involvement was a set-up. Right from the start. Someone wanted the plans spiked. They have an insider in the government department. Must have.'

'I'll sort out protection for your daughter right now. Details please.'

Rae left the room, heading for the incident room. She called Barry's wife, Gwen, a fellow detective sergeant in Southampton city police.

As she glanced out of the window, she spotted a squad car draw up close to the entrance. Rose Simons emerged, gripping the arm of a man in handcuffs. This must be the notorious Ronnie Delphic. Rae hurried down the stairs and found a corner seat in the reception area. She wanted to watch his behaviour as he was checked in, observe his reactions, see what kind of person he was.

Delphic was smartly dressed, just as Jackie had described after her brief encounter with him at Billy Pitt's flat several weeks earlier. He wore a neatly pressed suit in pale blue, a white shirt teamed with a red tie, and gleaming black shoes. He oozed confidence and wealth, although his dark eyes seemed guarded. He looked around him, as if assessing the lie of the land, and answered the questions from the custody officer quietly. Rae guessed that an expensive lawyer would be arriving soon, one adept at trying to give the police the runaround.

Rae waited until Delphic was taken inside the custody suite, then had a quiet word with Rose Simons.

'Did everything go smoothly?'

'Pretty well. He didn't give us any trouble, if that's what you mean. He's not the type. Too clever.'

'What was he doing when you arrived?'

'In an office, talking to one of the club managers. He was on the phone. Said it was a conference call, but I think he's lying. I'm sure I heard him say the word cops when he spotted us just before he closed the call.'

Rae frowned. Would he have had a chance to issue a warning to anyone? She headed back to the incident room, thinking hard. She'd need to warn Barry. Maybe Tommy too. Forewarned was forearmed.

She was quickly back in the interview room, facing Val Potter. 'Your daughter will be fine, Dr Potter. I've had a conversation with an experienced detective sergeant in Southampton police, someone we know well. She's arranging protection at this moment. I'm happy for you to phone your daughter and explain to her what's being arranged. Do you want to do that now? But keep the conversation short and the details to a minimum. Just say it's a security issue related to a sensitive aspect of your work.'

Val did so. Rae watched and listened carefully.

'Tell me about your previous visit to Parantos, Dr Potter. As a gap-year student on that ecology project twenty-six years ago. I understand there were problems then.'

There. That should be enough detail to imply they knew a lot more. Val looked stunned, yet again. Would she be more ready to spill the beans now?

\* \* \*

Rae joined Barry outside the second interview room. 'Val Potter's opened up,' she said. 'She says that they put the screws on her by threatening her daughter. She's at university in Southampton, so I had a quick chat with Gwen to arrange a watch. I'm sure you'll hear about it from her later.'

'I'm a bit mystified how these thugs made initial contact, though. EcoFutures got the contract and that was probably publicised. But how did they latch on to the individuals so quickly? How did they know who to target?'

'Well, it gets messier, boss. It's a timescale thing. Val was across in Parantos during her gap year, as a nineteen-year-old. But she also went back a few years later, after graduating. That was twenty years ago. Her daughter is nineteen. The father is a local over there, working on the river. The daughter returns occasionally to visit. Do you see how it's starting to fit together? Someone from the Perez gang must have got to hear about her, maybe years ago. My thoughts on it are that Val was being intimidated, through her daughter. They started to put the screws on recently. She wonders whether the guy she had a fling with all those years ago, the father of her daughter, might be on the periphery of the gang.'

'Why do they want the location switched? Did she say?'

'The development as it stands would make things harder for them. It would open up a derelict area that they currently

246

use. It's convenient for them to keep it as it is. That's what she thinks.'

'What did she say about Delphic?'

'That he's an opportunist with links to international organised crime, including in Parantos. She says he hosted a party for them in his villa there. He's an obvious contact point for anyone wanting to do a bit of unpleasant intimidation around here. He's not a nice person, boss. Not from what Val Potter said. But I don't understand why she went along with it, right from the start. Was the threat against her daughter made really early on?' She shrugged. 'I don't know.'

'But she's a devious liar herself, isn't she?'

Rae gave a thin smile. 'Absolutely right, boss. But I still think the nastier one is the O'Neil woman.'

'My thoughts too. She was doing it for the money. And the thrills, in a warped kind of way. Until she got too greedy, and they decided to put the frighteners on her.' He paused. 'Let's go and see what we can get out of Delphic.'

The two men already inside the room looked calm and alert. The lawyer was tall and thin, almost gaunt. He wore an expensive-looking charcoal-grey suit. The lenses in his spectacles gleamed. His eyes were wary, flickering over the two detectives. Ronnie Delphic was of average height, with smooth skin and dark hair, oiled back.

As soon as the two detectives sat down to start the interview, the lawyer spoke.

'My client is happy to co-operate with the police to help solve these very unpleasant murders. He denies any involvement. If you make any such suggestions without clear evidence, I will advise him to withdraw that level of assistance.'

Barry stared at him but didn't answer. Instead, he turned to Delphic. 'This is a double murder enquiry, Mr Delphic. It's important that you understand the serious nature of the crimes we're investigating. In particular, the murder of a man near Golden Cap. He was staying in a cottage rented from you. We think the killer was also staying there. Would you care to comment?'

'I don't get involved with the rental process. A letting agency does that.' Delphic's voice was smooth and measured.

'Yes. Lyme Coastal Cottages, in Charmouth. In my experience, Mr Delphic, when a let or loaned property has been used as the base for some kind of criminal activity, particularly a murder, the property owner shows immediate interest. You've shown none. Care to comment?'

Delphic shrugged. 'Doesn't involve me. Why should it? What people get up to is their business.'

'Not when it's murder. Then it becomes very much *my* business. Who cleans the cottage?'

There was a curious pause. 'The agency does it.'

Rae interrupted after checking her notes. 'So why the change on this occasion? The letting agency have said you altered the arrangements. Apparently, someone called Paula has been doing it for the last week or two, by request from you.'

Delphic frowned momentarily.

'Is Paula the cleaner the same person who acts as your own housekeeper?' Rae asked.

Delphic suddenly looked tense. Barry wondered why that would be. It was when the name Paula was mentioned. Or her role as a housekeeper. Maybe Delphic hadn't banked on them finding out about her. Or possibly it was the mention of his own house. Yes, that would be it. He didn't want their attention to switch to his own home because Isabella Perez was in hiding there.

'Yes,' he finally murmured.

'That's up at your own villa, off the Sidmouth Road?'

Delphic nodded, warily.

'Will she be there at the moment? Your housekeeper, I mean. Paula.'

'No. She only works mornings.'

Rae nudged Barry's leg. He thought back a few days. Hadn't Jackie's *ad hoc* visit to the house been in the late afternoon? And she'd spoken to the housekeeper, this Paula woman. Delphic was obviously nervous about the probing into his own house.

'Paula sometimes does some cleaning of my cottages. It gives her a bit of extra cash.' Delphic was clearly trying to switch the conversation back to the cottages and away from his villa. Interesting.

'Do you live there alone?'

'What?' Delphic had lost some of his composure. Tiny pinpricks of perspiration sparkled on his forehead.

'In your own home? Are you mostly there alone? Does someone else sometimes stay? Would there be anyone there at the moment?'

'No.'

'I want to ask you about your holiday home in Parantos, Mr Delphic. How long have you owned it?'

Delphic turned to his lawyer and shook his head.

'My client feels that he's been co-operative enough. Either charge him or let him go.'

'In that case, we'll be charging him with being an accessory to murder,' Barry replied.

* * *

Tommy Carter replaced his phone and turned to George.

'That was my boss, Rae Gregson. She wonders if the Perez woman might have got a phone tip-off that Delphic's been brought in for questioning. If so, she might well do a runner.'

'What can we do? Check the place over?'

Tommy thought for a few moments. 'You stay here, keeping an eye out. I'll walk down the hill past the house and have a look. Anything from the listening devices?'

George touched his earpiece. 'Still music playing. Latin-American. No voices.'

Tommy climbed out of the car. 'Back shortly.'

He ambled down the hill, trying to look like a tourist. There were no signs of life in Delphic's house, but that had been the case all day. What should he do? In the event, the need for a decision was taken away from him. An angry-looking man came hurrying out of the neighbouring house.

'Did you just run through my back garden?' he asked, accusingly.

'No,' Tommy replied, sounding somewhat mystified.

The resident didn't seem convinced. 'Someone did, I'm sure.'

He glared at Tommy, who took his warrant card out of his pocket. 'I'm a police officer,' he said to the man. 'What did you see?'

'I was in my back room watching the teatime news. I saw a dark figure running along the back of my shrubbery.'

'How long ago?' Tommy asked.

'Just a couple of minutes. I went out for a look. Someone trod on my begonias. They're ruined.'

'Right, sir. All noted. I'll try to find out who.'

Tommy hurried back to the car. 'I think she might have got out through a back entrance and sneaked through several neighbouring gardens. If it is her, where's she gone?'

George was examining the road ahead carefully. 'Look down the hill in front of us. You see where that van's parked? Someone sneaking out of that neighbouring house would be in a blind spot from where we are. If they suspected we were here, that's where they'd head for.' He checked the map. 'That's where that path is, the one Rose reported. It leads to the cliff top. I'll go to check. You phone in. Didn't the chief super say that our suspect would probably try to run?'

He was out of the car and striding down the hill in seconds, a little voice of warning niggling in his ear. *Take care. Don't do anything rash. I don't ever want to lose you.* It was the voice of his girlfriend, Jade Allen. He slowed as he reached the cut-through between the houses. Take it slow, he told himself. This is a killer you're following. Armed and with nothing to lose. He started down the path, the early evening sunlight coming in low on his right. A blackbird was singing from a tree in a nearby garden. Was that a good sign? He walked forward carefully, watching the surface he was treading on. He didn't want to alert anyone to his presence by stepping on a dry twig.

## CHAPTER 41: TEARS OF HAPPINESS

Sophie Allen was furious with herself. What was wrong with her? It was obvious that Rae had meant nothing malicious by that comment she'd made about Sophie's singing. Yet she'd snapped out a reply that was both vindictive and completely uncalled for. She'd seen the look of shock on Rae's face and knew instantly that she'd overstepped the mark by a mile. Even Barry had looked astonished. And then she'd chosen to turn tail and flee rather than apologise.

She knew what the real problem was. Tomorrow was decision day. The day on which she'd be meeting her consultant for a detailed discussion about her long-term prognosis. She was dreading it, feeling deep inside herself that the news would bring an abrupt end to the career she loved. What use was a crippled police officer? Maybe her fantasy alternative, becoming a singer in a nightclub, would need to be considered rather more seriously, though not if Rae's throwaway comment about the quality of her singing voice had any truth in it. A sales assistant in a cake shop? She almost smiled to herself. Who'd have guessed, some five years after she'd told that tiny doll-like woman Lily Dalton about a vacancy in a coffee and cake café, that she'd be considering a similar career change? Oh, how the mighty have fallen.

Martin was coming across this evening so he could be there to support her on her very own day of judgement. She looked at her watch. Goodness. Was it that late? He would be in Lyme soon. She really ought to head back down the hill to her hotel and get ready.

She looked once again at the panoramic view in front of her, from Golden Cap in the east, along the hilly shoreline to the Cobb below her, that massive arm of stone curling out into the blue waters of Lyme Bay. She felt uneasy, a result, she guessed, of not knowing what the future held for her. By this time tomorrow she'd know rather more about her options. Whether there was any point in hanging on to desperate hopes that she still had a realistic future in the police. She could still feel the ache in her thigh, that dull throb that seemed to be ever present, despite the painkillers she took religiously every day. Was the pain easing over time? She told herself so, and everyone who asked. On a day like today, though, she wondered if she was really just kidding herself. But at least she was feeling easier in her mind now. An hour or two up here on the clifftop path had somehow lifted her spirits enough to allow her to start processing her conflicted feelings. Maybe she should be getting back. Martin would worry if she was nowhere to be found when he arrived.

Her phone signalled an incoming message. Paul Baker, her contact from Scotland Yard. It was short and simple. *Maria Castillo. Her uncle has links to the Perez gang.*

Sophie scrabbled through her memory for the names of the people Barry and Rae had met at the High Commission. They'd only mentioned three women. An assistant to the man they'd been dealing with. But wasn't her name Angelika? The catering woman, Julia. The only other one was the receptionist. Yes, that was her. Maria. Problem solved.

She sent back a reply. *I'll let Barry know. That solves a problem he's been fretting about.*

She backtracked along the coast path and turned into the narrow cut-through between the houses, a hedge on one side and a fence on the other. A figure appeared further along the path, turning onto it from a residential road and walking purposefully in her direction. A woman, short, with cropped dark hair. Her large, hooped earrings caught the sunlight and glinted as they swayed to the same rhythm as her steps. Isabella Perez, without a shadow of doubt.

Sophie unobtrusively pressed the release button on her wheelchair's restraining belt. Then her grip on the speed controller seemed to slip and the wheelchair appeared to shoot forward rather too fast, lurching to the side, where its front corner hit a fence post just as the drive wheel on the other side gained grip. The chair seemed to balance on two wheels for a fraction of a second then tipped over, sending her sprawling across the path in front of the chair. She slipped a hand inside her bag and transferred a small container to her pocket, unseen by Perez, now approaching warily. Sophie gave a heartfelt groan. The tumble really had jarred her injured shoulder. Luckily her good leg had borne the brunt of the fall on the lower part of her body, as she'd planned. She shuddered to think of the effect if the force of the impact had been on her damaged leg.

She turned slightly to gain a better view of the approaching woman and continued to emit a low, regular moan. She saw the figure slow, hesitantly. The narrow path was completely blocked, impassable until she and the wheelchair were moved to an upright position.

'Help,' she whimpered. 'My leg's broken.'

Perez stopped, glancing around her. Sophie could see the uncertainty on her face. Her brain must be cycling through the options open to her, considering each in turn, weighing them up before accepting or rejecting them. She glanced back along the narrow path for a moment as if a return to the road might be the best choice, but then seemed to stiffen and move forward.

She righted the wheelchair first, as Sophie had hoped. It was the logical choice, after all. It now provided somewhere on which to prop Sophie once she'd been moved from her sprawled position blocking the narrow path. She felt Perez's arms slide under her armpits on both sides, starting to exert an upward pull as she hauled hard on Sophie's torso, trying to gain enough purchase to lift her sideways onto the chair in order to free up space to squeeze through and gain her freedom. Sophie planted her feet more firmly on the ground and her fingers closed around the canister of incapacitating spray in her pocket. She suddenly swivelled and raised the spray.

'Police,' she said, before pressing the release button.

A jet of spray shot forward into Perez's face and she shrieked, releasing Sophie as her hands clawed at her eyes. She staggered backwards against the fence, temporarily blinded and coughing. Sophie used the arm of the wheelchair to lever herself upright, reached inside her bag for the handcuffs and slipped them onto the woman's raised right wrist. She then punched the moaning woman as hard as she could in the stomach, causing her to partially double up, before locking the cuffs onto her left wrist too. She stuck her foot behind Perez's ankle and gave her a hard shove, causing the woman to tumble backwards onto the ground.

Sophie crouched down as far as her injuries would allow and quickly felt the woman's outer clothes. A handgun, in her jacket's right-side pocket. A knife, in her cargo trousers' leg pocket. Sophie pulled them both out and tossed them into the pannier on her wheelchair. She then sat in the wheelchair, panting hard. She felt exhilarated, for the first time in nearly three long, hard months. She still had what it takes. She lifted her phone to her face to call Barry. By the time she'd finished the short message, she was crying. They were tears of happiness.

That's how George found her a few moments later. Sitting on her wheelchair, gazing out to sea, blinking through the tears, with Isabella Perez sprawled beside her on the narrow, rutted path, still groaning, her nose running, a trickle of saliva leaking from her open, gasping mouth, and Sophie's foot pushing down into the small of her back.

Sophie turned to face him. 'I've still got it, George. I'm not ready to give up yet.'

## CHAPTER 42: EXETER

Exeter had always been one of Sophie's favourite cities, though she wasn't sure if that feeling still applied. She'd spent several pain-filled weeks in the hospital here following the assault that had shattered her leg and broken her shoulder. Dark days that still haunted her.

The hospital visit got off to an unexpectedly good start. As she and Martin arrived at reception, a familiar figure leapt up out of a nearby chair and flung her arms around Sophie.

'Hannah!' Sophie gasped. 'You've come all the way from London. Are you mad?'

'That's always been the case, Mum. And I think I must be, really, considering that I had to catch the early train from Paddington. I still can't believe the time I got up this morning. But I wanted to be here for you.'

'Well, let's hope it hasn't been a wasted journey.' She looked at Martin. 'Were you in on this, you rascal?'

Her husband smiled warily. 'I knew, though I didn't arrange it. But I thought I might need some comfort and support to help me through a difficult morning.'

'Double rascal!' Sophie replied, giving him a hug.

The receptionist watched them in a bemused way. 'I think Ms Hopkins is ready for you, if you want to go through.'

The consultant greeted the trio warmly when they entered her room. Sophie, now feeling more phlegmatic, looked around her. The décor of the room hadn't changed, of course, but a vase of colourful blooms stood in the centre of the low table around which they were directed to sit.

'Lovely flowers,' she murmured, to no one in particular.

'I'm glad you like them,' Dr Hopkins replied. 'A present from my new boyfriend. It's his way of wooing me, I guess. I happened to mention on our first date that I liked to see bright colours in flower beds. It was a throwaway comment, but he obviously took it seriously. It puts the pressure on though. I suppose I'm going to have to get him a gift for our next date. Where will it all end?' she sighed.

Sophie couldn't help but laugh. 'And you worry about something like that? If you were a close friend, I'd tell you to get a grip.'

'Yes, well, that would be a very pertinent comment. What's the saying? Fair dos? Anyway, down to business. Do you want the good news or the good news?'

Sophie suddenly looked confused. 'Pardon?' she said.

'I've had a chance to look at your scan results, I've read through all the reports from your other doctors, therapists and the like, whoever and wherever they are, and I can reassure you that the outlook is good. Very good. The bone is actually knitting together better than I'd hoped. All that effort that you've undoubtedly put in has been worth it. You're on the mend, I can confidently say.'

Sophie closed her eyes and took several deep breaths. Martin and Hannah both had their mouths open.

'Did I hear you right?' Sophie asked, her voice unsteady.

Martin and Hannah both flung their arms around her at the same time, causing a minor clash of heads and a tangle of limbs.

'I can't quite believe it,' Sophie said when they separated. 'Are you sure?'

'Do you think I'd try to kid you over something like this?' came the reply. Dr Hopkins looked at Martin. 'I'd think of breaking out the bubbly when you get home. Make it the proper stuff.' She turned back to Sophie. 'You're not out of the woods yet. You still need to stick to the process and do all the therapy, otherwise it could all go pear-shaped. But having got to know you over the past couple of months, I have no doubt you'll manage that okay. Don't push yourself too hard, though. It's a question of finding the right balance.'

'Can I hug you too?' Sophie said.

* * *

They arrived back in Lyme in the late afternoon and all three of them climbed the stairs to the incident room, Sophie on elbow crutches. It was empty, apart from an administrative assistant sorting through files. A single note lay on Barry's desk. *Gone to the pub!* it read.

'You have a very sensible team around you,' was Martin's comment. 'My guess is that it's an instruction for us to join them.'

The sun was shining as they walked the short distance to the nearby Appletree Inn. Martin pushed the door open, peering into the slightly gloomy interior. He was followed by Hannah, holding the door for her mother. The WeSCU members were spread out around a large table near the bar and had fallen strangely silent when they'd spotted who had entered. They all knew about Sophie's earlier appointment with her specialist.

Sophie was unable to speak, but her smile said it all.

'Mum got a great result from the consultant,' Hannah announced, beaming. 'Everything's going brilliantly. We've been ordered by the doc to break open the bubbly!'

Sophie finally found her voice. 'Bugger the bubbly,' she said. 'It can wait. A pint of Dorset Gold for me. I need something to calm me down.'

Barry was first across to put his arms around her, then to shake Martin's hand. 'That's wonderful news. I'm just so relieved.'

'I think you speak for all of us,' Martin replied. 'And there's no doubt about one thing. We need a holiday.'

Rae followed on and embraced Sophie. She was in tears. 'Ma'am, I'm so sorry for what I said about your singing. It was totally crass. You know how I feel about you really, don't you?'

'You caught me at a bad time. Anyway, how could I ever feel bad about you? You saved my life, remember. I'll never forget that. Never.' Sophie took a deep swig from the pint glass that had materialised at her elbow. 'God, that's beautiful.' She turned back to Rae. 'But having said all that, I would appreciate the opportunity to sing at some future celebration of yours. I've been taking singing lessons, you know. And the windows are all still intact.'

Hannah interrupted. 'Yeah, but you set off all the neighbourhood dogs, Mum. Haven't you noticed?'

## THE END

# GLOSSARY

**Bloke:** guy
**Ecology:** the study of the relationship between living things and their environment.
**Home Office:** a ministerial department in the UK Government, responsible for immigration, security and law & order.
**Home Secretary:** One of the three "great" offices of state in the UK Government, other than Prime Minister.
**Hydrotherapy:** the use of water as a medical treatment.
**Pear-shaped:** gone wrong
**Mobile phone:** cell phone

**UK Police Ranks (in descending order of seniority):**
Chief Constable (or Commissioner in London's Metropolitan Police force)
Deputy CC (Deputy Commissioner in London)
Assistant CC (Assistant Commissioner in London)
Chief Superintendent
Superintendent
Chief Inspector
Inspector
Sergeant
Constable

Detectives hold the same ranks but with a prefix before the name (DC, DS etc.) There is sometimes career movement back and forth between detectives and uniformed ranks.

# ACKNOWLEDGEMENTS

Writing a novel such as this can be, at times, a very solitary, sometimes lonely, time. But lots of people help in many different ways and deserve a mention.

To all the staff at Joffe Books for their help, particularly the editorial team for working on my original text so thoroughly. They always do a great job. Special thanks to Kate Lyall Grant and to my meticulous editor, Rachel Malig, along with Kate Ballard and Julia Williams. A mention also of Gemma Carr, my contact in the marketing team at Joffe. The biggest thanks go to the boss, Jasper Joffe, to whom I owe so much.

Any errors in this book are mine. If you spot a typo, please email Joffe Books and they'll do their best to correct it.

A big thanks to my closest friends in the crime-writing community: Joy Ellis, Janice Frost and Helen Durrant. What a pleasure to meet up with you all for coffee and a party on a sunny spring day in London!

At home in Salisbury, thanks are due to my personal friends, those who help to keep me going just by being around. Ruby and Nicky; Sam and Rachel; the local CAMRA members, all of whom are so friendly and encouraging; my lovely, supportive family (Stephen, Malcolm, David, Kate, Kat, along with my six grandchildren). Also to Sandra and Tereza, who I've known for almost fifteen years since we met on a crime-writing workshop in London. Above all, to my darling wife, Margaret.

I need to own up to the fact that I really dislike social media, the misuse of which causes so much harm to so many people. I like email, though, and I'd like to reassure readers that if they email me direct at michael@michaelhambling.co.uk, I will always respond as quickly as I can. Please visit my website at www.michaelhambling.co.uk. It went through a bit of an overhaul a while ago, though I need to remember to post stuff on it more regularly! It does carry relevant information and a selection of free-to-read short stories.

You may like to read the novels I've written for teenagers, the Misfit books. The stories are about a small group of unorthodox young people in Dorset who try to solve low-level, anti-social crimes that have a habit of escalating into something more serious. Rae Gregson, who appears in the Sophie Allen novels, tries to keep an eye on the group in her spare moments, and acts as an unofficial adviser. Available from Amazon.

# AUTHOR'S NOTES

*Location*

Lyme Regis is situated at the western end of Dorset but lies about a third of the way along the famous "Jurassic coast", a 125-mile stretch of coastline that includes parts of East Devon and has revealed many fossils over the years. The town's most well-known former resident is probably Mary Anning, a person famous for both palaeontology and her belief that a woman has every right to pursue the same interests in the natural world as a man. It has also appeared in many famous works of fiction, from Jane Austen's *Persuasion* to John Fowles' *The French Lieutenant's Woman*.

The nearby town of Axminster, also featured in this novel, is across the border in Devon.

I featured the area around Golden Cap, owned by the National Trust, in *Ruthless Crimes*, the ninth novel in the Sophie Allen series. I make no apologies for using the location again. It really is a landmark.

We stayed in the Alexandra Hotel in Lyme Regis while researching locations for this novel. It's a lovely place for a break, with great views eastwards along the coastline and down onto the Cobb. Great food too!

*Food and Drink*

Dorset produces a variety of fine food and drink, from local lamb to cheese, beer, cider and wine. It has many fine pubs, many of which can form the basis of a country ramble.

I've kept rather too quiet for too many years about the fact that my favourite pub in the UK is the famous Square & Compass in the small village of Worth Matravers, near Swanage. I don't want it spoiled! But Charlie Newman, the owner and licensee, is such a great character that he deserves a mention. His pub is unique, in so many ways. It has its own Fossil Museum, displaying unusual artefacts as well as fossils collected locally (and legally) by the Newman family. It serves beautifully kept ales, direct from the barrel. Charlie also makes his own ciders. But please note that the pub doesn't have a bar (drinks are served from a hatch) and it doesn't have a restaurant. It does have two small sitting rooms and a large garden, usually filled with ramblers, cyclists and nature-lovers. Food is restricted to pasties and pies, but they are first rate ones. The pub is best enjoyed after a five- or six-mile walk along the coast path from Swanage (we find the upper coast path easier). You'll have earned your drink then!

If the idea of Caribbean food, mentioned in this novel, has grabbed your attention, then another Purbeck pub might interest you. The Scott Arms in Kingston hosts a "Jerk Shack" in its garden during warm weekend days in the summer months.

*Salisbury*

My fellow author Ruby Vitorino Moody, mentioned in the dedication, has written a detailed A–Z history of Salisbury's most famous pub, the Haunch of Venison, published by Hobnob Press. I would urge Wiltshire folk interested in local history to buy a copy. Even better if you visit the pub to soak up its unique atmosphere and taste the beer. Churchill and Eisenhower reputedly paid a visit to the Haunch during a break from the planning of D-Day. Much of that planning took place in the Double Cube Room at nearby Wilton House.

# THE JOFFE BOOKS STORY

We began in 2014 when Jasper agreed to publish his mum's much-rejected romance novel and it became a bestseller.

Since then we've grown into the largest independent publisher in the UK. We're extremely proud to publish some of the very best writers in the world, including Joy Ellis, Faith Martin, Caro Ramsay, Helen Forrester, Simon Brett and Robert Goddard. Everyone at Joffe Books loves reading and we never forget that it all begins with the magic of an author telling a story.

We are proud to publish talented first-time authors, as well as established writers whose books we love introducing to a new generation of readers.

We won Trade Publisher of the Year at the Independent Publishing Awards in 2023 and Best Publisher Award in 2024 at the People's Book Prize. We have been shortlisted for Independent Publisher of the Year at the British Book Awards for the last five years, and were shortlisted for the Diversity and Inclusivity Award at the 2022 Independent Publishing Awards. In 2023 we were shortlisted for Publisher of the Year at the RNA Industry Awards, and in 2024 we were shortlisted at the CWA Daggers for the Best Crime and Mystery Publisher.

We built this company with your help, and we love to hear from you, so please email us about absolutely anything bookish at feedback@joffebooks.com.

If you want to receive free books every Friday and hear about all our new releases, join our mailing list here: www.joffebooks.com/freebooks.

And when you tell your friends about us, just remember: it's pronounced Joffe as in coffee or toffee!

Printed in the USA
CPSIA information can be obtained
at www.ICGtesting.com
LVHW031243091224
798679LV00017B/1088